Dennis Russell was born in Portsmouth, and educated at the Grammar School and at Brasenose College, Oxford. After National Service as a pilot in the R.A.F., Dennis joined a London advertising agency, where he was taught to write by Julian Yeatman (of *1066 and All That* fame). Later he worked in Marketing and General Management for major companies such as Nabisco, Cerebos, Ranks Hovis McDougall and Reed International. In 1988 he completed one of the earliest management buyouts, of a company called 'Mr Plumber', which claimed to have launched the DIY plumbing business in the UK. More recently, he was Regional Director for a London outplacement agency, and then Director of Client Services for Praxis, one of the most successful agencies in the rapidly developing field of temporary management. He is the author of the standard book on the subject, *Interim Management*, published by Butterworth-Heinemann in 1998. **Carew** is his first published novel. He is currently working on a thriller.

CAREW

A STORY OF
CIVIL WAR
IN THE WEST COUNTRY

Dennis Russell

AIDAN ELLIS

First published in Great Britain by Aidan Ellis, 2000

Reprinted 2001

A CIP catalogue record for this book is available from the
British Library

ISBN 0 85628 298 7

Set by TW Typesetting of Plymouth

Printed in England by Biddles of Guildford

Aidan Ellis Publishing, Whinfield, Herbert Road, Salcombe,
Devon TQ8 8HN, England
http://www.demon.co.uk/aepub

Contents

For Averil

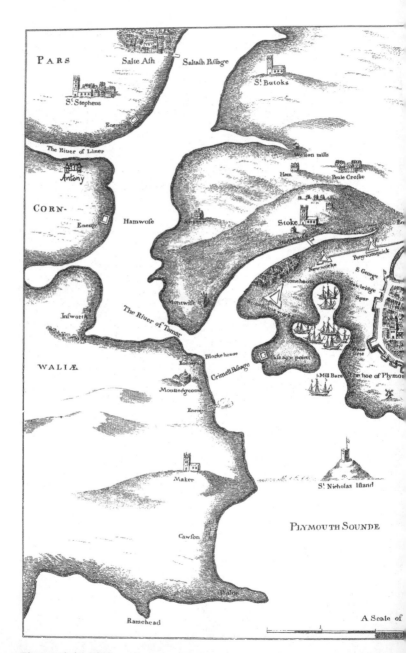

Plymouth in 1643
By kind permission of Plymouth Library Services

A TRVE MAPP AND DESCRIPTION OF THE TOWNE
of Plymouth and the Fortifications thereof, with the workes and
approaches of the Enemy, at the laſt Seige A.º 1643

Eg Buckland

Enemy
Enemy
Compton
Enemy
Lipſon mill
Holiwell
Lipſon mill worke
rdlya
Lipſon
Reſolution Fort
Leerie point worke
OVTH Maidenbrad
The Leerie
Plymton marie
Eaſtgate

Catdowne
Saltrum
Catdowne
Prince rock
Beckley

Fiſhers noſe
Catwater
Pomſlit mills
Enemy
Plymstock
Enemy
Mount
Batten
Hoo
Radforde

Wenburie

The Carew and Edgcumbe Families

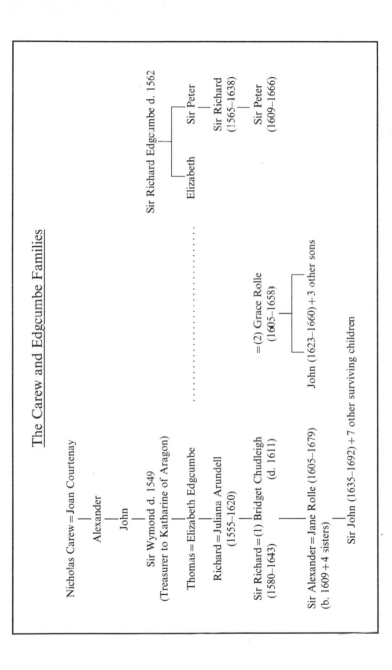

Nicholas Carew = Joan Courtenay

Alexander

John

Sir Wymond d. 1549
(Treasurer to Katharine of Aragon)

Thomas = Elizabeth Edgcumbe . . . . Sir Richard Edgcumbe d. 1562

Elizabeth   Sir Peter

Richard = Juliana Arundell   Sir Richard
(1555–1620)   (1565–1638)

Sir Peter
(1609–1666)

Sir Richard = (1) Bridget Chudleigh   = (2) Grace Rolle
(1580–1643)   (d. 1611)   (1605–1658)

John (1623–1660) + 3 other sons

Sir Alexander = Jane Rolle (1605–1679)
(b. 1609 + 4 sisters)

Sir John (1635–1692) + 7 other surviving children

Our Bastion in the West

'Surrender. I think we should consider most seriously the advisability of surrendering the city, rather than . . .'

Thomas Ceely's words were drowned out by a roar of conflicting voices. He was Mayor of Plymouth, a small, scholarly man in his mid-fifties, with an old-fashioned short square beard. In this January of 1643 he knew that his authority hung by a thread, but he was determined to make one more attempt to have the Council see sense. He waited for the hubbub to die down, then spoke again.

'Sir William Ruthin, our Garrison Commander, disregarded our advice when he marched off with our troops and our guns to attack the King's army in Cornwall.'

There were murmurs of agreement on this point, and Thomas pressed home his advantage.

'At Braddock Down, at Liskeard, and now yesterday right across the river here at Saltash, he has suffered defeat after defeat. Our troops are killed or captured, and we must presume that the enemy now has all forty of our cannon. Within the week they will cross the Tamar somewhere higher up, and come down on us, this time with our own guns blasting breaches in our ancient walls, so that four thousand Cornish savages can pour through and sack our city, as the Rules of War allow them to do if we resist. Is that what you want to happen? To see women raped, children butchered, ourselves executed as traitors? We have no army now to defend us. Nor can we expect any help from London. It makes no sense to become martyrs. We should therefore seek out the King's commander in the west, Sir Ralph Hopton, and negotiate at once for honourable terms of surrender. I know Sir Ralph, and he is a most civilised gentleman . . .'

'NO!'

From the murmur of talk that had continued while Thomas was speaking, one voice rose out, strong and challenging. Alexander Carew, Plymouth's Member of Parliament, stood up from the long bench at the side of the Council Chamber, and pushed his way through the crowd towards the platform where Thomas sat with the senior members of his Council. Alexander was thirty-four, tall, slim, with fair hair that fell in waves to his shoulders and fine delicate features. His bright red cloak, worn over a fashionable black doublet slashed with red silk, and red hose, contrasted strongly with the provincially sober dress of the rest of Plymouth's Council. The hall fell suddenly silent as he stepped boldly up onto the dais, and stood before them.

'I say "NO". No to turning belly-up to a rabble from Bodmin, St Austell or Penzance, most of whom can't even speak English. Why have they joined the King? I'll tell you, it's because he has promised to bring back the old religion, that's why. Is that what we want? Popery and incense? Hocus-pocus in Latin?

'NO!

'The stake erected again in the market square to burn our Protestant Martyrs? England ruled from Rome?

'NO!'

'Is that why we've fought the Spaniard for a hundred years? To hand over our city once more to the torturers of the Inquisition?

'No, No, NO!'

Alexander's oratory had been honed by the months of passionate debate in Parliament, and by the fiery preachers on London's street corners, and the effect on his audience was instantaneous. They roared out their answers to his challenges, and stamped their feet in emphasis. He held up a hand.

'Thank you for your support. I promise you, Parliament will not forget or abandon its friends in Plymouth. As soon as I heard the news of yesterday's tragedy in Saltash, I sent off two men at the gallop to Exeter to seek assistance. Even now, I am certain that Lord Robarts and the Earl of Stamford are marching to our aid, and sending ships with more cannon for us. All we have to do is keep our nerve . . .'

The wide doors at the side of the Council Chamber crashed open to interrupt his speech.

'I hear there's been talk of surrender?'

Colonel Sir William Ruthin spoke quietly, with a soft Scots lilt to his voice, but there was no mistaking the steel in his tone. A short slight figure, his big thigh-boots flapped thick with mud as he strode into the chamber and stepped up beside Alexander, where he threw his black hat and cloak onto the table. He stood facing the assembly, one hand on the hilt of his sword, the other inside the fold of the heavy black leather jerkin that was brightened by the orange sash of Parliament. For several seconds he stood in silence, turning a fierce gaze from face to face as he assessed the mood,

'I heard Mr Carew ask you to keep your nerve. I trust that's not in doubt amongst the sons and grandsons of the men who defeated Philip of Spain?'

A dark, burly man with a beak of a nose and a greying beard pushed his way to the foot of the platform,

'No doubt at all, Sir William, no doubt at all. Just tell us what we have to do, and we'll fight to the last man, and to the last woman too, I promise you.'

All around him men clapped and stamped in support, and the chorus of shouts coalesced into his name.

'Francis, Francis, Francis for Mayor! Ceely out, Ceely out!'

Philip Francis found himself hoisted onto the platform, where he stood almost shyly between Alexander Carew M.P.

and Colonel Sir William Ruthin, each of whom shook his hand. Alexander held up both hands for silence.

'Members of the Council of Plymouth. If you are deciding now to choose a new mayor to lead and represent you, it must be done in the proper way, by election. The proposal is for Mr Francis to replace Mr Ceely as mayor. All those in favour please raise your hands.'

About half the hands went up. From the gallery above, packed with citizens who had no vote in this decision, there was a great roar of cheering, accompanied by shouts of 'Hang the King's men,' and 'Down with Property'.

'Those against Mr Francis?'

A handful of Plymouth's Councillors dared to put up their hands, but most of the rest stood unmoving, not wanting to risk the rage of the mob above them.

'I declare Philip Francis duly elected Mayor of Plymouth. If you would yield the chair please, Mr Ceely?'

Thomas stood up and kept a stony face against a renewed surge of booing from the gallery. Phillip Francis took his place in the high gilded chair, and smiled as a shaft of winter sunlight suddenly flashed through one of the tall windows of the Council Chamber, and brightened their end of the great room, with its red hammerbeam roof above.

'I see that Heaven has decided to throw some light on our darkness at last!'

There was a ripple of laughter across the assembly, and Philip took advantage of the moment.

'Well then, Sir William, we are at war, so we should pay attention to soldiers, should we not? Your campaign into Cornwall has gone badly, but we should not forget the way you led those same troops out against the Cornish who laid siege to us last Autumn, and beat them soundly back to their own country. So what must we do to save our city this time?'

The Colonel bowed very slightly to acknowledge the authority of the city's new Mayor.

'Our situation is difficult, but not as desperate as Mr Ceely would have had you believe. I have come back with half my mounted men in good order, that is some seven hundred dragoons and cavalry. No doubt over the next week we may expect as many again of the foot-soldiers to make their way in to us, having evaded capture. We have ample powder and shot, matchlocks and a few cannon still in the castle. We need to send at once to Exeter . . .'

'I have already done so, Sir William.'

'Thank you, thank you Mr Carew. I am sure the weight of your name and authority will make them stir their stumps. Now, the important thing is to prevent Hopton hitting the city and our walls with his cannon. To do that, we must hold him up at least half a mile from the walls.'

'Is that possible, with just a few hundred troops?'

Philip's question was quietly spoken, but was heard in every corner of the now silent Council Chamber.

'We can, Mr Francis, we can. Or rather you can, the people of Plymouth. You have four or five thousand able-bodied men in the city, and no doubt four or five thousand women too. I want you to put everyone to work, and I mean everyone, starting at first light tomorrow, to dig for us a great ditch and rampart. My captains will go out with the Council straight from this assembly to mark the line. It will run in an arc around the north of the city, from the deep-water inlet of the Tamar opposite Stoke on the west, to Lipson Mill at the Catwater on the east. Eight feet deep, with the excavated earth used to build a rampart behind the ditch eight feet high, by my estimate four thousand yards long altogether. Of course we must have a few roads through this line, and here will be our forts where we will place cannon. From the top of Plymouth Castle we will be able to observe any concentrations of enemy troops five or ten miles before they reach our fortifications. I can guarantee that they will not carry our ramparts in a month, no not in six months, even if our only defence is a few hundred troops and the stout hearts of the town militia. And once Plymouth is reinforced from Exeter, we will be impregnable again.'

'If the city is to endure a long siege, keeping open our

lifeline to the sea will be vital. Like the old Athenians with their Long Walls.'

'Just so, Mr Carew, a very exact parallel from naval history. In our case, the key to the city is the island of St. Nicholas, in the middle of Plymouth Sound. It must be held for us by a man of total integrity and reliability. May I, therefore, suggest that you undertake that charge personally, together with the fort below the Castle that covers the actual entrance to the Pool?'

The shouts rose again from the citizens, mingling excitement and relief.

'Francis and Carew! Francis and Carew! Carew! Carew!'

Alexander warmed to the glow of popular acclaim. He had been foolish perhaps to imagine that he might become Mayor of Plymouth, a position that Sir Francis Drake had been proud to hold only fifty years before. He had never thought it appropriate for a Carew to take any part in the city's complex politics. But he had his place now, and would do his duty.

As Sir William had predicted, the Great Ditch proved an formidable obstacle for the Royalist army. Sir Ralph Hopton had recruited the Trained Bands as a militia from the towns of Cornwall, but now they stood on their legal rights and refused to enter the county of Devon. Some were persuaded to re-enlist as paid soldiers, but the insuperable problem was the incessant heavy rain of that February, which slowed down all movement to a crawl. Deep mud filled the narrow lanes on each side of the Tamar, making it impossible to move the cannon at all.

After the initial challenge and excitement of taking charge of the garrison and guns of St. Nicholas island, Alexander quickly became bored with his duties. Parliament had the Fleet, so there was no real danger of an attack from the sea. Rather the island itself was the threat; if the enemy were to seize control of it, no ship could enter or leave Plymouth without running the gauntlet of its cannon at point-blank range. To pass the time, Alexander took to spending long hours with a telescope on the roof of the lofty keep of Plymouth Castle. To the north and east the horizon was filled with the steep slopes of Dartmoor. Often invisible in low cloud, the brown hills would reappear when a storm had blown through, brightly lit by the slanting winter sunlight, and for two weeks were capped white with snow. To the west the land rose again beyond the wide Tamar river to the bleak uplands of Bodmin Moor, while to the south was Plymouth Sound and the open sea, sometimes sparkling blue, but mostly grey and windswept. About seven miles due west, up the Lynher river, he could make out the roofs and chimneypots of his father's house, Antony. Sir Richard Carew was famous for his apple and pear orchards, which occupied the land on the north side of the house, running down to the Lynher.

Early one morning in March Alexander climbed the now familiar wooden ladders to reach the castle roof, and found that Colonel Ruthin was there before him, apparently excited about something he was watching through the spyglass.

'Mr Carew, I'd heard this was your daily habit. Now, your young eyes may see a wee bit better than mine. Would you come and take a look?'

Alexander clambered around the battlement to reach the north side. Through the crenellation he could see straight down to the courtyard far below, where two tiny troopers were meticulously grooming a miniature horse. He took Sir William's place behind the telescope.

'Use the glass to follow the line of Drake's Water northward across our ditch. Have you got that?'

Drake's Water was a combination of natural stream, canal and aqueduct, contrived by Drake to bring fresh water into Plymouth. So far the enemy had left it undisturbed.

'Keep moving north up the Water, about a mile past our ditch, then look just to the right. Do you see the village with the church tower?'

'I have it. That's Queen's Buckland, if I'm not mistaken?'

'It is. Look now into the churchyard, what do you see?'

'It's . . . difficult . . . there are so many trees in the way . . .
but there seems to be a ring of wagons in the yard, covered
wagons. And there's a lot of movement, soldiers leading
horses and donkeys into and out of the ring. It must be . . .'

'Precisely, Mr Carew, it must be a main provisioning point
for Hopton's army. But what provisions? What are they
collecting, can you see that?'

'No, the saddle-bags are all closed. Flour, meat do you
think? No, wait a moment . . .'

He adjusted the focus fractionally.

'That's better. That's it, two small barrels on each side.
That must be . . .'

'Powder, Mr Carew, powder. You've been able to see what
I was only guessing at. So if that's the place where the powder
is kept, perhaps stored in the church itself, it could be the key
to breaking the siege.'

'You mean if we could blow it up they'd have nothing left
to fight with?'

'Certainly a lot less than they have now. The King's
powder mills are in Sussex, safely in Parliament's hands now.
Hopton's only real port is Falmouth, and I hear that our
Lord High Admiral, the Earl of Warwick has that
well-blockaded. I am ashamed to have to admit that, when I
was forced to abandon our guns at Saltash, my orders to
spike the cannon and put fire to the powder were not carried
through, so Hopton has those supplies. And likely that's what
is in that churchyard.'

Alexander's reaction was immediate.

'Let me try, Sir William. I've hunted deer all my life in
those Tamar woods, and I could find my way up the Water
blindfolded, and . . .'

Sir William reached up a hand to Alexander's shoulder to
check his eagerness.

'Mr Carew, I thank you. Your enthusiasm and your
courage do you credit. But this is a task for a specialist, one

of our troopers or a corporal perhaps, with experience of handling a lit slow match. He cannot take the chance of alerting a sentry with the sound of flint on steel, so he must carry the match already lit across two miles of thick country at night. He needs to know instinctively the likely routines of sentries, and how to apply the match where it will do most damage, but still give him the chance to get away. A task for a very brave man, Mr Carew, but also a very skilled one. And it has to be admitted that there is a significant chance of failure, even death. How would I explain to Parliament if I allowed one of our leading men to lose his life on such a hazard? I understand how tedious it must be for you, sitting behind these walls, after all the excitement of the great events at Westminster. But your courage is not in doubt, Mr Carew. You have already saved Plymouth for Parliament when you stood against Thomas Ceely. Can you bear to leave soldiering to us soldiers?'

'Mr Carew, Mr Carew sir, would you wake up sir please? Wake up sir!'

It was two nights after the munition supply centre had been identified. Sir William and one of his captains had spent many hours, day and night, observing the patterns of movement, and especially marking the watchfires.

'What time is it?'

'Three hours after midnight sir. Sir William sent me to request the pleasure of your company on the roof, if you are so inclined.'

Alexander was immediately alert, and emerged out onto the roof five minutes later. As he climbed the ladder he saw the stars of the Plough twinkling in the dark sky. The narrow lead-lined gully between the conical roof and the battlements was slippery with hoarfrost. Sir William and the young captain were stamping their feet and swinging their arms.

'Thank you for calling me, Sir William. I assume you are expecting something to happen soon?'

'Aye, very soon, Mr Carew. Our brave corporal left our lines two hours ago, so if he has got through to Queen's Buckland we should see the result within the hour. May I introduce Captain Hallsey, who produced the plan of the enemy bivouacs and sentry posts from our observations?'

Alexander was shaking hands with the tall, thin rather lugubrious Dragoon when he heard the ladder rattle, and a muffled curse behind him. Someone had clambered up onto the roof and immediately fallen to his knees. Alexander had time only to recognise the swarthy features of Plymouth's new mayor, Philip Francis, when the night sky to the north was torn by a rippling flash of light that reached as high as the Plough itself, before subsiding into the great red tongues of flame that leapt up in its place. There was a silence that seemed to go on and on, but could only have been a few seconds, and then there was a long growling roar, mingled, of all things, with a jangle of church bells.

'The tower, look, the church tower!'

As they stared, the light of the fire was bright enough to show the dark silhouette of Queen's Buckland church tower itself sway and then topple into the inferno below.

'The poor devils, the poor devils. I doubt they'll find enough pieces to be worth the burying.'

The note of pity in Sir William's voice was only too genuine. As a soldier he had seen often enough the devastation a single barrel of gunpowder could wreak when ignited by accident. He could only guess at the carnage resulting from a whole depot going up. A breath of warm wind reached their cheeks, and an acrid smell of charred wood and of something else. Alexander and Philip stood silent against the parapet, their eyes fixed in amazement on the burning ruins that had been the village, trying without success to imagine the horrors that lay beneath the dancing flames.

'Come gentlemen. Mr Carew, Mr Francis, I've had my fill of this for tonight. I'll leave the captain here for another hour with the telescope, and he will take note of any developments. I'm for my bed. A most satisfactory night's work.'

There was a tremor in Philip Francis's voice when he finally managed to speak.

'Sir William . . . it is difficult for me . . . I have, had . . . a married sister in Queen's Buckland. I wonder . . . do you think it possible . . .?'

He appeared to make a strong effort of will to control his fears.

'My wife . . . that's Lucy, my second wife . . . I asked her to prepare for us some good soup and a warm wine with brandy. Will you be my guests for an hour?'

Colonel Ruthin shook his head.

'My compliments to your wife, Mr Francis, but I must beg to be excused on this occasion. It's been two days and nights since I put my head down. You got your people to do a wonderful job with our ditch. I'll say good night to you now. Perhaps we should meet again tomorrow — I should say this afternoon, to be exact.'

Alexander watched him disappear down the ladder.

'That's a good man, Mr Francis,' he said quietly, 'We're lucky to have him.'

He looked out again at the line of flames that were still consuming the little village, and thought with shame of his naive eagerness to be charged with that awful task.

'He told me I should leave war to the soldiers, and I begin to understand what he meant. Come Mr Francis, I couldn't sleep now, that is certain. May I accept your kind hospitality?'

Philip Francis lived in a fine timbered house with an upper storey that jutted out, like its neighbours, into Plymouth's High Street. Alexander followed him closely in the dark as they picked their way through the noisome filth that covered the cobbles. Philip pushed the black iron-studded door that opened directly into a cosy, wainscoted parlour, lit only by a good fire of crackling logs that filled the room with dancing shadows.

'Lucy? Lucy my love, are you there?'

From the deep recesses of a huge padded leather chair a slim figure uncoiled quickly, like a startled cat. Lucy Francis was twenty, the daughter of one of Philip's oldest friends and political allies, Peter Keckwick. She wore a high-necked velvet dress of pale blue, cinched in at the waist with a yellow cord. Her tousled mop of fair hair was pushed back shyly from her forehead as she stood to greet her distinguished guest with a little curtsey. Alexander took her hand as she rose, and looked into her elfin face. Was it a trick of the firelight, or were those huge eyes really tawny yellow?

'I am very pleased to meet you, Lucy. Mr Francis tells me that your mulled wine and brandy are famous.'

Alexander's father was dead. That much at least was certain. There was the polished oak coffin with the wrought-iron handles, occupying its place of honour on the raised platform at the end of the Great Hall of Antony House. Above it was the big window that looked north onto his beloved orchards, and beyond them a glimpse of the Lynher river that flowed east into the Tamar, just a mile downstream. On that day, 10 April 1643, the early morning sun was still struggling to lighten the gloom of the cosy, now old-fashioned house the Carews had built a hundred years before. Already there had been half a dozen visitors, all tenants, come to pay a last respect to Sir Richard Carew, Baronet.

Alexander was the eldest son, sole heir to the title and the estates, but at that moment he was feeling that the situation had moved beyond all reasonable management. The hall echoed to his booted footsteps as he stalked restlessly down its flagstoned length and back to the dais, where he flung himself irritably into a carved chair, set beside the coffin. His hand moved over the coffin's new wood, feeling yet not feeling its polished smoothness, tension and indecision only too apparent.

'I really don't know what to do for the best.'

His words seemed to be addressed at large to some invisible audience that filled the hall before him, but Jane Carew decided to accept them as meant for her. She was thirty-five, a year older than her husband, small dark and pretty in a matronly way, where he was tall, fair, and remarkably good-looking. In the ten years of their marriage she had borne him nine children, seven of whom had survived, and was bringing them up in her sturdy, no-nonsense style that conflicted sometimes with Alexander's moody sensitivity.

'It's obvious to me that you should not have sent out the news of Sir Richard's death to all and sundry quite so soon. You must expect the county and the tenants to be anticipating a proper funeral.' She stood up from the seat at the other end of the coffin, and walked gracefully down the hall to warm herself by the fire that consumed a log as thick round as a man. 'It's still only April after all. Cool enough away from the fire too. He'll keep all right, won't he? Why not set a date for the funeral fourteen days from now? That will give time for our preparations and for the messengers to get around the county. There may well be some who'll want to come down from London and elsewhere though. Do you think we should allow four weeks? A month today say?'

Alexander exploded upright again, and slapped his hand on the coffin to relieve his temper.

'The county? London? Two weeks, a month? Dear Jane, don't you understand that we are in the middle of a war? I was eleven when grandfather died, and father led me every step of the way through the preparations for that funeral. I know what is expected, in the normal way of things. But things are anything but normal, as you must know.'

Jane had ample experience of her husband's moods, and sat quietly by the fire whilst he worked off a little of his bad temper pacing up and down the length of the hall again, his hands clasped behind his back, and his handsome chin thrust aggressively forward. Eventually he calmed down enough to stop by the fire to throw on another log, a final kick sending a shower of sparks glittering up into the wide chimney. It was apparent to Jane that he was coming to some sort of decision, and she kept patient silence as he stood at the mantelpiece above her, tracing with his index finger the carved outlines of three lions in the Carew coat of arms. At last he heaved a long sigh, and sat down opposite her.

'I'm sorry if I roared at you. These last few day . . . and then last night with our vicar . . .'

'I saw him arrive after supper, but then you closeted yourself with him in your study. You haven't told me yet what he had to say.'

'You were asleep when we finished, and I didn't want to wake you.'

Jane judged that the moment was right to show some sympathy. She took the cushion from her chair and sat curled up on the floor beside him, resting her dark head against his knee.

'Whatever it was, he shouldn't have worried you with it at a time like this. After all, we pay for him and his church. He owes you every support when you need it.'

Alexander ran his fingers through her thick dark curls. 'Jane is so sensible, so clear-thinking', he thought, 'if only life could be so uncomplicated!'

'I said as much to him last night. Not in so many words, of course. I mean, he has his pride you know. But I told him I was quite certain that my loyalty lay with Parliament. "Not that our quarrel is with the King himself", I said, "but rather with those wicked advisers, who have told him that he can and ought to rule in England in the same way that the French king rules in France, and the Spanish king rules in Spain. But England isn't France or Spain," I told him, "Englishmen are used to being consulted or persuaded, about taxes especially, not ordered about like naughty schoolchildren. What's more . . ." '

Jane shook her head free of his caressing hand, 'Now don't start going over all that again. It's not me you've got to persuade is it? Could you just tell me the conclusions of this discussion? If there was a conclusion?'

'Oh, there was a conclusion all right. A very definite one. But you're not going to like it much.' He reached for the poker and stirred the fire again, 'I asked his advice about father's funeral. You know Grandfather had that grand tomb in the church, and father always expected to go in there when the time came.'

'Of course he did. You're not suggesting . . .'

'I'm not suggesting anything. I'm just telling you what the vicar said. It's because of the war, you see.'

'But there's a truce, isn't there?'

'For how much longer? It's just a local agreement you know, and we've had weeks of it already. By the time a proper funeral could be arranged, the truce might be over. So how could I ask anyone to travel?'

'I see that, of course. We shouldn't even ask them to take the chance. So, let's make it a quiet family affair, just family and a few close friends, and the tenants from the estates if they want. That would certainly be fifty . . . perhaps a hundred even. That would be enough to give Sir Richard a proper send-off. We could arrange that for next week if we make a start today. I'll find your steward and tell him to begin.'

She stood up decisively, and kissed his cheek. But he sat quite still, staring into the leaping flames as though to divine the future.

'I'm afraid it's not going to be as easy as that.' He sensed that Jane was beginning to boil with impatience at his lack of action, but kept his tone very calm, 'Sit down again, Jane. Please?'

She obeyed, and sat down, this time back in the big oak chair on the other side of the fireplace.

'The vicar spoke at length about his decision to support the King, "The Lord's Anointed", and of his most profound regrets if this should set him in opposition to the Carews. "Your father was my dearest friend for forty years," he said, "and it grieves me more than I can say that I may inconvenience you and your family at this difficult time." '

'Inconvenience. There's a fine word. Is he saying that he won't bury Sir Richard?'

'Not in so many words, no. In fact I'm sure he will do whatever we decide.'

'I should think so.'

'But he is advising most strongly against anything in the nature of formal funeral celebrations along the lines we've considered.'

'Advising? Against? Does that mean threatening? It certainly sounds like it. Alexander, you're head of the Carew family now, and they've possessed these estates for two hundred years. The Edgcumbes are just a few miles away. Sir Peter is your oldest friend. I know he's for the King, but he'll stand by you to bury Sir Richard properly. So what should you fear?'

'Insult. Riot, perhaps, even injury or murder.'

'Really, Alexander, I think you exaggerate the danger. The people around here are our people or Sir Peter's. Your father went among them as a friend all his life, and his father was Cornwall's greatest benefactor. They're not going to start a riot at his funeral!'

'Some of them might. Because of the Ordinance.'

'What Ordinance?'

'There was an Ordinance, in Parliament last month, to empower Commissioners "to seize and sell off for the benefit of the Cause" the lands and property of "Notorious Delinquents", which means in practice anyone opposed to Parliament.'

'But nobody's doing that around these parts'

'Indeed not, because father and I were named as the Commissioners.'

Jane opened her mouth to speak, but no words came out. At a stroke those idiots in Parliament had destroyed the relationship of trust and friendship that the Carews had built up over centuries with the tenants and electors. And for what advantage?

'You never said anything about this Ordinance before. When did you know about it?'

'Last week, when I was still in Plymouth. The ship *Bonaventure* came in from London, and Captain Thomas gave me the private letters of appointment for father and myself. Then your man arrived with the news that father was ill, and I forgot all about it.'

Jane had recovered now from the cold shock, and her practical brain began working.

'But Alexander, you know it can't be enforced in these parts. Parliament's writ doesn't run half a mile beyond the gates of Plymouth. Only last autumn you came down from Parliament with the writ to "Raise the Militia". And what did you do with that?'

'I read it out in the Council Chamber to the Mayor and Council.'

'With what effect?'

'Outside of Plymouth itself, no effect at all.'

'Exactly. You didn't try to enlist the tenants then, did you?'

'No, but . . .'

'Nor will you try to dispossess them now.'

'Of course not.'

'So, where's the problem? It was a private letter to poor Sir Richard and yourself, and in the circumstances of the truce you have simply decided to postpone any action, in order to preserve the peace.'

Alexander fixed his eyes on the leaping flames of the fire. There was a long silence before he spoke, and then it was without raising his gaze to his wife.

'I'm sorry, Jane, but I think the risk is too great. The Letter of Commission itself was sealed, but the appointments were announced in London, and Captain Thomas said it was common knowledge there. The vicar knows too, and God knows how many others of the people around here.'

'And is he intending to lead them to oppose you?'

'I rather doubt that he will be a leader. He is an old man, and just longs for a quiet end to his life. But he says he has consulted his conscience, and believes it can not be right to go against the King with force of arms. King Charles raised

his banner at Nottingham last year, and those who stand
against him are simply traitors, in the vicar's opinion. And he
said he was telling our people just that.'

'From our pulpit?'

'No, he told me he would not do that. "In God's church,"
he said, "I will confine myself to interpreting God's word."
But outside the church he is his own man, and will speak
accordingly.'

'And the funeral?'

'He . . .'

Alexander's reply was interrupted by a rattle at the great
door behind them, and the entry of a visitor. Alexander was
glad to escape his wife's challenges for a few minutes.

'William! It's good to see you here! Jane, you know Will
Plumley, of course.'

'Of course. You were here only last New Year, with
Elizabeth. How is she? And the children? Come over by the
fire and warm yourself, the wind's so cold still isn't it? Will
you take a cup of ale? And I have some cakes still warm from
the oven too.'

Will Plumley was a solid, square-faced man with black
curly hair and a pointed beard. He was a year younger than
Alexander, but his quiet, restrained manner gave him a
natural authority that made him seem the elder. The Plumleys
had been tenants of their three hundred acres around Antony
for a hundred years before the Carews first came into
possession of the estates by a fortunate marriage into the
Courtenay family. As children, Will and Alexander had
played together, as young men they had hawked, hunted and
fished together. But when the time had come for Alexander
to go up to Oxford to be educated, and later to go into the
Inns of Court in London to study the law, Will had stayed
behind to become totally absorbed in improving the yields
from his family tenancy. He noted with quiet approval that
the Carew family portraits had already been covered to mark
the mourning, and accepted a place by the fire from
Alexander, who dragged up another chair for himself.

'I must learn to call you "Sir Alexander" and "Lady Carew" now, mustn't I?'

Alexander shrugged his shoulders, 'Only in company, Will, only in company. Between ourselves we can be plain Alex and Will. Nothing's changed, not really.'

Will looked quizzically at Alexander, then introduced a safer topic.

'Do you remember, last September I think it was, us talking about a plan to change the three-field system?'

'You mean about not leaving one third fallow in rotation? Father was much against, I remember. He said "a field needs its rest, just like a man on the Sabbath." But you've given it a try?'

'Indeed I have. Sir Richard was widely-known to be the best man in the kingdom with apple trees. But he was honest enough to admit that, when it came to fields and farming, his opinions were based on tradition rather than experience and science. So he allowed me to make my trial.'

'And do you have a result?'

'Of a sort, yes. I took Sir Richard's advice, and planted up just ten acres of this year's fallow. I ploughed it, and set a crop of those turnips, to be feed for the animals when the hay is finished and the new grass is not yet ready.'

'Has it worked?'

'Very well, so far. We've a fine new crop from land that would only have produced thistles and very rough pasture if we'd left it. Of course the danger may be that the land becomes tired with constant producing, and what we've gained with this year's turnips we lose from next year's wheat. So I think I should stay with just the ten acres for at least a couple of years, and keep a careful record. There's the benefit to the feeding of the cattle to be reckoned in too. It might be five or even ten years before we could be definite one way or t'other.'

Five years! Ten years! Alexander was filled with envy of Will's ability to focus on his land with that kind of intensity. Sir Richard had been like that with his trees, as a visitation from old King James himself had affirmed. Alexander felt more akin to his grandfather, who had been a restless, many-talented man of business, scholar, historian and even poet. As they talked he and Will made their way to the dais at the north end, where Sir Richard's coffin rested on a simple table that was covered in a black cloth. Tall candles burned at each end, their light now almost extinguished by the brilliant spring sunshine that illuminated the scene. Will knelt by the coffin, and pressed his hands together in silent prayer. After a minute he rose.

'Have you fixed the day yet for the funeral?'

Alexander glanced back down the hall. Jane had discreetly withdrawn, and there was no one to overhear. A thud and crackle punctuated the silence as one of the logs burned through. He decided to take Will into his confidence, and told him what the vicar had said. 'So you see how difficult it could be, Will. What would be your advice?'

Will stood with a hand resting on the coffin, as though to take an oath, and paused for what seemed an age before answering.

'We've been close for thirty years now, haven't we Alex? And the Carews have always been straight with us. I remember my grandfather telling me that in Queen Bess's time some of her clever lawyers tried to change the rights of the freeholders and leaseholders of Cornwall, to make more money for the Crown. And your grandfather, old Richard Carew, led the deputation from the county. He it was that wrote the petition that persauded the Queen to call off her hounds. All Cornwall owes the Carews a debt of honour for the stand he made, and I say that I'll walk behind your father's coffin whatever the vicar, or anyone else says. And God help anyone who tries to interfere.'

'So, should we invite the neighbours and tenants to the house here, and walk the mile together to Antony church with Father?'

By now Will was seated by the fire again with his legs well spread, sipping the cup of strong ale and nibbling on one of

Jane's cakes. Alexander stood anxious and ill at ease before him, and the casual visitor could easily have come to the wrong conclusion as to which was landlord and which tenant.

'My congratulations to Jane. Or was it the cook that baked these? I'm sorry, Alex, I've not been thinking straight. You want of course to give your father a proper send-off, in the Carew tradition. So the question is, can we trust people to behave themselves? On the whole, I'd think we can. We're not very political around here, not unless something annoys us that is. All mixed up really. I mean, I'm for the King I suppose, but I'm damned if I want to go to war for him against you or our friends in Plymouth. But I'm a bit of a Puritan as far as religion is concerned, so I'm against the vicar and the King too for that. The vicar says we should obey the King, but I've heard him say himself that the Members of Parliament like yourself and Sir Richard here should be the ones to decide what taxes the King can have. Mind you, there are some hotheads around. I can think of half a dozen straight away that rode off to Bodmin as soon as the harvest was in, and enlisted for the King. And if they've had a few of them killed in the fighting, they might not be in a friendly mood. With the truce holding up they'll be home now . . . Aye, there could be trouble there . . .'

He took a final pull from his cup, and stood up.

'Well, Sir Alexander, I thank you and Lady Carew for your most gracious hospitality.'

Alexander made a mock bow in response, and opened the Hall door for his guest.

'Seriously now, Will, what would you advise?'

'Seriously Alex, I suggest you put off deciding. Wait two weeks, no a month. If the truce still holds then, even the most bigoted will be cooling off, and I think you could safely plan the full ceremony, and lay to rest Sir Richard with his father, as is proper for a Carew.'

They embraced on the steps, and Alexander was pleased to see his groom appear promptly with Will's black mare.

Wait? A month? He knew that plans were already being made to take the King's army by surprise in two weeks' time. He shivered in the cold April wind, and turned back inside the house.

Two days later the small clinker-built sailing craft *Juliana* was launched into the Lynher River from the beach beneath Antony's famous orchards, and the brisk westerly breeze filled her sail to carry her on a run downstream towards the Tamar. Seated in the stern, Sir Alexander Carew handled the tiller nervously, and deferred to the experience of his steward, Walter Goodman. In the bow, Walter's thirteen year- old son Peter trailed his fingers in the cool green water, and kept look-out.

'We're coming up to the Tamar now, Walter,' said Alexander.

'Aye-aye, sir. That's Saltash up to the left, sir. You want to keep on well over to that far bank of the Tamar before we turns, sir. Tide's running out fast, and right foolish we'd look if we got *Juliana* aground on one of them shoals.'

Alexander duly waited until they were almost onto the east bank of the Tamar before gybing the boat ninety degrees onto a southerly course, down river. Walter ducked quickly under the boom as it came over and shifted himself to the starboard side to balance the wind's press. The *Juliana* accelerated on a broad reach, foaming water rattling past the gunwales. Alexander moved onto the curved bench alongside Walter with the morning sun full on his face, and warm now.

'This is the life, isn't it, Walter? Who'd be a farmer when you can get afloat?'

'Indeed sir, very nice today. Not so nice when you've got to go out fishing and the sea's freezin' your fingers to the rigging, and the storm's blowin'up fit to lay you flat in the water.'

Alexander kept close to the wooded lee shore where the deep channel ran, and sailed down the Tamar towards Torpoint, where they would turn east again for an easy run into Plymouth.

'Walter, I wonder if you know how many of our people went off to enlist for the King in Sir Ralph Hopton's army?'

Walter was silent for a minute, apparently paying attention to the trim of the sail.

'If you was to let the mainsheet out a bit, sir, we'd be a sight more comfortable. Enlisted for the King? Not many of our people, as I recall. Young Jamie Bridpole went off from Home Farm, and I suppose I've 'eard of another six or seven daft buggers like 'im from amongst the tenants. Just boys for the most part, out for a bit of excitement after the 'arvest. I can do without that sort of excitement m'self sir, and I've told young Peter 'ere that 'ed feel the weight of my 'and if 'e as much as talked to any of 'em.'

'What about amongst the freeholders?'

' 'Fraid I couldn't say with much certainty, sir. But I know Sir Peter Edgcumbe 'as been encouraging his people to volunteer. I did 'ear that they 'ad a bit of a parade, two or three weeks back, when the enlisted men came 'ome for the truce. Fifty or sixty men in the muster I 'eard, and they're to turn out again next Sunday.'

'Fifty or sixty. So many?'

Alexander's voice was soft, as though he were speaking to himself. He concentrated on managing the boat through the Cremyll Passage, the turn to the left where the Tamar narrows as it meets the broad sparkling waters of Plymouth Sound. On their starboard bow now sat St Nicholas Island, dark and squat against the sun. Walter followed the direction of Alexander's gaze.

'That's an 'eavy load they laid on you when they give you the island, sir. We always say it's like a cork in the mouth of the Sound. If the enemy gets it, Plymouth is done for.'

Alexander shaded his eyes. 'I can see a sentry parading on the wall, so they're keeping a good watch, thank the Lord.'

He could make out now the black mouth of one of his culverins, run out and ready. It could hurl a sixteen-pound ball to smash any ship that tried to get at Plymouth. Ahead and to the left of *Juliana*'s bow he could just see the tower of his fort at Fisher's Point, on the south-east corner of Plymouth Hoe itself. Walter was right, between fort and island he had the safety of Plymouth in his hands.

Alexander handed over the tiller to Walter, who threaded his way expertly through the crowd of ships, both anchored and under way, in Plymouth's Sutton Pool. It was almost low water as they bumped alongside Town Steps, and Peter took the painter in hand as he jumped out onto the bottom step, still wet and slimy with weed.

'Mind 'ow you go, sir, it's very slippy.'

Alexander wore a broad-brimmed black hat now, black trousers tucked into high boots, and a favourite long doeskin jerkin dyed black for the mourning. His arrival was noted by a good number of interested people on the quay and on the ships.

'You've got the list of purchases Lady Carew made out? Pledge my credit where you can, Walter, we must conserve our cash. I'll be staying over two nights, so send young Peter up to the Castle for me at this time the day after tomorrow.'

He climbed carefully up the stone steps. Peter followed a discreet distance in the rear, carrying Alexander's box on his left shoulder with a certain amount of pride. At the top they turned left along the Hard towards Plymouth Castle. Alexander felt his spirits lift again as he surveyed the bustling scene. To seaward, the Sutton Pool was full of masts as merchants made every possible use of the uncertain truce. Prominent at the southern end he noted Captain Thomas' *Bonaventure*, with two wherries alongside, and great barrels being hoisted high by a yardarm and swung into her. Salted pilchards and mackerel probably, bound for London. She would leave on tomorrow afternoon's high tide, and the captain would carry with him to Parliament the assessment of Plymouth's position, and their immediate plans for resuming the war.

In the years immediately following the defeat of Spain's first Armada, the coasts of both Devon and Cornwall had suffered from the attacks of Spanish raiders, based in Brittany, much as Spain's colonies in the Americas had been pillaged by English privateers. Both Penzance and Newlyn had been sacked during those bad times. When Alexander's grandfather, old Richard Carew, had prepared his famous petition to Queen Elizabeth, he had made much of the fact that 'these attacks', from both Spanish fleets and Arab slave-traders in unholy alliance, were likely to weaken seriously, if not destroy altogether, the West Country's principal contribution to Her Majesty's wealth and security – her 'fighting seamen'. So Plymouth's fortifications had to be strengthened. King Henry's Castle, at the south-east corner of the town, had been doubled in size and provided with cannon, and this was Alexander's destination. Tall black warehouses and poles strung with nets came right down to the edge of the Hard, and the morning air was heavy with the odour of fish. Alexander doffed his hat six or seven times in a hundred yards to acknowledge respectful greetings. He warmed to the thought that these were his people, just as much as the tenants on his lands. They had looked to him for political judgement and support, as their Member of Parliament, and now they depended on him to protect the town and keep open its lifeline to the sea. He would not let them down!

His boots thumped across the drawbridge and the Captain of the Guard turned out in person.

'Good morning, Sir Alexander, I trust you had a pleasant journey to us this morning? The others are here already. I'm sure you know the way to the Commander's quarters. I'll see your box is taken to your room, sir, and make sure there's a good fire kept in.'

Alexander made his way into the dark winding staircase

that led past the guards' quarters and up into the Gatehouse
Tower, where the Garrison Commander, Colonel Sir William
Ruthin had his rooms. He rose and welcomed Alexander
warmly.

'Come in, come in. You are the last, but only just.'

He spoke in a soft, Lowland Scots accent. In his late forties
now, his red hair was beginning to fade into grey, and the
deep crinkles around his eyes were evidence of years in the
open air. He was a professional soldier, with a lifetime's
experience in the army, most recently in Ireland.

'I believe you know the other members of our Committee
well enough?

Philip Francis had been Mayor of Plymouth for three
months now. His predecessor, Thomas Ceely, had been noted
for his adherence to the King and to the old religion. Philip
had replaced him, thanks to the support of Plymouth's strong
Parliamentarian and Protestant majority. He was a stocky
barrel of a man in his early fifties, running now to fat. His
swarthy complexion and fierce beak of a nose suggested that
there might be some truth in the old slander that there was
Spanish blood amongst his ancestors, indeed he was
commonly referred to as 'Don Philippo' behind his back. He
pushed back a lock of dark curly hair as he rose.

'Sir Alexander, I welcome your presence at our little
council of war. I was distressed to hear of the death of Sir
Richard. A good man, a most honourable man. My wife
asked me to convey my condolences to yourself, and also to
Lady Carew, the poor widow. How is she, by the way?'

'Bearing up quite well, I believe. At my suggestion she has
taken advantage of the truce to visit her family at Heanton
Satchville. Nowhere is truly safe of course, but that corner of
North Devon may be less disturbed by the troubles.'

Alexander did not wish to be impolite to the town's mayor,
but his attention had been captured by the second guest.

'Don't you know me, Alex?'

The big man pushed his chair aside as he rose. His head
almost touched the blackened beam in the ceiling, and he held

out huge hands with a broad smile. Bright blue eyes, pink
cheeks, fair hair that fell in waves to touch the broad
shoulders clad in a black leather jacket, with lace at the throat
and silver buttons down the front . . . Alexander screwed up
his eyes in disbelief.

'It's James, isn't it, little Jamie Chudleigh?'

'Not so little now, as you see. It was your wedding day
when we last met. Ten years ago? I was only fifteen and very
quiet.'

'And very small and very skinny, I remember. Whatever
they've fed you on since, I'd like the recipe to fatten my
bullocks!'

Sir William reached up to put a hand on each of their
shoulders.

'Gentlemen, we should make a start, please. There is wine,
by courtesy of Mr Francis, and cold beef on the table to
sustain us. Major-General Chudleigh, would you take the
position of honour on that side with Sir Alexander? Mr
Francis and I will each take an end.'

He opened the door to check that his sentry was at his post
at the top of the staircase.

'No one is to approach this door without my permission,
sentry. That includes yourself. If you need to approach, shout
first and wait for me to come to the door.'

He closed the solid oak door behind him. It was a pleasant,
airy room over the main gate of Plymouth Castle. On two
sides mullioned windows looked out over the ramparts and
the blue waters of Plymouth Sound. The plastered walls had
been newly whitewashed, and there was a plaited rush mat in
front of the fire.

Alexander and James were first cousins – James' father, Sir
George Chudleigh, was the brother of Alexander's mother,
Bridget. She had died when Alexander was just two, leaving
him to be brought up with three older sisters and one
younger. They gossiped over the beef and wine about their
families and mutual friends. After two cups of wine
Alexander grew playful.

'Mr Francis, you're a great man for Parliament I know, but were you aware that the General here can claim kinship with the great John Pym himself? There's a challenge for you, James. Can you make the connection?'

'Of course I can. Father taught me the whole family tree, years ago. Let's see now ... it's not exactly a blood relationship though ... our great leader, John Pym, is the son of Philippa Pym. She was widowed early, and married again to Antony Rous of Halton, that's near Saltash here. His first wife Elizabeth had been a Southcote from Bovey Tracy, and she was the sister of Mary Southcote. And Mary was also my grandmother, on my mother's side. How's that!'

He sat back in his chair and laughed in triumph. Alexander joined in.

'There's more connections. My father told me that his father, old Richard Carew, was a close friend of Antony Rous, and he often met young John Pym at Halton. So you see we Parliamentarians are all one big happy family!'

'No doubt the King's men say much the same for their side,' Sir William interjected drily. 'Shall we get down to business?'

He unfolded a map on the table.

'Unfortunately, Mr Saxton omitted to draw in the roads when he produced his map, probably because he didn't know where they were. But this is the best we have for now. Mr Hollar's scale is here at the bottom, five miles to the inch. What would you expect for an army, General, two or three inches a day?'

James immediately became serious. A career soldier, like Sir William, James had performed brilliantly with the royal army in Ireland, and had earned spectacular promotion for his leadership and skill.

'Ten, perhaps fifteen miles a day? Depends on the terrain, the victuals, the cannon of course, but that's a reasonable day's march. So tell me, Sir William, where are we likely to find Hopton's army?'

Alexander intervened. 'Is it settled then? The truce is to be broken? Those are your orders?'

James sat back in silence and looked around the table, not wanting to reply directly to Alexander's questioning. Sir William kept his eyes down, so James turned the other way, to Philip Francis, who was only too keen to respond.

'I wouldn't call our plan "breaking the truce", Sir Alexander. My understanding is that it was only to be forty days from the middle of March. You must have heard the same reports I have, of Hopton moving troops in small numbers, by night. Surely he is getting ready to strike at us again next week, when the forty days will be up, and this fine drying weather lets him bring down those cannon.'

There was no mistaking the passion in his voice as he continued, with beads of sweat breaking out on his dark forehead.

'I say we should attack Hopton and his Cornish army before he gets stronger. Plymouth is surrounded by enemies, and my people would rather get out and fight than stand a siege. Don't forget Hopton still has the forty cannon Sir William had to abandon at Saltash. Mind you, I'm not criticising Sir William here. He and his men fought bravely enough against the odds. I just want you to understand that our citizens will not take kindly to being pounded by our own guns. Attack is the better option, in my opinion.'

He bared his teeth in a little grin that revealed his nervousness, and mopped his brow. Alexander accepted the inevitable, sick at heart at the thought of his still unburied father, and of the fury of war that would soon be ravaging through the quiet lands of Antony.

'I did not mean to oppose either the citizens of Plymouth or the General here. Of course not. But I have had no direct instructions from the Committee for Public Safety at Westminster that the negotiations with the King are at an end. Might we not be seen as endangering that process if we attack the Royalists so precipitately?'

'Quite the opposite, I would say,' said James, with a calm authority. 'Our Commander for the West, the Earl of Stamford, was severely criticised from London when they

heard of our truce, and he is under no doubts whatsoever
about his instructions for action next week. I do not pretend
to be a master of high strategy, but I rather doubt if Hopton's
preparations are for an attack on Plymouth, Mr Francis.
More likely he is hoping we will leave him alone to assemble
a greater army to march east for the King, perhaps for an
attack on Bristol. What a prize that would be! It is clear that
the King is still under the control of those evil advisers, who
have encouraged him to pretend to seek peace during the
winter, while at the same time we know that the Queen is
across the water, seeking to raise money and mercenaries to
fight for him. My orders are to interrupt and delay the
movement of troops from Cornwall.'

Despite his personal misgivings, Alexander was impressed
by the importance of James' mission.

'I can see that your command has a task of some
significance in the scheme of things. Will the Earl move with
his whole army to assist your attack? We have heard that
Hopton has some three thousand men assembling at
Launceston. The Earl's army is much bigger, isn't it?'

'Twice as big, but he is not ready to move yet from Exeter.
In fact he is ill himself, which is why I have come on ahead
to Plymouth. He suggested that, if you all agree, I should take
half the garrison, and attack Hopton on 23 April if possible.'

Philip was on his feet in an instant

'Half the garrison? Take them all, General, take them all!
We have our walls, we have the outer ring of ditch and bank
now completed. As long as you are engaging the King's army,
they cannot come at us with the cannon, so what have we to
fear? Sir Alexander's fort and the island protect us from the
sea, and we have replenished our stores of food and
ammunition. Let us strike with our strongest force at these
Cornish invaders and drive them back where they belong!'

Colonel Ruthin introduced a note of calm common sense
into the fervour.

'With respect, Mr Francis, I fear you may not fully
appreciate the problems of moving troops. The winter has

been very long, and very wet. In fact these last few days have been the first dry spell since Christmas, as I recall. The only road, if you can call it that, from Plymouth up to Launceston follows the valley of the Tamar, and is mostly a sunken lane, running with mud. To attempt it with our whole garrison of three thousand men could be a total disaster. I know, because I've campaigned in these parts since October, and as you reminded us, it's only too easy to come to grief.'

James agreed to take all five hundred dragoons and a thousand of the best infantry. The troops would be moved out of the city in small groups on the morning of 22 April, as though to occupy the ditch and bank fortification that had been thrown up in February, but not yet manned. There they would be rested for the day, to march after dark the twelve miles to Tavistock before pausing again for a few hours, intending to attack Launceston, ten miles farther on, the next day.

'Our objective is to disrupt his preparations and capture or destroy his supplies. With any luck it should be all over in an hour.'

Privately Alexander thought that there were plenty of opportunities for the scheme to go wrong, but having no military experience he said nothing.

He spent the afternoon visiting his Deputy Commander at the Fort, right on the sea beside the entrance to Sutton Pool, Plymouth's main anchorage. On the following day Sir William lent him a gig manned by four tough sailors to row him the half mile out to St. Nicholas Island. Both his deputies seemed to Alexander to be keen and competent, though both complained of being bored with the inactivity. He took this seriously, and encouraged them to develop a rota whereby the garrisons of fort and island could exchange duties, week in and week out, allowing the fort garrison to sleep in the town for a few nights, and join in the practice drills also.

One question was asked everywhere, 'Will the truce be renewed, Sir Alexander?'

Alexander longed to be able to share the burden, but

replied, 'I hope so. Like every sensible Englishman I pray for peace. I heard only today that the King and our Parliament are still in negotiation, so we may hope for the best.'

'I wait not at the lawyer's gates,
Nor shoulder climbers down the stairs.
I vaunt not manhood by debates,
I envy not the miser's fears.
But, mean in state and calm in sprite,
My fish-full pond is my delight.'

Alexander pushed back the chair from his dinner table with a small sigh.

'My grandfather wrote those words. He was a great man. Have you read his "Survey of Cornwall"? I know most of it by heart. He travelled all over, and loved Cornwall and its people. How can they come out against us?'

Antony House was tucked into the peninsula of Torpoint, which also contained Edgcumbe House, the home of Alexander's friend Sir Peter. The Carews' lands were in the County of Cornwall, but because of the proximity of Plymouth just across the Tamar, their natural connections and loyalties were to Devon. Having discussed the tactical situation with James Chudleigh, Alexander had concluded that, as long as Plymouth was not taken, Antony would probably not be threatened by anything more than the occasional cattle raid by a foraging party. On the other hand it had become clear that troops coming up from Cornwall to join the King at Oxford would naturally march north of Dartmoor. So the family home of the Rolles at Heanton Satchville was now squarely in the path of danger. He had sent a rider from Plymouth with a letter strongly urging Lady Carew, his stepmother, to return to Antony, and Grace had arrived at midday accompanied by her two brothers, Henry and John Rolle, who were both also Members of Parliament. Eleven years after Alexander's mother, Bridget Chudleigh had died giving birth to his sister, his father had married Grace Rolle. Alexander was thirteen, and Grace only four years older. The twenty years of her marriage seemed to have treated her harshly, and although she was so close in age to Alexander she seemed already to be bowing into middle-age. His wife, Jane, was Grace's sister, younger by only three years, but she appeared positively young by comparison. Alexander wondered idly if there might be some connection with the fact that Jane had given him children almost every year, whereas Grace had given Sir Richard four sons in the first five years, then no more. Grace's temper, never very genial, had been positively waspish over dinner, and it was obvious that she took the delay in arranging her husband's funeral very badly. It was Grace who took it upon herself to reply to Alexander's question.

'Of course they loved your grandfather. They loved my poor Richard too, and no doubt you could be loved as well. If you were to ride around Torpoint by yourself now I dare say none will raise a hand against you, or even speak ill of you behind your back. But this isn't where Sir Ralph Hopton has raised his army, is it? He's gone around collecting the dregs of Penzance and Falmouth, Newlyn, Newquay and Bodmin. There they don't speak English, do they? They cling to their old Popish ways like children scuttle into their mothers' skirts, and they'll kill anyone who tries to change them. Wasn't it in Queen Bess' time that they had to send in the army, and hang a few of them, vicars and all, because they wouldn't give up the Latin Mass and follow the Prayer Book?'

'The young King Edward's, I believe.'

'There you are then, still less than a hundred years ago. They're foreigners really, as foreign as the Welsh or the Irish, and that's where Hopton has got his troops. More like beasts than men, I shouldn't wonder.'

Alexander recalled how difficult it had been when he had

first told his father that he wanted to marry Grace's sister. But Jane and he were of an age, and their marriage had been good. It had been his father who had been the unusual one, taking so young a second wife, and starting a second family in his forties. His father had been scrupulously even-handed between Alexander and his four sisters on the one side, and Grace's four sons on the other, and Alexander had told Grace that nothing would change. John, the eldest of her sons, was completing the traditional Carew education in one of the London Inns of Court, and by all reports was an active Parliamentarian, one of those who took an extreme position favouring the abolition of the Monarchy. Alexander called to mind the history of the Greek and Roman republics that he had studied so diligently at Oxford. Had they set their feet now on the road that led inevitably to the destruction of all the old forms, then to the mob-rule that Plato had so abhorred, and back again to a Tyranny? His reverie was interrupted by a movement on the other side of the table as Henry Rolle helped himself to another glass of wine from the silver jug.

'Come on now, Alex, surely you can tell us a bit more about why it was so important for Grace to return to Antony this week? Is the war to be renewed?'

Henry and John Rolle could have been twins, so alike were they. Henry was a year the elder, and ten years older than Alexander. Both were short, burly Devon men, with their fair hair close-cropped, and sporting small, pointed beards. Like everyone else at the table, they wore black out of respect for Sir Richard Carew. Alexander thought for a moment, to be sure he had the day right, then said.

'I dared not say more in my letter to Grace, for fear that it might fall into Royalist hands and be the cause of the deaths of many good men.' He paused for a few seconds 'This morning my cousin, General James Chudleigh led his troops out of Plymouth, and they will attack Hopton at Launceston tomorrow. If they are successful they could cripple and scatter the Cornish, allowing time for the Earl of Stamford to bring up the main force from Exeter and complete their destruction. In two or three weeks Plymouth could be safe, and Antony with it of course.' There was no mistaking the fervour in his voice, 'On the other hand when I was looking at the General's map I realised that I had sent Grace home to Heanton, only twenty miles from Launceston, and I feared for her safety there if the attack were not completely successful. So I sent my letter to Grace, and I thank God that she understood my meaning enough to come, and that you were able to escort her. By the way, how is my sister Mary? Could she not have come to Antony with Grace, as I suggested?'

Mary was two years older than Alexander, and was married to the eldest Rolle brother, Samuel.

'Mary is well, but seven months gone with child, so she could not possibly travel. I wouldn't have expected her to leave Sam at such a time anyway, and of course his place is beside Father. But can we talk some more about the war? It's a bad business, breaking the truce, don't you agree?'

John was quick to correct his brother, 'It isn't breaking the truce, is it Alex? Today is the last day of the agreed forty days.'

'It is, and I'll warrant there are a good few of the militia on both sides who've rejoined having done the same as ourselves, ploughed a field when the rain let up and sown some wheat this past week.'

'On the hill slopes perhaps. Our valley is still very wet . . .'

Jane interrupted with a polite cough, 'I hesitate to disrupt this flow of men's talk, but before you get down to the weather there are one or two urgent matters to be decided, if you will oblige?'

The smile on Jane's face lifted Alexander's mood, 'Dear Jane, always with her hands on the essentials. Do go on my love.'

'Thank you, Alex. First question; can we assume that, having heard about the war starting up again, Henry and John will stay at Antony until we have news that it is safe to ride back?'

'Of course. I . . .'

'Definitely not.' Henry's rejection of the invitation cut in sharply, 'I'm sorry to have to leave you, Alex. You and Jane have been good hosts today. But with the war getting close to Heanton, my place and John's is back there, as soon as possible.'

The early evening sun was shining full through the long west window of the family dining chamber, which opened off the Great Hall where Sir Richard lay. With his back to it, Alexander's face was in deep shadow, so that only Jane could recognise his disappointment. He had hoped that Henry and John might have contributed greatly to the protection of Antony and his family from wandering pillagers.

'I can understand how you must be feeling, so I will not argue with you. We have a big wherry which could take you and the horses a good way up the Tamar on the rising tide tomorrow morning. You should get round Tavistock before midday, and clear Okehampton in the afternoon. I'll see you're well-provisioned and draw you a bit of a map that should keep you away from any fighting at Launceston, and get you home to Heanton by dark.'

Henry and John Rolle retired early to bed as soon as the preparations for their departure at dawn were in place. Grace kissed them tearfully.

'I thank you both for bringing me safely back to Antony. I pray God that you get through to Heanton tomorrow. I have this awful foreboding that we may not meet again this side of Heaven's gate.'

It was obvious that she was almost fainting with fatigue after the rigours of two days on horseback, but she insisted on joining Alexander and Jane upstairs in the parlour, where the candles were reflected now from the polished wainscoting, and a warm fire crackled. The thick red damask curtains had been drawn, and Grace sank down with a sigh into her favourite chair of green padded leather on the left of the fireplace.

'Before I put my head down I want to hear from you,

Alexander. What do you intend for your father's funeral? I had expected that the invitations would have been out by now, but no message had come by the time I left Heanton.'

Alexander sensed the unspoken criticism. He stood in front of the fire.

'These are not normal times, Grace, and we must adjust to them as best we may. I remember last year while I was still at Westminster, Father wrote to me with some advice. "We have need always in all our actions, both great and small, to use all the foresight and circumspection our understanding can provide, so that we avoid every kind of danger. We are duty-bound to preserve ourselves if we can." '

Grace looked up at him with mild disapproval. 'Sir Richard was a man of principle, but some of his principles were open to question, and that sounds like one of the less heroic kind. Anyway what does it have to do with a funeral?'

Alexander explained the vicar's caution, and quoted Will Plumley's advice to delay.

'Nothing has happened since to improve the situation, Grace. Of course if the Royal army is soundly defeated tomorrow at Launceston, then Plymouth will be safe, and Antony will be safe. We could invite everyone to a proper ceremony in Father's honour. But if we are defeated, Plymouth could fall, and we could well lose Antony itself.'

Jane stood up in alarm from her chair on the other side of the fireplace.

'For Heaven's sake, Alex, surely that's not a possibility? You are wicked to frighten us all like that. You've only done your duty. Why should you expect to be singled out for punishment?'

Alexander stood between them, gazing fixedly into the leaping flames as though he divined some vision of the future there.

'Plenty of reasons. Strafford for one; if you remember, two years ago we decided to get rid of one of the worst of the King's advisers, the Earl of Strafford. I was one of the leading speakers against him, and put my name gladly to the Bill of

Attainder that resulted in his execution. I heard that the King grieved mightily that he could not save him, and kings have long memories for things like that.'

Jane stood beside Grace, an arm about her shoulder.

'I had no idea the danger was so personal. It's . . . so near to us all . . . it's truly terrifying, Alex. Is there no way you could become less exposed, less visible? Look at Sir Peter Edgcumbe, for example. He's known to be for the King in a general way, but he's not playing any active part. If our side wins, I can't see him being greatly penalised.'

'You don't think so? Nonetheless, if I had the power to carry out that Ordinance I told you about, Peter's estates would be high on the list of those to be seized and sold off to pay the expenses of the army. And you can be sure that he knows that.'

Grace stood up, 'I'm for my bed. No doubt we can wait a few more days to decide about the funeral, and I trust you to do what's right, Alexander.'

The worries of the day seemed to be shut out by the thick, dark blue curtains around the bed, and Jane Carew fancied that the embroidered deer and lions had a life of their own in the flickering light of the two candles above her head.

A few months earlier Jane had felt that baby Thomas ought to be her last, and had cautiously asked Grace for advice. Grace had given Sir Richard four sons in quick succession, but there had been no more children in fifteen years. 'Was this perhaps a decision of Sir Richard himself?'

Grace had laughed, 'Oh no, nothing like that. Sir Richard was always loving and affectionate, until his health began to fail at the end. Very affectionate indeed sometimes! But Alexander had his four sisters, and I'd had our four sons, and when my fourth was born it went hard with me, and afterwards Sir Richard asked me straight, "Did I know of a way that might limit our family, and yet be acceptable to the Lord?" '

'And did you?'

'Not at the time, no. I'd heard stories of devices and methods they used up in London, but I didn't know anything specific, and anyway I doubted if Sir Richard could square his conscience for anything like that. So I didn't know what to do. Of course I was still nursing and sleeping with the new baby, but I couldn't see things going on like that for much longer.'

'So what did you do?'

'Did you ever meet Goodie Wallgrave?'

'Never. I've heard tell of her of course.'

'Just about that time I heard she was down in the village. Sir Richard would have nothing to do with her, "In my father's time they would have stoned her as a witch." he said, but I told him there was no harm in having my fortune told, and he let me go down to her.'

Here Grace had decided to pause for effect, and to tease her younger sister.

'Oh please go on, Grace, this is so important to me.'

'She was wonderful. I can hear her croak now. She told me I would outlive our new King Charles, but that I would never see his successor on the throne. I've often thought about that since, but I still can't understand what she meant. Then she told me I had four fine sons, but would have no more.'

' "How should that be," I said, "seeing I am still a young woman and my husband is strong and loving?"

' "Because you don't want any more," she said, "and you wants my advice today on 'ow to fulfil your purpose." '

'And what advice did she give you?'

'Give? Nothing at all. But I paid her a shilling for my fortune, and another for her advice. And I told her she could come back to Antony for another five shillings each anniversary, provided her advice proved effective.'

'So you've paid her every year since?'

'Five, no six years, I think. Then I heard she had died in Exeter, so I sent that year's money to the Cathedral, to pray for her soul, God rest her in peace.'

At length, Grace explained Goodie Wallgrave's 'advice'. It required Grace keeping a careful calendar of the arrival of her monthlies. Grace imitated Goodie's words.

'Keep nursing the baby for as long as you can mind. That's good for the 'ealth of a strong woman like you. Now, you 'as to understand that a woman waxes and wanes like the moon. Not with the moon, mind, but like it. Each of us 'as the two weeks each month when we's waxin', and two weeks when we's wanin'. When you're waxin', then if your'usband makes love to you you're likely to start a baby. But when you're wanin', you're not. It's simple really, once you can tell the two 'alves apart. Course you needs to 'ave an understandin' man too, But I've found that most men is only waiting to be told these things by a wife that 'as the knowledge.'

Suddenly a head appeared through the curtains at the foot of Jane's bed. Alexander grinned at her as she stifled a little scream.

'It's all right, it's only me. Is tonight . . .'

She sat up and held her arms out to him.

'Of course it is, Alex. It's been ages hasn't it dearest?'

Okehampton, 26 April

My dear Cousin Alexander,

Believe me, I understood very well how concerned you were when our Council of War at Plymouth Castle decided that the fighting had to be renewed. It is easier for me, I am a soldier by profession, and you could say that I have done very well out of the business of war. But you do not share that experience, I know, and without it any enterprise of this kind must seem hazardous in the extreme.

And yet there was no doubt whatsoever in my mind that, in complying with our orders that we should attack Sir Ralph Hopton, we have also adopted the policy most likely to secure Plymouth itself and your beloved Antony.

So far our little campaign has gone well, better even than we

could have expected, and my purpose in writing today is to set
your mind at rest for the moment, and also in the hope that
you will communicate this account of the events of the last few
days to Mr Francis and Sir William, with the expectation that
they will, in their turn, be able to encourage the garrison and
citizens of Plymouth to maintain their high position as
Parliament's Bastion in the West.

Huge relief flooded through Alexander as he read the
opening paragraphs of James Chudleigh's letter, which was
obviously written with an eye to history and public
consumption. Plymouth was safe! Antony was safe! He read
on avidly.

As we had agreed, our force was divided into ten troops of
one hundred and fifty, and two troops marched out to each of
five points on the defensive bank – Lipsom, Holwell, Maudlyn,
Pennycumquick and Millbridge – during the morning of 22
April. The intention was to give any Royalist spy the
impression that our purpose was merely to man our defences.
Each man had a good breakfast, then at midday I sent a
squadron of dragoons ahead to scout the Tavistock road, and
we began our march. Our infantry were well-armed with pikes
and matchlocks, and a fine, cheerful army they made. After
four hours we rested in a valley just outside Tavistock, which
we avoided anyway so as not to announce our advance to
Hopton. Then we marched on along the Launceston road,
which was happily a good deal drier than I had expected. It
was an hour after dark when we forded the Tamar, and we
made camp soon after near Lawhitton, which I estimated to be
one hour's march from Launceston.

During the night two of our lieutenants, Mr Charles and Mr
Wearwell bravely volunteered to go into Launceston itself and
spy out the land. They reported that all was dark and quiet,
which I took to be a good omen for our purpose.

We fed and rested for a few hours, and marched again
before first light. My plan was to surprise Hopton with a bold
attack. It was a disappointment therefore to find that, as we
approached within half a mile of Launceston, the alarm was
raised and their troops came out at a run with drums beating,

to oppose our advance. I could see that we were already outnumbered by those before us, so I decided that we must give up hopes of a sudden victory. Instead I asked Captain Hallsey to lead his dragoons in a charge against the enemy, before they could get set in their ranks with their pikes. This he most gallantly did, and dealt great execution amongst them, so that their centre fell back before him in confusion, and his charge was stopped only by the gates of the town itself being closed against him. This diversion allowed me to lead our infantry over to the north-east, along a sunken lane which issued onto the Okehampton road near Liftondown. There the road passes through a valley, and we took up a position barring this road, on the east bank of the Tamar, which the enemy would have to cross if they wanted to attack us. If you will look again at Sir William's map, you will see that from this place we could also threaten Hopton's flank if instead of coming after us he chose to move on north towards Barnstaple.

Before midday we stood to arms again, as our scouts reported that the whole Royalist army was coming out of Launceston onto the Okehampton road. My captains were prepared to stand and fight our position, but I saw that, as well as being heavily outnumbered, we were likely to be cut to pieces by Hopton's cannon without ever getting a blow in, and as our orders were to delay and impede the enemy, rather than fight to the death, I decided to withdraw towards Okehampton, a distance of some nineteen miles. In this manoeuvre the danger always is of being overtaken on the march, but I kept the dragoons skirmishing behind us, and there was no strong pursuit. We marched in good order and good spirits, and entered Okehampton after nightfall, weary from the long march but proud too of our good discipline. We were welcomed in a friendly way by the Mayor and his Council, and our men were lodged in the church and some barns, thus avoiding the unpleasant business of billeting on private citizens.

The next day we rested and were well fed with sheep roasted, given freely to us as a mark of goodwill and respect. Early in the afternoon my scouts came in with the news that Hopton was moving towards us again with his whole army. I calculated that their slow pace of advance would not allow them to attack us before dark. Hopton would stop short of Okehampton in order not to overstretch his troops, and come on the next day expecting us to await a siege.

The Mayor was naturally most concerned at this possibility, and begged us to consider if there might be any way that the town and its citizens, who had received us most generously, could be spared the awful consequences of battle in their streets. At this I conceived a plan, and told the Mayor to send two of his most distinguished aldermen on horse to meet with the enemy, under a flag of parley. They should tell Sir Ralph Hopton the truth, that we were in the town and determined to fight, but that the Mayor and Council were trying to persuade us to withdraw or surrender. Therefore Sir Ralph should, in the morning, approach the town and call for its surrender according to the Rules of War, before beginning bombardment and assault. I explained to the Mayor that Sir Ralph was an experienced officer and a civilised gentleman, and would certainly abide by the rules of seige, which allow a town to be promised protection, and an occupying army to withdraw with their weapons, provided the gates are opened when the besiegers demand. Meanwhile I gave orders that our men should make ready to march or defend themselves at a moment's notice. By the time the delegates returned it was getting dark. Sir Ralph, they said, had received them kindly, and given his assurances that, if our army did not resist, the town would be placed under his personal protection and none would be harmed. An hour later my scouts returned with the report that the enemy had, as expected, made camp for the night on the road near Bridestowe, four or five miles from us.

I held a Council of War with our officers, and was pleased to find that everyone was for attack, as I had hoped, rather than the alternatives I put to them of standing the siege, or withdrawing again towards our main force at Exeter.

I set a close watch to ensure that no spy might leave the town, and we moved out quietly two hours after midnight. It was a very dark night, cold and with a stiff breeze blowing from the south-west. 'Rain before morning' we thought, just what was needed to cover the sound of our approach and to make their sentries keep their heads down. The dragoons were held behind in the town to give us an hour's start on the march and to reduce the sounds of our progress until we were ready for the assault. After two hours' march we came into a wide valley, and could see their campfires ahead of us and hear the sound of their horse carried to us on the night wind. As I waited Captain Thomas Hallsey came up as planned, having left his dragoons a mile back. I showed him how the fires marked where they enemy slept, and told him to bring his men up as quietly as possible, and charge as soon as he was ready.

His dragoons came through us at a quiet walk, and as the sky began to lighten behind us we saw them manoeuvre into a broad front, less than half a mile from the enemy. In the morning's first light I saw the captain's sword go up, then go down with a flash as the signal to charge. Every man gave a shout of our watchword – 'For King and Parliament' – and we felt the ground shake in front of us as the dragoons thundered in, with our infantry at the run close behind.

The surprise was total. Everywhere I saw enemy troops being killed, wounded or surrendering where they had slept. The High Sheriff of Devon himself was seen in his nightshirt, fleeing on horseback on a borrowed nag (many are saying that he dressed in woman's clothes to avoid capture, but I believe my account should be as factual as may be, and I have found no one who actually saw him so).

After the first charge had carried the dragoons right through the enemy encampment Captain Hallsey was able to rein in his victorious cavalry – no easy task, as I know from experience, when the blood is up in a hot pursuit – and he brought them back in a second charge to take in the rear the large number of enemy troops who were attempting to make a stand around Sir Ralph, Sir Bevil Grenville, and Lord Mohun. Pressed from the front with our pikes, the enemy were utterly broken when the dragoons crashed into their rear, and ran off in disarray leaving us in full command of the field after less than two hours.

We counted two hundred and ten enemy dead, and twice as many wounded, and these together with some six hundred prisoners have been sent back to Exeter. Our own losses were just twelve dead and twenty wounded, and we gave thanks to the Lord who strengthened our hand and protected us.

We have captured no less than forty cannon, and these together with a prodigious quantity of shot and some powder have been set on the road back to Plymouth, where I know you will put them to good use to make the town impregnable.

Sir Ralph Hopton and his commanders escaped us, as our horse was too exhausted to make proper pursuit. But we did find Sir Ralph's despatch case, abandoned in his tent in their headlong flight. Included in his papers was a signed order from the King, commanding him to use the truce to re-assemble his army with all quiet discretion, and rendezvous with Prince Rupert in Somerset, no doubt with a view to an assault on Bristol, as we had previously anticipated.

It seems likely now that Sir Ralph will attempt to rally his scattered army again, probably somewhere well away from us, in order to renew his march north, through Barnstaple. We are resting here for a few days, and then will march towards Bude, in the hope that we may impede his passage once again, while we await Lord Stamford with our main force, which will for sure come out of Exeter when they receive my despatch.

Well cousin, I hope that my plain soldier's narrative will allay your very proper concern, and that the news of our victory will encourage the stout hearts of the people of Plymouth – though I'll warrant the cannon will do the trick anyway! I beg you, give my warmest personal salutations to Sir William, and to Mr Francis.

Your loving cousin,

James Chudleigh

P.S. I should of course have included in my letter my deepest sympathy once again to you on the loss of your dear father. When you told me of the uncertainties you felt about the arrangements for his funeral, I felt ashamed that our Army of the West had not been able to provide enough security for even the common decency of civilised burial for one of our most distinguished citizens and supporters. My earnest hope is that, with one more push, we may destroy forever that Cornish army, and I look forward with confidence to being at your side, together with Sir George my father, when Sir Richard is at last laid to rest with his forebears.

Sincerely, J C

Alexander finished reading the letter as he sat by the window of his room in Plymouth Castle, glad of the warmth

from a crackling log fire. He looked out over the waters of
the Sound, now dark and grey with the sudden onset of
another April storm that drove the whitecaps racing in serried
ranks to attack the shore below him, and that rattled his
casements with great irregular blasts.

His immediate feelings of joy and relief at receiving James'
official report of his victory at Bridestowe had been overtaken
now by a mood of restlessness and inadequacy. Alexander
was intuitive enough to recognise the envy he felt for his
younger cousin. James was not married, and had no
responsibilities outside of his chosen profession of soldiering.
And how he was glorying in it now! Alexander was not
deceived by the studied modesty. He could imagine the huge
swelling of pride and exhilaration that the soldier experienced
after a battle so gloriously won. James would expect
recognition, promotion and glory on his return, and rightly
so. But what was Alexander's place to be? He had put his life
and property at risk by opposing the King at Westminster,
and had accepted proudly the duty in Plymouth of keeping
the town as Parliament's Bastion in the West. But Jane had
been right also, when she had said that he could have played
the game with more circumspection. Was it just vanity that
had made him take the lead in condemning Strafford? Vanity
too that had allowed him to accept the role of Parliamentary
Commissioner, charged with seizing the property of other
Englishmen? Or was it principle? He had heard the
Republicans, like John his half-brother, arguing that
Monarchy had ceased to serve the people, and should be
abolished. How far did he want to go down that road? It was
obvious that war was the business of soldiers, and when the
war ended it would be the generals who would naturally be
left in control of the State. Would they then meekly step aside
for some untried elected authority? Once Caesar had
demolished the Roman Republic, the army had been the real
power in Rome for the centuries that remained before the
barbarians came. Would it come to that in England?

There was a knock at the door.

'Beg pardon, sir, but Mr Philip Francis is most anxious to see you.'

During the space of a few weeks of the year 1625, Philip Francis had buried his first wife, his father, his mother, and last and most agonisingly, his only daughter, just two years old. All of them, together with a quarter of the population of Plymouth, had died when the Duke of Buckingham's army had been billeted in the city to await the fleet that was to carry it on the young King Charles' first foreign expedition. For a few months the citizens of Plymouth were actually outnumbered by the King's army, and the consequence was the grinding horror of the plague.

Philip held the King and his ministers responsible for the destruction of his family. He turned to the politics of revolution as an absorbing diversion from the overwhelming pain and grief that had almost cost him his sanity in the earlier years. Just recently he had moderated the fiery republican oratory that had been a feature of his youth, and begun to follow the official line of the Parliamentary side, which said that 'the King himself was not necessarily evil, but weak, and misled by evil counsellors'. As a result Philip now spoke for the great majority of his fellow-citizens, and so was a potent force for good or ill in the town. The Army held Plymouth, but Philip and his people held the Army too. Philip was secretly rather proud of his nickname, Don Philippo. Of course no one called him that to his face, but he thought it was an affectionate recognition of his authority, as well as a comment on his swarthy complexion and beaky nose.

'Good morning, Sir Alexander, I trust you are well? I hope you will forgive me for calling on you in this unceremonious way, but I heard that a trooper from General Chudleigh had brought you a letter, and I wondered if it confirmed the rumour we had heard of a glorious victory?'

Alexander indicated that Philip should take the padded chair by the fire, and pulled up another one for himself.

'A victory? Yes, no doubt of that, a great victory to be sure. Here, the General's letter is meant for us all to read.'

He re-assembled the closely-written sheets, and stirred the log-fire to send the flames shooting up the chimney again as he watched Philip devour the letter. He noticed that his lips moved and a thick forefinger followed the words across the pages. But there was an expression of keen intelligence and attention on his face that revealed something of the real Philip beneath the bombast and bonhomie. Alexander had seen Philip principally as a demagogue, at the mercy of the worst elements among the anti-royalists, men who wanted to tear down every institution and tradition that held the country together. He wondered if there was more to Philip Francis than met the eye.

'Excellent, truly inspirational! I like especially the news about the forty cannon. Certainly the General has saved Plymouth, don't you agree? Of course I'm no soldier, but I would expect Sir William to be able to place those guns on the strong points of our fortification so that we are impregnable on the landward side, and your St. Nicholas Island guarantees our access to the sea. We are safe!'

'As you can see, the General intended the contents of his letter to become known to all the citizens . . .'

'I will see to it personally, this very day Sir Alexander. It will be set in type and printed off as a pamphlet, which my people will circulate across the whole town. It will be posted on street corners and read out in full in every church of course. I will discuss with my Council the possibility of a great Service of Thanksgiving. In the open air perhaps . . . What do you think of the idea?'

Alexander could only admire the speed with which Philip could transpose his mood from anxiety to relief and now to excited calculation. What should he say was his attitude to having the church bells rung for Cousin James?

'The General seems to expect a second, decisive battle

within a couple of weeks. Might it not be more appropriate to delay the celebrations of victory until after that? Perhaps then we could expect the General and the Commander of Parliament's Army of the West, Lord Stamford to attend. That really would be a memorable celebration, don't you agree?'

Part of the reason for Philip Francis' success as a politician was that, beneath his bluff Devon manner, he concealed an intuitive ability to assess men and motives. He sensed the latent rivalry between Sir Alexander and his cousin, and wondered how it could be put to use ... There was one interesting prospect ...

'I bow to your superior judgement, Sir Alexander. There is another matter that I would like to discuss with you, but my people are desperate to hear the good news, and I will put in hand the printing first. May I return in an hour or so?'

Alexander was intrigued by Philip's air of mystery.

'Come back and eat with me. I have a piece of venison from Antony, being roasted at this very minute downstairs.'

When Philip returned his manner was brisk and business-like. He ate and drank sparingly, complimented Alexander on his well-hung venison, and turned the conversation to the matter that was obviously uppermost in his thoughts.

'I wonder, Sir Alexander, if you have calculated what it costs to maintain our garrison in Plymouth?'

'I can't say that I have, no. I do know that I've had to pay the men under my command myself twice now, because Parliament's funds had not arrived and our Council had run out of cash.'

'The full three thousand men cost six hundred pounds a week in pay, plus the keep for the horses and the cost of powder and shot and so on. I estimate that the total is equivalent to the entire weekly income of the town in times of peace when trade is good. Even if we are able to get in the wheat we've planted, the price in the market is likely to double. Plymouth is likely to be hungry next winter, very hungry indeed. And how shall we remain "Parliament's Bastion in the West" if we can't feed ourselves?'

Alexander wondered where the conversation was leading, but felt flattered to be included in the mayor's deliberations.

'But we are only a few weeks from a total victory, as General Chudleigh forecasts, and then everything will be different. To start with, we will not need to support a garrison of three thousand – just a few hundred to service the cannon, with time to improve the skills of our own militia. That would cut the costs. And I know we all have more fields we could plant, which will itself bring down the price of wheat. One of my tenants was telling me about these new turnips . . .'

'Indeed yes, Sir Alexander, indeed yes. If the army wins its total victory, and the Cornish cannot raise another army. If the King does not send another army into Devon, then all may be well. But in the meantime men of prudence and foresight, men like ourselves who are exposed to great personal danger, Sir Alexander, such men must plan for every eventuality. Every eventuality, if you take my meaning?'

He paused, and waited for a response, Alexander searched Philip's florid face, with its great hooked nose and dark eyes glittering beneath black brows, for any clue as to his exact intention.

'Is your meaning that we should consider even the possibility that the King might eventually win? That Plymouth might be taken?'

A little sigh escaped Philip's lips.

'You take my thoughts precisely. If Plymouth fell, and you and I were taken, do you think we would be pardoned?'

Alexander slowly shook his head, like a man who could see his worst nightmare coming true.

'No, Mr Francis, we would not be pardoned. Other men who have taken a lesser part, who have merely followed our lead, they could look for pardon. A fine perhaps, but not the axe. The King will want peace and reconciliation more than revenge. But that would not apply to you and me. He would want to make examples of us, to serve as a warning to the others. Lands and possessions forfeit, family in beggary or exile, and our heads on poles paraded around the streets.'

'My fears exactly. So, because the danger for us is greater than for other men, do we not have a right, a duty even, to protect ourselves as best we may from the awful consequences of catastrophe, no matter how unlikely? I speak as a man, like yourself, Sir Alexander, whose loyalty to Parliament is beyond question. But we do have that right, don't you agree?'

This time there was no doubting the sincerity of his thoughts, and Alexander replied as Philip had hoped he would.

'Of course we have the right. We are the ones taking the greatest risk on behalf of the people, so we must have the right to try to protect ourselves and our families. But how can it be done?'

Philip reached inside his jerkin, and produced a plain pine box, about eight inches square and four inches deep. He placed it with a small flourish in Alexander's lap.

'Open it, Sir Alexander, open it.'

Alexander weighed the box in his hands. Two pounds at a guess,.

'What's in it?'

'Our security, I believe. Open it, and see for yourself.'

Alexander pushed his thumbs against the front of the lid, and eased it open. Inside he saw the folds of a bag made of black leather, closed with a silk drawstring. He untied the knot, and pulled open the neck of the bag.

'Pearls, by the Lord, a whole bag of pearls!'

He thrust his hand into the bag and brought out a handful, which he allowed to trickle back, one by one. They seemed to be all of the finest quality, lustrous and unblemished. The smallest were about a quarter inch in diameter, most a good deal bigger, as big across as his thumbnail.

'Where did these come from? Whose are they?'

'You had not heard of their existence already?'

'No. The proceeds of a sequestration?'

'Just so. About two months ago a couple of our troopers

intercepted a coach which proved to be carrying the Earl of Marleborough. There was some sort of scuffle, and the Earl was unfortunately killed, as well as the three retainers with him. The troopers very reasonably took his resistance as proof that he was a royalist, so the coach was brought into Plymouth. You were away in Antony at the time, Sir Alexander, or you would have most certainly been consulted. Anyway our Committee of Sequestration conducted a search personally.'

'You had the proper quorum?'

'In addition to myself there were Peter Keckwick and Charles Vaughan, our treasurer. We found the pearls in this box, hidden under the driver's seat. Naturally the Committee concluded that the pearls should be seized and sold.'

'I heard absolutely nothing about this.'

'It was decided that nothing should be said to anyone in the town until now. After all, we had only assumed that the pearls belonged to Lord Marleborough. He was no longer alive to be questioned, and there might be other claimants. And there was certainly no one in Plymouth with enough money to pay a fair price for them anyway, so we thought they would need to be taken up to London.'

'But that has not been done yet?'

'Yes, it has. As soon as the truce was declared, we agreed that Peter Keckwick should give us a surety, and take the box himself up to London with our authority to negotiate a sale.'

'How much surety did he give?'

'Two hundred pounds. Not much perhaps, set against the value of the pearls, but the Committee was desperate for money to pay the garrison, and that was all the money Peter could raise.'

Alexander picked up another handful, and watched them slide back again as he opened his fingers. The pearls seemed to possess a life and warmth of their own, altogether different from the cold glitter of other jewels.

'Why didn't Peter sell the jewels in London then? Why bring them back here?'

'Peter had them valued by four most reputable London goldsmiths . . .' Philip paused to consult a slip of paper, 'Messrs Jarvis Andrews, Nicholas Gould, William Markham and Thomas Smith. They advised him that the pearls were not from English oysters, but most likely from the West Indies or South America.'

'Spanish then? The booty of some privateer from the days of Queen Bess?'

'Very possibly. Anyway they are today literally priceless. Without the King and his Court in London, there is no proper market for them now. Peter said that the goldsmiths had all given him the same advice, "not to sell until the present emergencies have been resolved". Alternatively he could consider offering them in Paris.'

'So he brought them back to Plymouth.'

'And into my hands for safe keeping, yes.' Philip sat in silence for a few moments, and watched Alexander as he continued to play with the pearls in restless fascination, then continued, 'Assuming the agreement from the other members of the Committee, I would like to ask you, Sir Alexander, if you would accept the responsibility for the safe-keeping on our behalf. It seems to me that, on St Nicholas Island, the pearls would be safe even if Plymouth was taken by assault. You would keep a boat there of course, so that you could make your escape if need be . . .'

Alexander was quick to see the implication, 'And of course rescue yourself also, Mr Francis?'

'As I said, Sir Alexander, those who have accepted the greatest exposure to danger have a duty to look to their own security in the event of a catastrophe.'

Alexander looked steadily at Philip's impassive face for a few moments, then smiled. 'Capital, capital, Mr Francis! And should I assume that you would want also some security from myself for the privilege of protecting our future from disaster?'

Philip lowered his gaze, so that Alexander did not see the naked triumph that glittered in his eyes. 'Certainly Peter

Keckwick would like the use of his two hundred pounds again, and we are desperate for funds to pay the garrison.'

'How much?'

'Peter said that, when the times are right again, the pearls will be worth many thousands of pounds.'

'He may well be correct in that view. But the times are most definitely not right. And may never be right again. Nor am I King Charles with the whole nation's tax money to spend, as you well know.'

'Indeed so, Sir Alexander, indeed so. You know well how great our need is. Could you offer a thousand pounds say, as the security? Against a pledge from the Committee to repay twelve hundred when the war is over and the pearls sold?'

Alexander dropped the last pearl from his hand back into the bag, tightened the drawstring and closed the lid of the polished pine box. 'I will pay as much as I can possibly afford into the Committee's treasury. In a project of this magnitude, Mr Francis, I need to consult Lady Carew, my wife. Indeed her dowry may have to provide the major part of the actual cash you need, and I value greatly her opinion and good sense.' He ran his fingers over the smooth surface of the box, as though longing to be handling the pearls again, 'You may safely leave these in my charge for the time being. I will go to Antony today, and return as soon as possible with the money. It will be every penny I can spare, I promise you. And then we will consult some more on the plan to protect us both from catastrophe.'

Philip was reluctant to give up the pearls without receiving the security, but saw that he could hardly resist Alexander without seeming to doubt his honesty. He stood up and held out his hand, 'I have absolute confidence, Sir Alexander.'

Later that afternoon Sir Alexander Carew sat holding the tiller in the stern of a longboat, as four sailors pulled steadily at the oars. The morning's April storm had blown through, and the setting sun flashed in his eyes as he steered into the Lynher river from the choppy tidal waters of the Tamar, with less than a mile to go to the landing stage below Antony. All the way from Plymouth Alexander had been trying to weigh up in his mind the scale of the risks he had been running. He recalled standing up in Parliament just two years previously, to speak for the Bill of Attainder that brought to execution the Earl of Strafford, the King's favourite.

'If it was certain that I would be the next man to suffer, on the same scaffold with the same axe, I would still give my consent to the passing of it!'

Brave words! And how pleasing to hear the roars of approval and stamping feet as he sat down! How intoxicating the excitement of being a leader in the cause of liberty and democracy! And now it had come to this, that his very life might depend on the military skills – or luck – of his young cousin, General James Chudleigh. Little Jamie, who had caught Sir Ralph Hopton once with a stratagem. Could he do it again? Alexander patted the leather jerkin he wore, to feel again the hardness of the wooden box he had tucked inside. Wasn't there something infinitely squalid, even dishonourable, about this arrangement with Mr Francis to purloin Marleborough's pearls? He tried to envisage how they might escape together if Plymouth were stormed. Where would they sail? To Antony first, to rescue Jane and the children. Then where?

The longboat bumped against the high wooden jetty, and Alexander climbed out.

'Pull the boat up over there, well above the highwater mark, then follow the path up to the kitchen. My steward, Walter Goodman, will see to it that you have food and will find you a bed, and you can return to Plymouth tomorrow morning.'

Sir Richard Carew's widow Grace, the Dowager Lady Carew, was addicted to the herb Savin. This was the cause of the premature ageing that Alexander had noted, and also of her notoriously sudden changes of mood. It had begun about fifteen years before, when Grace had become one of Goodie Wallgrave's clients, in order to prevent further pregnancies. Goodie had instructed Grace in the lore that connected a woman's fertility to the phases of the moon, and in addition had provided Grace with a pungent herbal tea to brew, 'You take a good strong cup o' this m'dear, each mornin' arter your 'usband bin lovin like, an' you'll 'ave no more o' them little problems to worry you. A spoonful in a glass of 'ot water's all you need.'

Sir Richard was a kind and loving husband. He found no problem in dropping into that monthly rhythm to suit Grace, and, if he noticed her morning hot drink, he said nothing about it. She had given him already a second family of four fine sons, and he felt that the future of the Carew line was well secured, even though Alexander was the only boy amongst the six children poor Bridget had borne him.

At first Grace had found it difficult to swallow a full glass of Goodie Wallgrave's bitter, oily tea, but after a few weeks she began to miss it on the mornings when Sir Richard had not been active. 'Another glass this week isn't going to do any harm,' she told herself.

Month by month the small sack of tea was depleted, and Grace found it hard to eke out the last spoonfuls through the weeks before Goodie was due again at Antony's village fair. When she finally arrived Grace pressed her very strongly, 'You're a witch, Goodie Wallgrave, and you know it. A word to my husband, and stoning out of the village is the least you might expect. So don't tell me you've sworn an oath never to reveal the recipe. You want my money too, I assume? You'll be paid just the same every year, as I promised, and you'll be saved the trouble of supplying me in the future.'

Eventually Goodie was persuaded to offer a list of ingredients. It included small quantities of marjoram, thyme, parsley and lavender, which were obviously there to make the taste more palatable, but the largest component was a herb

called Savin. Grace had never heard of it, so she looked it up
in the Herbal in Sir Richard's library.

Savin *(Juniperus Sabinus), commonly called 'Covershame',
a notorious restorative of slender shapes and tender
reputations. Use the points of the leaves to make a drink. The
berries may also be used, (like Juniperus communis) to
infuse and soften raw spirit, (Hollander).*

A 'restorative of slender shapes' – that was plain enough!
Sir Richard was a considerable authority on horticulture,
particularly on growing apples from cuttings and graftings,
and his orchards had been the subject of a special visitation
from no less than King James himself. He was delighted to
show Grace his experimental techniques.

'Juniper you say? To make a fragrant bank? Charming
thought. There are many varieties you know, but you will
find them growing wild here in Cornwall.'

Grace had the benefit of Goodie's description, 'It grows flat
to the ground, dark green leaves like the tamarisk', and soon
the cuttings from the bush were thriving so well that within
three years she was independent of Goodie for supply, even
though she was taking it at night in wine, as well as each
morning in her tea. She wondered sometimes at the strength
of her need for it, the feeling that she could not start the day
nor sleep the night without it.

'It's just a habit, I suppose. Harmless really. I could cut
down, but why bother?'

Her short temper evidenced itself as soon as she heard of
Alexander's return that evening. She hurried down the stairs
from the solar, and met him in the hall while he was still
pulling off his boots.

'Alexander, you're here at last! Have you any idea what it's
been like here for Jane and myself, waiting for news? Has
James won a victory? Are we safe? Do you realise that it's
been two weeks since your father died, and I've heard nothing
about a funeral? We really couldn't keep him up here in the

hall any longer, and we've had to move the coffin down to the cellar. How do you think I feel about that?'

Alexander was in the habit of deferring to his stepmother, but his own nerves were too raw with worrying to permit of a soft answer.

'For the Lord's sake, Grace, I've only just got one boot off. Is this a proper way to receive me? Where's Jane?'

'Out walking by the river somewhere, with the children. I'm surprised you didn't see them. They'll be so pleased to see you again.'

Alexander sensed the shift in her tone, towards conciliation.

'I'm sure they'll all be here soon, it's getting dark. I'm hungry, and I'll tell you all the news over supper. It's good news, and I promise we'll decide about father tonight. Could you stir the kitchen up please?'

During supper Alexander went over the details of James' victory for Jane and Grace.

'So you see that James believes that he can hold up or slow down Sir Ralph Hopton, to allow The Earl of Stamford to come up with our main Army of the West from Exeter, and so destroy the Cornish once and for all.'

Jane reached across the table to squeeze his hand.

'And we'll be safe at last. I've been so worried, Alex. Will you have to go back to Plymouth again? Couldn't you just stay here and wait for the news?'

Dear Jane! So loving, so gentle! He could feel the weight of anxiety and terror that lay behind her pleading. Were not his responsibilities for his family, for Antony, at least as important as his duties in Plymouth? If he decided to stay, who could demand that he go? 'Only myself,' he thought, 'only myself.'

After supper he called for a candle, 'I'm going down to see father for one last time, Grace, and tomorrow we'll arrange the funeral.'

The door to the cellar opened off the kitchen, which was still bustling with activity as he entered. He congratulated Mrs Twemby, the cook, on the fine piece of roast beef they had just enjoyed, and asked the scullery maid, Bessie, about her new baby.

'He's fine, thankee sir. An', with your permission sir, we'd like to 'ave 'im christened Richard, seein' as 'e came into the world on the day good Sir Richard left us.'

'Of course, most fitting. And if my duties permit, perhaps I might be a godparent.'

He opened the cellar door, and held the candle before him as he stepped down into the gloom. The cellars at Antony occupied the entire foundations, and had been built on the new principle, two thirds below ground and one third above. As Alexander moved carefully down the broad steps his eyes became adjusted to the chill moonlight that filtered in through the three shallow windows opposite. To his right he could see arches and alcoves disappearing into the distance. This was the source of the familiar smells of apples, root vegetables and salt meats. From the left, equally in arched darkness, came a different smell, sickly-sweet and overpowering.

He found the coffin in the farthest vaulted alcove, resting on two trestles. He paused for a moment to summon up his courage, and his hand shook as he rested the flaring candle on the coffin lid. One end of the lid was separate and hinged, and Alexander closed his eyes as he lifted this portion, his whole body now trembling with mingled fear and disgust. Yet when he finally opened his eyes it was to see the calm, pale face of his father again, with the hands folded across his chest, apparently unchanged since he had last seen him two weeks before. He knelt in the dust beside the coffin.

'Forgive me, father, I am weak and unsure what to do for the best for you and for our family in the midst of so many and great uncertainties. Give me, I pray, a measure of your calmness, your wisdom and your strength.'

He could not bring himself to kiss his father one last time, but he touched the cold forehead, as though for luck. Then he took from inside his jerkin the polished pine box, and placed it beneath the red cushion on which rested his father's head. He closed the lid quickly, and foraged around to find a stone, which he used to tap home the oak dowels that secured the lid. He was swallowing back the bitter taste of vomit as his feet carried him up the cellar steps into the warm brightness of the kitchen.

'Goodness, Sir Alexander, you look real poorly!' Mrs Twemby was all solicitude, 'Sit yourself 'ere at the table sir, an' I'll get Walter to pour you a drop of brandy.'

Thankfully Alexander allowed himself to be fussed over, slowly recovering his spirits by the fire, now damped down for the night, with its intricate array of turning spits and hooks. Beside him on the table was a sugar loaf, partly crushed for use, and he nibbled a piece as he thought about Mrs Twemble and her scullery maids. He had been almost overwhelmed himself down there. What must it have been like for little Bessie, sent down for the carrots?

Grace Rolle had been just seventeen when she had married Richard Carew, who was then a widower of forty two. Of course it was hardly a love match, but Sir Richard was gentle, scholarly and kind, and as devoted to the new family of four sons that Grace produced as he was to Alexander and his sisters. When Richard succeeded to the Carew estates, Grace was still only twenty four, young enough to relish being the lady of a great manor. Now, after fourteen years of having her own way, she was finding it difficult indeed to learn to yield to Alexander. Particularly difficult in the matter of her husband's funeral, which should have done so much to consolidate her new position as the Dowager Lady Carew amongst all her friends and relatives, but which now promised no such comfort. That evening, as Alexander explained his plan, she rose suddenly from her seat beside the fire, and stood looming over him, her eyes blazing with indignation.

'Let me be sure I have understood you aright, Alexander. You are proposing to dig a shallow grave for your own father, Sir Richard Carew of Antony, *in the orchard*? And bury him there like a pet dog? Jane dear, tell him this cannot be. I absolutely forbid it. I'll throw myself into the grave, rather than allow us all to be made a laughing stock in such a way. My dying curse will be on your head, Alexander, and on your children, and on your children's children. Do you hear me? I FORBID IT!'

Behind her the log crackled and broke in the fire, sending tall shadows leaping around the panelled room as though to lend substance to her threats. Alexander had been thirteen when Grace had first come to Antony, and she had been more like another older sister than a step-mother. But he had always treated her most respectfully, as his father had expected of him. Resistance did not come easily. He kept seated, without meeting her eyes directly.

'I didn't make the war, Grace, that's between Parliament and the King, and we are being ground down because of it. Nothing would give me more pleasure than a proper funeral for father, but just now it is impossible, you must see that. Within the week I must be back in Plymouth to attend to my duties there, and I have concluded that, even if James is successful, it must be another month before we can feel sufficiently secure to put on a great event. Frankly, father cannot be kept that long, can he? Not in the cellar, for certain. Already there's a problem when you open the cellar door. Have you been down there? I do not recommend it, really I do not. And within another three or four days it will be absolutely unbearable. I'm sorry to have to speak so coarsely, but that's how it is. He will be buried tomorrow with all the dignity and reverence we can muster, and with the family and the servants to follow him, and the vicar to speak the words of the service of course. Father loved his apple trees – I think the proudest moment of his life was when King James came over to Antony especially to see his orchards, and have father explain his discoveries and

methods. His spirit will rest easy there, I know, and when the
war is over we can still arrange a reburial alongside
grandfather, as we all want.'

'You're a coward, Alexander. I think it must come from
being brought up with just sisters after your poor mother
died. A disgrace to the Carews, a degenerate unworthy of
your ancestors, I . . . I . . .'

She swayed as she spoke, and her sister Jane jumped up to
put an arm around her 'Grace, please Grace, it's just for a
little while. Alex is only doing what he thinks is right and
best . . .'

'Damn you, damn you both!' Grace thrust aside Jane's
supporting arm and moved to the door, 'Damn you, damn
you to hell!'

'Oh Richard, Richard, why did you have to leave me?'

Grace sat by the small fire in her bedroom, poured a little
hot water onto her Savin to infuse the 'tea', then filled the
glass to the brim with good Malmsey. She stared into the
flames in stillness for several minutes, then drained the glass
with a sigh. Shocked and enraged beyond measure at
Alexander's unexpected refusal to bend to her will, her
thoughts were of revenge, and even murder.

'Poison. Why not poison? There were several poisons
identified in the Herbal, I recall. I could find the opportunity,
given time, I could do it. But what's the point? Alex has four
sons himself, so I could scarcely expect to work through the
whole accursed brood. And even if I did, could my John
inherit? That's the nub – what do I have to do to destroy
Alexander and at the same time disinherit his family?
There was something in that letter that came from John last
week . . .'

She rummaged in the wooden box beside her bed, 'Damn
these candles, they're nowhere near as bright as they used to
be . . . Ah yes, this is it.'

. . . Thanks to the letter of introduction father wrote last year,
I have been invited to assist Mr Pym as one of his secretaries
. . . we are determined that, when the war is won, active
supporters of 'that man of blood', as the King is called, will be
rooted out and deemed traitors. Their lands will be forfeit and
their heads subject to the axe. Certain of our own generals and
commanders will find themselves caught by this same
Ordinance, if Parliament is not satisfied that their loyalty is
absolute and their diligence total . . .'

Grace prepared another glass of the Savin and Malmsey,
and felt a lightening of her mood as she undressed for bed.
There had to be a way!

Sir Richard's famous orchards occupied most of the land on
the north side of his manor, between it and the Lynher river.
The next evening was dull, and a blustering wind whipped
through the trees, with a threat of rain before dark.
Alexander had chosen a place near the centre of the orchards,
beneath a grove of the tall Russet apples that had been one
of his father's first successes, and which now towered forty
feet above. The blossom had fallen a week before, but still
carpeted the thick grass, and beneath the heavy, close-grown
canopy it was as dim as in a cathedral. At the head of the
grave the vicar was intoning the burial service.

'Ashes to ashes, dust to dust . . .'

As at a signal the handfuls of gravel and earth rattled onto
the lid of the coffin, which lay about two feet below the level
of the long, petal-strewn grass. Alexander stood at the foot,
facing the vicar, with Jane at his left, holding tightly onto the
hand of his eldest son, eight years old and trying hard to hold
back the tears. On Alexander's right his steward Walter
stood, with his wife next to him, accompanied by Mrs
Twemby the cook, Bessie the scullerymaid and her man
William, who was one of the gardeners, and half a dozen

other servants. Grace had taken to her bed, being 'too poorly to come out for the interment'.

'We brought nothing into this world, and it is certain that we can take nothing out of it . . .'

Alexander smiled grimly to himself as he thought of Marleborough's pearls lying safely beneath his father's head. Not even Achilles went down to Hades with more treasure in his tomb!

As they scrambled back up to the grey stone house the first fat drops of rain were blowing in from the darkening west, and Alexander stooped to swing his son onto his shoulders, and hurried behind Jane through the kitchen door into the light and warmth.

Grace watched the funeral procession in secret, from the window of the upstairs parlour. The previous night's fury had been replaced by a colder purpose, and she sat now by her bedroom fire putting the finishing touches to a letter to her eldest son, John, care of the House of Commons, Westminster. He was now twenty, officially still a student in the Inns of Court, but in fact engaged full time as an assistant to John Pym, leader of the Parliamentarian cause.

'. . . I will therefore say no more now about Alexander's disgraceful treatment of your poor father. However there is one matter of great concern to us all, John, which I hesitate to mention in a letter, but which is of such great moment that it cannot be left unsaid.

You know of course that we Rolles have a long and consistent tradition of opposition to Royal tyranny. Your uncles Henry and John were amongst the first Members of Parliament openly to refuse to pay the forced loans demanded without precedent by King Charles, and thus they put themselves at the centre of resistance. And you are yourself carrying on that tradition now under Mr Pym. However I feel that Alexander is not so honest in his principles, nor so dedicated in his actions. His connections and loyalties are, I fear, to Cornwall and the old religion. I tremble therefore to think that he has the defence of Plymouth in the palms of his slippery hands. I have no 'chapter and verse' that I dare put in this letter, my dear, but I know you will grasp the importance of this matter, and will speak at the right time to the right people, those with both authority and discretion . . .'

Philip Francis, Mayor of Plymouth, was uncomfortably on the defensive. Knowing that Peter Keckwick would be pressing him again at any time for the return of his £200 surety, Philip had called a meeting of the Committee for Sequestration to tell them that Sir Alexander Carew now had the pearls in his possession. But as he did not intend to share with the committee his plan for escape from the town, if the need should arise, he was compelled to dissemble.

'I cannot say how Sir Alexander came to hear about Marleborough's pearls. Plymouth is not so large a place, and Sir Alexander is a powerful man with many friends. I can only repeat that he raised the subject when I went to ask him for the news from the battle, and offered to consider putting up a larger surety himself.'

Peter Keckwick was the owner of Plymouth's largest fleet of fishing boats, and incidentally the father of Philip's young second wife, Lucy. He was a big, red-faced man in his early fifties. He had seven boats working for him, and was an important – and relatively rich – contributor to the business of feeding the town and bringing in money by sending salted fish round to Exeter and London.

'That £200 of mine would pay twenty of my fisherman for a year or more, Mr Francis. I thought I was doing the right thing for our cause when I lent it, but now I have neither money nor pearls nor even a note of hand to say what I'm owed. I take it hard now to learn that you've decided by yourself to hand our pearls over to Sir Alexander. He's a great man, no doubt. So was his father and his grandfather before him, to my own knowledge. But those pearls must have a value great enough to be a temptation for any man, and I take it amiss that you've betrayed my trust in this, I really do. If I offend you by my plain speech, I'm sorry, but that's how I see it.'

Philip Francis sat at the end of his old oak table, in the timbered bay window that jutted out over Plymouth's bustling High Street. He felt his temper rise in response to Peter's challenge to his honesty, but bit back the angry retort that could only serve to harden Peter's suspicions. Instead he pushed back his chair and stood to look out of the window behind him in a long silence. When he spoke his tone was quiet and measured.

'Peter, my old friend, will you come and stand beside me and look down on our citizens, please?'

The two of them looked out onto a street of half-timbered houses like the one they were in, the timbers brightly painted for the most part in reds and greens as well as the more sober browns and white. Below was the usual hubbub of street cries, a horse drawn wagon rumbled across the cobblestones, and the people of Plymouth were going about earning a living. Philip opened a casement to allow into their meeting Plymouth's special combination of loud noise and the smell of fish, fresh and salted.

'How many people can you see in the street, Peter? A hundred, maybe two? If you were to arrest every one, and torture them till their life's blood ran out, I doubt if you could squeeze out your two hundred pounds. Sir Alexander is the only man in Plymouth who could find that sort of money for us. So when he asked me for the pearls, I gave them to him, and rejoiced. And extracted a promise, of course.'

'For how much?'

Philip closed the casement, and the noise of the town dropped back again to a distant rumble.

'I'll be honest with you, Peter, I asked him for a thousand pounds. We know the pearls are worth more, when the market returns, and Sir Alexander admitted as much. He said he would consult with his family, and loan us as his surety as much as he could afford.'

'That may mean anything. Or nothing.'

Charles Vaughan, the third member of the Committee and its treasurer now joined the challenge. In times of peace he had been Plymouth's leading moneylender. Small in stature, with a narrow face and a dark complexion, he had met with a good deal of resentment when he had first taken on the work of treasurer, with Philip's patronage, because many citizens had first-hand experience of the ways he could exert pressure, and they were only too willing to question his honesty as well. He had in fact surprised the Council by his ability to produce exemplary books of account, and he was now widely accepted as a reliable adviser on all matters relating to money. His dry comment was as much of a threat to Philip's authority as Peter's bluster had been, but this time Philip decided that attack was the best defence.

'Mr Vaughan, I think you know better than I do what a dead asset is. Those pearls were useless in our keeping, I couldn't afford to offer Peter here two pounds towards his outlay, let alone two hundred. I had to decide there and then, face to face with the man who is our Member of Parliament and commander of our fort and island, whether to trust him – and show our trust – or whether to offend him. I chose to trust him, and so give ourselves the chance of getting something in exchange for this dead asset. Would you care to propose a motion of censure to be put to the Council? Perhaps they will agree with you, and then again perhaps they won't. Do you want to put it to the test?'

Charles had the moneylender's professional indifference to public opinion, and rose from his seat as though prepared to call Philip's bluff, if bluff it was, but Peter intervened before the quarrel could become an open breach.

'Now then, you two, you're starting to hop and squawk like a couple of fighting cocks working up for the bout. It's my money that's at risk, isn't it? So it should be me that decides whether Philip has done the best he could or not. And

I say I'm satisfied, at least for now, and I don't want the Council brought into it. When might we expect Sir Alexander back?'

'Within the week. He has to see to burying his father, and then he'll be back. He gave me his word.'

'Fair enough. Now then, Mr Vaughan, how does the town stand for money? When are we to expect more from Exeter or London? It's all very well being called "Parliament's Bastion in the West", but if we don't see some funds soon I'm going to sail up to Westminster with my fleet and teach them to cry stinking fish, you see if I don't.'

Despite his earnest protestations to Philip Francis, Alexander had no intention of even mentioning the business about the pearls to his wife. Philip himself had refrained from putting a value on them. But Alexander recalled buying a few pearls in London to have a brooch made up for Jane, on the occasion of the birth of their first son. Multiplying up from the cost of those, he estimated that, when the times were right again, the pearls would sell for a price equivalent to the value of his house and all the estates of Antony put together. So huge a sum was indeed a temptation for anyone, and Alexander decided that Jane would be safer if she could honestly deny ever having heard of them. So he had kept his grisly secret to himself, but ensured that Sir Richard was not too deeply buried.

He landed back in Plymouth on 14 May to find the town boiling with expectation. James' optimistic letter had been printed as a broadsheet, and widely distributed. Every church in the town and in the nearby villages had a copy, which was read aloud to the congregations on Sunday. Taverns had copies pinned up, which the literate read out for the benefit of the rest. As a result the talk had been of nothing but the forthcoming great victory, which was seen as not just another skirmish in a long war, but as bringing the final defeat of popery, or property, or injustice, or whatever it was men believed they were fighting against. Alexander was widely recognised as he walked through the fish market. He had decided that there had been enough mourning, and instead of black he was wearing a favourite yellow jerkin and a red doublet.

'Mornin' Sir Alexander. Is there any more news yet from General Chudleigh? One more push an' we'll be rid o' the King for good an' all!'

The morning's catch had already been landed and sold, and in the warm spring sunshine the people had time to stand and listen, as well as to talk. Across the back of the open quay a row of hefty wooden pillars supported a broad roof in front of the warehouses and provided a covered way. This was a popular place to find the town's demagogues haranguing their fellow-citizens, and today was no exception. Alexander found himself drawn into the crowd, with their alternating cheers and jeers, that surrounded Isaac Weaver, a tall thin man with a bald head and beetling black eyebrows. Non-conformist preacher, one-time soldier and reputed ex-pirate, Isaac was a familiar figure to his audience.

'The King's priests have told us we should be contented with the station in which the Lord has placed us, and look for justice in Heaven. But is there any reason that we should not seek to re-arrange the world so that we have a foretaste of Heaven here, as well as hereafter? Men may look up to heaven, but while they do so their eyes are blinded by those same rogues and popish thieves that have deceived the King's Majesty, so that we can no longer perceive our own birthright. I tell you friends, the world will not be set right until each man, aye and each woman too, takes a full share of the responsibility of deciding who shall govern us, and who will lead us into our Promised Land. Are we sheep that we must have dogs to drive us?'

This last sally was answered with a huge shout of 'NO'. Suddenly Alexander found himself the centre of the crowd's attention, as Isaac called to him directly.

'Sir Alexander! Sir Alexander Carew of Antony! Make

way, make way there. Please, Sir Alexander, I know you for
an honourable man, our trusted Member of Parliament.
Come forward, please sir, and give us the benefit of your
learning and judgement. Is it not true that God wants each
of us to accept our share of the burden of government?'

Alexander found himself being patted on the shoulders and
propelled up to the front, to stand beneath the upturned
fish-barrel that supported Isaac. He recalled an aphorism that
his father liked to quote:

'Our Christian tradition is that men of business best serve
God by becoming more godly. These new Puritans would
have us serve God by becoming better at our business, and
so improving the world.'

He thought this was no time to be either supporting or
opposing Isaac's Leveller politics which were for many the
moral driving force that led them to volunteer to serve in
Parliament's army against the King. He turned to face the
expectant crowd.

'I believe that there are many important issues that should
be debated, and I regard it as one of the great hallmarks of
our cause that the people of Plymouth should be able freely
and openly to discuss such matters, without fear of
censorship or arbitrary arrest. But I have to say to you that
the Cornish army, and its wicked leaders, are not yet
defeated, and Plymouth's peril is real and imminent until the
final victory is won. I beg you therefore to allow me to go
about my pressing and immediate duties. Even now, our
Mayor, Mr Francis, and our Garrison Commander, Sir
William Ruthin are awaiting my arrival. We have great things
still to do!'

There were a few good-natured cheers as he reached up to
shake Isaac's hand, and as he made his way up to the Castle
he heard Isaac behind him.

'Sir Alexander is right, the war is not yet won. But men
that must go out to fight, and perhaps to die should give

thought to the justice of the cause for which they fight and die . . .'

Philip escaped from his awkward meeting when a soldier came from the castle to say that Sir Alexander had arrived, and 'would be grateful if Mr Francis would come up to share his dinner at four o'clock'. Charles Vaughan was cynical.

'If he's inviting you to share his dinner, it's because he's not going to keep his promise to you.'

Philip was troubled with the same presentiment, but put a bold face on his anxiety.

'Sir Alexander only ever promised to take counsel of his wife, who seems to hold the purse strings at Antony, and to offer us, as security for the pearls, as much cash as he could afford. It would assist me greatly, Mr Vaughan, if you could prepare a small summary of the present position as far as funds for the garrison are concerned, so that I can answer any question Sir Alexander may want to raise. May I call to collect it from you a few minutes before four?'

Charles and Peter took their leave, and Philip poured himself a glass of wine and reviewed his strategy.

If General Chudleigh crushed the Cornish, all the West Country would be secure in Parliament's hands. He could retrieve the pearls from Sir Alexander, and take ship openly for France, perhaps with a small official escort. Once in Paris the pearls could be properly sold for a very great sum, and it might be good policy to cover all possibilities by donating a proportion to the royal cause, in secret of course. Charles' Queen, Henrietta Maria, or her agents would certainly be in Paris looking out for just such support, and would be suitably grateful. He would then return to Plymouth and present the Committee with money and an official receipt, made out for some plausible fraction of the full price.

If on the other hand the battle went badly, he would have

to share the pearls with the Carews. But at least he would know that his escape would not be opposed by the guns on St. Nicholas Island. All in all, he thought, it was as good a plan as could be constructed in the current uncertainties.

'I can appreciate your disappointment, Mr Francis, but the sum of one thousand pounds, as you originally proposed, is quite beyond the capacity of Antony.'

Alexander was once again seated at his table in Plymouth Castle with Philip, dining together frugally off cheese, bread and pickles with a jug of beer.

'My wife's dowry, you recall, was a possible source, but she reminded me that I have already had most of it to pay our garrison when we were short, and until that can be repaid . . .'

He opened his hands as though to show that they were empty. Philip was a veteran of many negotiations, and waited patiently to see what would be offered. He remembered that special lust for possession he had seen Sir Alexander reveal on the last occasion.

'However, we are anxious to do the very best we can for our beloved town and our cause. I therefore have a suggestion which I believe will meet the need.' He reached into a side pocket of his yellow jerkin and pulled out a heavy leather bag, 'I have brought today two hundred and twenty pounds in gold. I know it is not as much as you asked, but it really is every penny that can be spared. In addition I have made an estimate of all the wheat still in our barns from last year's harvest. It is not an exact weight, but I believe there is something in excess of two hundred quarters. I am proposing to offer this to the Committee at forty shillings for the quarter, which is below the current market price, and very much below what the price may go to if this year's harvest is restricted again.'

'But Sir Alexander, you well know that the Committee has no funds to buy your wheat, no matter how great the potential profit.'

'I will, of course, accept your signature on a note, after delivery. Payable when times allow.'

Philip went through the motions of arguing that the cash was too little, and the price of the wheat too high for so large a quantity, but Alexander would not be moved, guessing that public opinion would feel his offer was fair, even supposing that Philip dared to bring it out into the open. On his side, Philip was relieved that there was enough to pay off Peter Keckwick, and so retain his invaluable support on the Council.

'The pearls, Sir Alexander, are they in a safe place?'

'As safe as can be.'

'May I know where?'

'I think not, Mr Francis, I think not. If you do not know where they are, you can swear on oath that you do not, even if, the Lord forbid, you were put to the torture. I think it is safest for both of us if I alone know where they are. Believe me, they are totally secure, even if Antony itself is torn to pieces.'

'And can be retrieved quickly, if need be?'

'Quickly enough. As to the rest of the plan, my wife is arranging to buy from one of her friends a fishing boat with a cabin, a boat large enough to carry us all to France if the need should arise. I will have it fitted out and kept at the Island with a crew. We could use it meantime for patrolling off-shore a few miles, keeping a watch for any enemy fleet, and incidentally keeping the crew busy and well-trained for us. Is there any news now of General Chudleigh?'

'We had a captain of his dragoons return here three, no four days ago. He had been sent to procure more powder and ball, with some urgency, and the captain gave us some news whilst we collected his supply and gave him dinner. Everything seems to be going to plan. Sir Ralph Hopton is said to have set up a camp down near Tintagel, and to be attempting to regroup there. The Earl of Stamford is reported to have recovered his health, and to have marched out from Exeter with the main army, advancing westward through

Okehampton. Our General Chudleigh is planning to occupy a hill near Stratton, from which he can command the coast road through Bude which Hopton must take if he wants to break out. And the general's father, Sir George Chudleigh, is pushing directly westward with a strong detachment of dragoons from the main army to cut off any retreat for Hopton, at Bodmin. I'm no military tactician, Sir Alexander, but it looks as though we have them in the jaws of a trap. The captain was most confident.'

'So am I, Mr Francis, totally confident.'

When James Chudleigh had won his victory at Bridestowe, two weeks previously, the rumours of a success had reached Plymouth by some means the very next day, and his letter to Alexander told the full story for everyone to read a few days later. The awful news of the disaster at Stratton on 16 May was heard for the first time in Plymouth only after a full week had passed, and was not fully understood for another week after that. The story filtered through only in small snippets, a bit here from a travelling pedlar, a piece there from a shepherd who had heard it from a soldier on the run, more when Sir George Chudleigh retreated into Plymouth from Bodmin, and more rumours later still when it was reported from Exeter that the Earl of Stamford had actually been summoned to a court-martial in London under pain of death.

When James' father, Sir George Chudleigh, clattered into Plymouth at the head of his dragoons on the evening of 23 May he was greeted at the gate of Plymouth Castle by Alexander himself. Sir George asked the first question, from the saddle.

'Has Hopton attacked Plymouth yet?'

Alexander looked at Sir George and his men, their horses lathered up as evidence of a hard ride, presumably straight from Bodmin – a good forty miles. His question seemed to confirm for Alexander the truth of the rumours that had been circulating around the town all day, and a cold apprehension gripped his mind, so that it was with difficulty that he kept a tremor from his voice.

'No, Sir George, we have seen no fighting here since the end of the truce, thank God. Come, let me help you from your horse, and welcome you officially to Plymouth. The Guard Commander will attend to your men. We are desperate here to know how things went at Stratton.'

Sir George dismounted stiffly from his mud-caked horse, and seemed glad of Alexander's supporting arm as he walked wearily under the portcullis of the castle, and up the stairs. Sir George was the brother of Alexander's dead mother, Bridget. A bluff, friendly man in his late forties, he was tall, with a mane of long fair hair – an older version of his son, though where James was clean-shaven his father sported a fine moustache and a pointed beard. As he came into Alexander's room he shrugged off his big black riding coat, and almost collapsed into the chair by the fire.

'So you've not heard what happened at Stratton? The worst, I'm afraid, an awful business. My son . . .'

'James? He's not been killed?'

'No, thank God, not killed. Nor wounded either.'

He seemed to retreat into some inner world, and Alexander decided, with huge reluctance, that he must put good manners and common sense before his own agonised desire to know the truth.

'Please, Sir George, I am forgetting the respect due to your years. If you will withdraw here into my bedroom you can rest for half an hour while I have a bath prepared for you in front of the fire here. No doubt your dragoons and their officers will be satisfying the town's curiosity, and I will content myself with waiting until you are refreshed.'

Alexander's room in the Castle looked south across Plymouth Sound to the low silhouette of St Nicholas Island,

the 'stopper in the bottle' as it was called, and beyond that to
the open sea. As he stood by the window the calm waters of
the Sound were still bright from the last of the evening sun
setting behind him, with the dark shadow of the castle
expanding moment by moment beneath his feet. Sir George
sat in the leather armchair by the fire, finishing a bowl of
lamb stew. He was refreshed physically, but the deep
depression of his thoughts was obvious from the slump of his
shoulders, and the way he paused again and again to stare
into the flames. At last the older man put down his bowl on
the small table next to his chair, and held out a hand.

'Come and sit beside me, Alexander, I can imagine what
you're going through at this moment. I went through it
myself when I heard the first rumours that reached us in
Bodmin, where we were quartered.'

Alexander pulled up an oak stool and sat in front of the
fire, wondering if there was any crumb of comfort or hope
that Sir George could offer. How soon might he have to
activate the escape plan? But Sir George wanted to get into
the story in his own way, and Alexander controlled his
impatience out of respect for his uncle, but it was a hard
struggle

'You're family, Alex, I was always your mother's favourite
brother, you know. Can you remember her at all?'

Alexander kept his eyes fixed on the glowing logs, which
were now the principal source of light in the room. Could he
remember his mother?

'I remember her dying. I remember because it was soon
after my sister Gertrude was born, and I wasn't allowed to
see my mother, and I was angry with Gertrude for that. My
father came out into the paddock, where I was sitting on my
pony in front of my sister Elizabeth, and he picked us both
together off the pony. Father was so silent and stern that I
was frightened and cried. When we got into the bedroom my
mother was lying on the big high bed, and her face was in the
dark behind the curtain. My father lifted me up to kiss her,
and I cried again because my sisters and nurse were crying.

Then my mother said said something, and I was carried out of the room and I never saw her again.'

Sir George put a hand on his shoulder, 'Not a happy memory to have, especially as your only memory. You don't recall those last words I suppose?'

'In a way. My father taught them to us later. In fact one of my sisters, Mary I think it was, sewed them into a sampler, and it hung above my bed when I was little. It said, "Lord, though thou killest me, yet will I put my trust in thee".'

There was a long stillness as Sir George put his head back against the high back of the chair, and closed his eyes as though to dream of his long-dead sister. Alexander too waited, and eventually his uncle sat forward purposefully, and spoke in a quiet voice.

'We will not be overheard or interrupted here?'

'Mine are the only rooms on this floor, and there are always two soldiers on guard at the foot of the stairs. We are quite secure.'

'Good. I have been putting my thoughts in order, and what I have to say is for your ears only. I have met with James.'

'With James? When, where?'

'Calmly now, Alex. Let me tell it my own way. There had been rumours reaching Bodmin of a battle at Stratton, where James was, but nothing definite until yesterday morning, when one of Hopton's lieutenants rode in, carrying a flag of parley on the end of a pike. He was led to my headquarters in the vicarage, where I was having a meeting with my captains to decide what to do. Our orders were quite precise, you know. We were to occupy Bodmin, and not move until Hopton's army tried to retreat past us, when our task was to break up and delay his movement so that the main army could totally destroy him. This lieutenant was a pompous fellow, nasty piece of work I thought, so offensive that I immediately forgot his name. Anyway, he said our army had been completely defeated, and thousands killed or captured. Sir Ralph Hopton was prepared to offer generous terms to us, but I must ride north with this fellow to Camelford for a parley, at once.'

'And you went?'

Sir George nodded. 'And I left orders that, if I had not returned by nightfall, my captains should carry out the plan we had already agreed on, to send scouts out after me as well as up to Launceston, and decide whatever they thought honourable and best for our cause. I rode with the Royalist lieutenant, accompanied by one of my own lieutenants and a couple of troopers.'

'Did you meet Hopton? Is he the perfect gentleman they say?'

'I didn't meet him, because he wasn't there. When we got to Camelford the village was deserted, except for a pair of silly women who flew into a panic as soon as they saw us and barricaded themselves in the church. We were told we should wait, but I was becoming suspicious. I found out later that Hopton's men had been through the village recruiting, and everyone else was hiding in the woods until dark. I was just about to break down the church door so as to question the women, when one of my men reported a small group approaching on horseback from the Bude road. And you may guess at my feelings when I saw my dear James at the head. And then almost immediately I realised that his three soldiers were all Royalist troopers!'

'You mean James was a prisoner?'

Sir George looked steadily at him.

'He was in command? Of a squad of . . . Royalist troops? He's . . . he's changed sides?'

Alexander thought of his last meeting with James. The perfect soldier, professional in every way. More than that, he had delighted in being genuinely proud of his connections to Parliament's cause, and seemed enviably free of the doubts and anxieties that had so pressed on his own thoughts, to the exclusion of almost everything else.

'Your astonishment is certainly no greater than mine, Alex. Anyway James had brought a loaf and some cold meat, and we two were allowed to withdraw a little from the rest, so he told me his story. You're sure we can't be overheard?'

Alexander went to the door of his chamber and checked
that the landing was empty. On his return he lit two candles
with a taper, and put them on the small table between them.
Sir George looked old, and unutterably weary.

'We are quite alone.'

'Forgive my caution, Alex, but I am thinking of your safety
as well as my own. James said that a week ago, on 16 May,
he was in place on Stratton Knoll. Do you know it?

'I'm afraid I don't, no.'

'It's to one side of the side of the road, very near Bude and
the sea, rising fairly steeply to three or four hundred feet, flat
on the top, three hundred yards across, half grass, half beech
and scrub. You can see for miles in every direction. That
morning as soon as it was light, the enemy could be seen
advancing in a great cloud of dust from the south. At the
same time James could see the Earl of Stamford's army, five
thousand good men, drawn up below him and just to the east
of the road. The agreed plan was that the Earl would engage
the enemy as they came up, and then, once they were fully
committed, James should charge down from the knoll and
take them in the flank. Good, simple plan, I thought.'

'How could it go wrong?'

'It didn't go wrong, it just didn't happen, because the Earl
did nothing. He just sat there with his army, and let Hopton
march right past him, about four thousand Cornish and a
couple of hundred cavalry. Of course they knew where James
was, and they marched straight on up the hill in five columns,
led by Sir Bevil Grenville. James said his men fought well, but
they were outnumbered three to one. The Cornish infantry
will follow Sir Bevil anywhere, and are truly ferocious
fighters. There was no sign of movement from the Earl's army
below, and James thought it was obvious that it was only a
matter of time before all his men were slaughtered. So he
decided to try to break out with the two hundred surviving
dragoons, and they charged full pelt across the knoll at the
enemy, with James at their head. They broke clean through,
but then the steep slope down was their undoing. They

discovered they had to ride down through massed ranks of
pikemen still coming up, and many of James' men were killed
in the melee. James dodged and twisted this way and that, but
eventually he found himself at a standstill in a steep gully,
surrounded by a hundred Cornish pikes, who would have
skewered him on the spot if Hopton himself had not come up
and saved him.'

'On condition that he changed sides?'

'Don't be too quick to condemn, Alex. No, James was
simply taken prisoner, as were most of the men he had left at
the top. Then Hopton turned his troops around to face the
Earl, but the Earl and his army simply melted away. James
said he was sickened by the cowardice of it, the way the Earl
had simply abandoned him and his men to be killed, after
agreeing to the plan of attack. It was the Earl, you remember,
who agreed to the truce in March, and severely criticised he
was for it at Westminster. Then the Earl had that mysterious
illness that prevented him leading his army out of Exeter until
he was shamed into it by James' brilliant victory at
Bridestowe. And now this latest proof that some treacherous
arrangement had been made.'

'Did Hopton confirm that?'

'James said not, but the facts speak for themselves, do they
not?'

Alexander wondered if anyone could ever know the truth
about a battle. That morning there had been rumours in
Plymouth about 'treachery in high places', but James had not
been named, as far as he knew. He thought his uncle had
suffered enough already, but he had to try to understand
James' reasons. Sir George answered the unspoken question.

'James said he believed the Earl had intended to change
sides himself with his army, but may have been prevented at
the last minute by the committed Parliament men among his
captains. But the result was much the same. Our Army of the
West is in tatters, broken up, gone home or fled back into
Exeter, with hundreds butchered and two thousand taken
prisoner. James said he had been treated most kindly by Sir

Ralph, and was particularly drawn to Sir Bevil. You know him of course?'

'We were friends at Westminster until that debate about Strafford. Bevil thought I was too impetuous in speaking so strongly against Strafford. But he's a good man, and I liked him.'

'It was Bevil who suggested that James could ask for a Royal Pardon. James said he just felt sick at heart. He didn't say as much, but I wondered if he also worried about me, cut off in Bodmin behind Hopton. I think he may have felt he was giving me a better chance to survive. I told him to say I had undertaken to go back to Bodmin to discuss surrendering with my captains, and then I brought the troops back to Plymouth.'

Alexander guessed that Sir George had been struggling to reconcile his own loyalties after his son's decision to rejoin the King. Perhaps he had only volunteered to join Parliament himself because his son had? Perhaps his captains at Bodmin had given him no choice but to return to Plymouth? Deep waters indeed!

'I'm very grateful, Sir George, that you have taken me into your confidence in this way. You may be certain that everything we have talked about tonight will be kept secret. And no word of accusation or condemnation of James will be spoken by me. Shall we get to bed now?'

After Sir George had withdrawn gratefully to the spare bedroom, Alexander sat in the comfortable chair he had vacated and tried to take stock of the position. Parliament's Army of the West was lost. What would Hopton do now? Probably follow his original orders, to join with Prince Rupert in Somerset, with an eye to capturing the great prize of Bristol. The King must be desperate for a safe port to bring in his foreign troops and supplies ... yes, definitely Bristol. Where did that leave Plymouth? Soon all Devon would hear of Hopton's victory and the Earl's treachery, and

the undecided majority would come out for the winners.
Recruits would flock to the King's colours, and there would
be men to spare to attack the towns across the county. Most
had stood by Parliament so far, but none, he thought, were
as committed as Plymouth. Probably most would open their
gates at the first serious challenge. Would Plymouth even
stand firm? Could it possibly stand alone even if it wanted to,
as the rest of the west country was submerged in a rising tide
of support for the King? How long before there was real
pressure behind the siege again? The Fleet, and all the ports
of any consequence from Hull round to Plymouth were in
Parliament's hands. They would surely try to sustain
Plymouth from the sea, as long as St Nicholas Island held.
As long as the Island held . . .

He stood up restlessly, and walked to the window. There
was the little island, dark now except for the pale glow of a
fire burning in the blockhouse guardroom. Time for another
visit tomorrow . . . he walked back to the fireplace and kicked
the log into a blaze of sparks and flames, then back to the
window again. *Plymouth is a prison, and I am to be sentenced
to death.* If the town was directly besieged again, it would
become too dangerous to visit Antony, indeed the house itself
might be seized. He thought of the Cornish troopers, and
their savage reputation. Would his wife and children be safe
in Antony? Was there any alternative? Bring them into
Plymouth perhaps – and abandon Antony to the looters? As
Mr Francis had said, the penalties for having backed the
losing side were too terrible to think about. He thought of the
brave words he had spoken in Parliament to support John
Pym in defence of the rights of Parliament, and again only
last January to help bring down Thomas Ceely in Plymouth.
How important were all those fine ideals about Liberty,
Equality and the right of every man to share in the
management of the country? Where did that really leave the
King? With the responsibilities of leadership, but without the
authority to govern. Did he want to see control of the
country in the hands of the landless mob? Because they were

certainly in the majority. The Greeks had tried total democracy, and Plato had surely been correct in condemning its mindless extravagances, as every would-be leader outbid the promises of every other in the contest for power. Did he want to be one of the makers of a Revolution, of a Republic even? Or did he just want now to be left in peace to enjoy his family and his beloved Antony, like his father?

Weary, bewildered, and sick at heart with a deep foreboding of inescapable catastrophe, Alexander closed the wooden shutters on his windows, pinched out the candles and dropped onto his bed, fully-clothed except for his boots.

Lucy

Early the next morning, Sir William Ruthin, Plymouth's Garrison Commander and de facto Military Governor, talked at length with Sir George, and invited him, together with Alexander and Philip to come to his room in the Castle at midday. 'Morale is the essence of the problem', he thought, 'In such circumstances confidence is everything. And it must flow from the top'.

'Help yourselves to some wine gentlemen. As it is such a fine, warm day I thought we would dine on cold beef and pickles, with an apple pie to follow.'

Philip Francis took a deep pull from a silver cup of wine, but would not easily be distracted from the gravity of the situation.

'Be straight with us now, Sir William. I have to think and speak for the lives and property of nine thousand souls here. Honest supporters of Parliament, most of them are. But ignorant of the realities of a siege, let alone a sack. Can we stand alone? Sir Alexander, will Parliament send an army to rescue us? How long before we have a Royal army at our gates?'

He sat down at the oak dining table by the tall lancet casements, and mopped his forehead in the brilliant light of the afternoon sun. Alexander thought he looked near to collapse. Perhaps he was anticipating only too vividly what his fate would be if he were taken with the town.

For his part, Alexander now felt strangely calm and

resigned. He had played out the hand he had been dealt, because honour would not allow him to do otherwise. He had played and lost, as it seemed, and now he must wait to see what the penalty would be. Back in Antony his wife, Jane, was supervising the fitting-out of the fishing boat to be able to carry passengers across the English Channel, but somehow the whole project had an air of unreality about it. Could he really see himself digging up his father's coffin to recover the pearls, and then sailing with his wife and children, together with Philip Francis and his pretty wife Lucy, into some desperate new life as exiles in France, or from there to Massachusetts even? Better surely to throw himself on the King's mercy and beg a Royal Pardon?

Sir William's response to Philip Francis was a sharp rebuke.

'Sir George, Sir Alexander, Mr Francis, I am Commander of the Garrison of Plymouth by the express commission of Parliament. There will be no despair, no talk of defeat at my table. Firstly, I had my scouts out yesterday, and one came back just a few minutes ago. He confirms that Sir Ralph and the Cornish army are indeed marching away from us, presumably towards Bristol. For the time being at least, Plymouth is not their objective.'

'Hopton may not be the only threat, Sir William. From what I learned of the events at Stratton Knoll, it seems more than possible that the Earl of Stamford has gone over, which must raise the possibility also that the remainder of the Army of the West could be turned against us.'

Sir George spoke from the table beside Philip, who was engaged carving thick slices of roast beef for them all.

'My information is far from complete on that matter, Sir George, but it does appear possible that your suspicions of the Earl's loyalty are perhaps misplaced. There have certainly been stories of his troops filling the roads to Exeter, and I believe it is safe to assume that his army has not changed allegiance, not at this time. So we will certainly send today to Exeter for reinforcements to replace the half of the garrison that General Chudleigh unfortunately lost, and we may expect to see them within a week or so.'

Alexander felt his mood of numb despair lifting, and tried to sound positive, 'We look to you as always, Sir William, to marshal our defence. What would you have us do?'

Sir William cut himself a fat slice of apple pie, 'Excellent, excellent. Spiced with cinnamon and nutmeg, I believe. We have your father to thank for this pie, Sir Alexander. He sent me a barrel of his best russets last Christmas, and these are from the last of it. Our castle dungeon has provided ideal storage this winter.'

He judged that the mood of his guests was more impatient than despairing now, and continued briskly.

'Now, as I see it, the strategic situation is quite clear.' He spread out his map on the table, and emphasised the logic of his assessment with his fingers, 'Point one; Hopton is under orders to join the Prince. Point two; the King's aim must be to get a convenient port to bring in his reinforcements and supplies, so Bristol is the target. Point three; Parliament, we have heard, has put an army already in the field to prevent that, under Sir William Waller. The Prince must defeat that army before he dares lay siege to Bristol, and he will find them a hard nut. Point four; Bristol will also be resolutely defended, and will not fall quickly anyway. So taking my four points together now, the King's armies will certainly have their hands full this summer, trying to fulfil their key objective, the possession of Bristol. If they are held off by the combination of Sir William Waller and the citizens of Bristol, there will be no force to spare to attack us this year. If, which the Lord forbid, they succeed at Bristol, it is still reasonable to assume that Plymouth will be seen as of no strategic importance, at least not worth diverting a large army with cannon to reduce. Therefore we may assume that we have time on our side. Does anyone care to dispute my calculation?'

There was a fierceness in his challenge that boded ill for anyone who cared to take it up. It was Alexander who broke the awkward silence.

'I'm with you, Sir William. We have time. Can we do more to help ourselves now?'

'We can indeed, a lot more. I turn again to you and your brave people, Mr Francis. Can you get them digging again?'

Philip seemed to drag himself back from a long way off, and the stress in his voice was only too evident.

'It's a matter of life and death for us isn't it, Sir William? I promise you they'll dig their way down to hell and back if that's what is needed to keep the Cornish out of Plymouth.'

'Not so far, not so far, thank the Lord. I want to be able to make best use of the forty cannon your son sent back to us, Sir George.'

'You have our full attention, Sir William. You need redoubts for the cannon?'

'Exactly. Have a look at this plan, and tell me what you think.' He unrolled a large sheet of white paper, and held down the corners with plates, 'You can see I've made a sketch map of Plymouth and the surrounds. Over here on the left is your country, Sir Alexander, separated from Plymouth by the Tamar river, so that protects our flank there. On the south here we have the Sound and the sea. That, too, is protected as long as we hold the Island.'

'We should probably increase the garrison there, in case a surprise landing is attempted.'

'We should, Sir Alexander, once there is an actual attack on the town. But until then I would rather not split my forces. And it's difficult to maintain good discipline and training with men cooped up on the Island.'

'I bow to your judgement, Sir William. I wonder though if I might suggest that an extra hundred men be allocated to my fort, with boats to move them?'

'Excellent tactics, a mobile reserve. And on the east side we have the Cattwater, which is also as good as a moat for us, and protected too by our forts across on Mount Batten and Stanfort. So, to sum up, any serious assault on Plymouth can only be attempted from the north side, where we have our ditch and rampart.'

'So that's where you'll want us to build the redoubts for the cannon?'

'I am gratified to see your grasp of our military needs, Mr Francis. Yes, we need five redoubts, one at each end of the ditch, and three covering the centre here at Holwell, Maudlyn and Pennycumquick. Each redoubt to be made double the height of the line, that's sixteen feet high, with a ramp going up from behind and sharpened stakes driven deep into the front to slow down any assaulting troops. I want the top of each redoubt to be flat, and hardened with stone and pebbles, hammered down so that we can manhandle our cannon even after a week of rain. Six cannon to go on each redoubt, the best ones, and the rest in reserve. We have powder a'plenty, with grape and canister shot. I pity any troops that try to assault our line!'

Philip Francis began to recover his shattered nerve, as he grasped the strength of Sir William's plan.

'Aye let them come, let them all come. We'll send them away with a bloody nose, just like Drake did with the Spanish! Tomorrow we start digging, and I will make the arrangements for that now. But this evening you're all to be my guests for supper. Sir Alexander, Sir William, Sir George – I have a new barrel of Spanish wine to be sampled, and Lucy and I look forward to welcoming you. Shall we say five o'clock?'

Alexander had drunk deeply of Philip's Spanish wine during the evening, and now he sat half-asleep by the fire. Beside him on the rug sat Lucy Francis, wearing a long pale green dress laced up to the chin with a white ribbon. After dinner Philip had persuaded his shy young wife to bring out her lute to entertain his guests. She sang a song of fishermen returning home from the sea, with a surprisingly strong, clear voice that echoed like a choirboy's around the oak-panelled walls of the upstairs parlour, now becoming shadowy in the gathering dusk. In turn she picked up the tune to accompany Sir

William in a Border ballad of chivalry and romance, and Sir
George seemed to throw off his melancholy for the evening
to offer a rollicking drinking song, which he sang in an
impenetrable Devon accent. Alexander's contribution was
Greensleeves, in a precise high tenor:

> Alas, my love, you do me wrong,
> To cast me off so discourteously,
> When I have loved you so long
> Delighting in your company.
> Greensleeves was all my joy,
> Greensleeves was my delight.
> Greensleeves was my heart of gold,
> And who but my lady, Greensleeves!

At the end he knelt in courtly humility at Lucy's feet, and
would not rise until she took his hand, to the accompaniment
of much banging of the table and roars of laughter at her
blushes. Soon afterwards, Sir George and Sir William took
their leaves, and Philip had just begged to be excused 'To
ensure there have been no problems in arranging for
tomorrow's work. See that Sir Alexander's cup is kept filled,
my dear.'

'Do you remember when you came to our house that night
in winter, after the great explosion at Queen's Buckland?'

Alexander turned to see Lucy looking up at him. Her long
fair hair was pinned back to frame her face, with its high
cheekbones, a small snub nose, huge tawny yellow eyes, and
a wide smiling mouth. She wasn't strictly a beauty, but her
youth and bright vitality were very appealing.

'When you came in I was as nervous as a baby deer. I'd
never met anyone so grand before, you being a Carew and
our Member of Parliament and all.'

'And how do you see me now?'

He knew at once that, just by asking the question, he had
in some strange way put himself into her hands, but it didn't
seem to matter. Nothing seemed to matter much now.

'You're not frightening at all, are you? You're like any man, you like to take a drink, and sing a song, and enjoy yourself.'

'And play the lover?'

Lucy looked at him in silence for a few, endless seconds, 'Play's the word I think, Sir Alexander Carew of Antony. I . . .'

There was a rattle downstairs of the front doorlatch, and she rose smoothly to her feet.

'Can I refill your cup for you, Sir Alexander?'

It had been at her father's urging that Lucy had married Philip Francis. Her father, Peter Keckwick, was by some distance the richest man in Plymouth, and finding a suitable match for his only child had been a matter of prolonged concern. They had been married almost a year now, and Philip liked his young wife. She was intelligent, attentive to his needs, and surprisingly well-read. Quick with figures, she was already largely in control of his wine-importing business, allowing him to devote ever more of his time to the town's affairs. On her side it was exciting now to be the mayor's wife, and there was a certain raw power about Philip's personality that excited her too.

She watched him from the high four-poster as he undressed beside the bedroom fire. He was almost fifty. His body was still strong, though his torso had thickened, with a mass of dark hair on his chest and belly, and across his thick-set shoulders. Lucy had a sudden vision of what they must look like, making love. Beauty and the Beast? Or perhaps she was Andromeda, and Philip was the Sea-Monster? She thought of Alexander Carew. He could be Perseus, come to rescue her . . . he would make a wonderful rescuer . . . would he be a good lover? 'What's amusing you?'

'Amusing?'

'You were smiling, Lucy, so I thought something must be amusing you.'

'Don't be so silly, I was looking forward to having you in
bed, that's all. These sheets are still cold.'

'What did you think of our guests?'

'I liked them all. Sir George was so sad to start with, but
he was very jolly later on. Do you know he patted my bottom
when I was serving his pasty?'

'Did he now? We'll have to watch out for him in future,
won't we? Sir William didn't lay hands on you, I trust?'

'Of course not. He's a proper Scottish gentleman, isn't he?
I loved that pretty ballad, though I didn't understand half the
words.'

'Sir Alexander made his meaning quite clear, wouldn't you
say?'

'He likes me, that's all. People from London have fancy
ways, Philip.'

'He does like you, that much is certain. And that could be
important for us both. Our lives could depend on him, as you
know. If the opportunity arises, you may encourage his
attentions . . . in a proper way, of course.'

'To hear is to obey, Great Lord. And now, how about your
husbandly duties?'

As Sir William had forecast, there was no immediate threat
to Plymouth, and throughout the long hot days of June
citizens and soldiers laboured side by side to construct the five
great redoubts that would so harden the town's defence.
Huge quantities of earth were dug by sweating men and
women to build each mound – fifty feet across, and as high
as a house. A ramp at the back allowed stones to be hauled
up to be rammed hard into the tops, and also the cannons,
shot and barrels of powder to be dragged up by teams of
horses. Later the ramps would be cut away for extra security,
and the ring of outward facing stakes driven in and sharpened
so that access would be by ladder only.

Two weeks after the work had begun Sir William was taken ill with a fever, and Alexander decided he could not leave the town, much as he longed to see Jane and the children again. He found himself in great demand to co-ordinate the planning and work of soldiers and civilians, and to arbitrate in the occasional dispute. He had become, *de facto*, the Governor of Plymouth.

Throughout the month there were rumours of Royalist raiding parties coming to threaten the town, and frequent alarms on St Nicholas Island when strange ships were sighted in the English channel. No shots were fired in anger however, and as warm day succeeded warm day, and the redoubts neared completion, Alexander felt the crushing anxiety gradually relax within him. He was at his favourite post by the telescope on the top of the tower of Plymouth Castle when a trooper rattled up the ladder and through the trapdoor to interrupt his reverie.

'Beg pardon sir. There's Mistress Francis below with her maid. Says she's brought a pie for your dinner.'

Alexander glanced up at the sun, high over the Island – midday already!

'Ask her to come up. No, I'll climb down, that ladder is a rickety climb for a lady.'

Before Alexander could follow the trooper down he heard Lucy's voice.

'Don't be a silly goose, Lizzie, of course I can climb the ladder. And this nice soldier here can bring the basket up for you, can't he?'

In a moment her blonde head appeared through into the sunlight, and Alexander found himself taking the cool hand she held up, and then putting an arm around her to steady her first steps onto the narrow battlement. She was wearing a loose cotton smock of palest blue, set off with white daisies embroidered on the full skirt and around the low neckline, which she emphasised for Alexander with a deep curtsy.

'I made a game pie this morning for Mr Francis, and then he sent to say he was detained on the Lipsom Mill redoubt.

He mentioned only last night how lonely it was for you, Sir Alexander, so I thought you would be glad of a little company, and a taste of my rabbit and venison pie?'

There was a challenge and an artless invitation in Lucy's matter-of-fact friendliness that Alexander found irresistible. The mention of her husband seemed to imply that he knew and approved of her visit. Still . . .'

'You are most welcome, Lucy, most welcome. But you should be chaperoned, don't you think? Call your maid. Ask her to come up and enjoy the view.'

'She absolutely refuses, Sir Alexander. She was my nurse, you know, and insists that respectable ladies do not climb ladders. I'm afraid that I am a terrible disappointment to her. Will you be too embarrassed if I stay up here by myself? She is within call, like your soldiers, if the need arises . . .'

Alexander bowed to hide the smile on his face.

'Well then, Lucy, what do you think of my view?

They went together from embrasure to embrasure around the four sides of the tower. Lucy knew every inch of the town, and delighted in telling Alexander the family history and scandals that lay beneath this plain thatch or that slated roof. She pointed out her father's fishing boats in the Sutton pool, awaiting the next tide that would bring in the mackerel shoal.

'Father tells me the price of fish is rising every week in London. Trouble is, no one has any money left, so it's all on credit. Everyone owes everyone else pounds and pounds, you know. How will it all end?'

Alexander's grasp of the economics of the war was only slightly more profound than Lucy's, but he applied himself seriously to answer her question.

'We all help one another, that's the important thing. Here in Plymouth you could say we are in the very front line of the war. We have soldiers to pay, horses to feed, ammunition and uniforms to buy. And the war itself restricts us, so our people can't earn as much from fishing and trading, the way they used to, and this year's harvest must be in doubt until it's safely in the barns. But Parliament can raise contributions for us in the way of taxes from other parts of the country, and send us the money to pay our expenses. Of course the people there don't like paying taxes, but at least that's better than having the King's army on their doorstep, so they do.'

By this time Lucy had found the telescope. Alexander showed her how to shut one eye so as to peer through the other, and how to follow a line feature like Drake's Water into the hazy green and brown distances of Dartmoor. She looked sadly at the ruins of Queen's Buckland.

'Isn't that terrible? There's no one moving there at all. Just a few blackened walls, and half the church. Philip's sister Charity died there.'

Alexander was adjusting the focus, standing close behind Lucy. He felt her tremble as his body touched hers. A half-turn of her head brought her cheek against his, and when he did not withdraw she turned completely, to be rewarded with the sudden warm pressure of his lips on hers, and a pair of strong arms holding her tightly. Eventually she gasped and broke away, to sit down on the parapet beside the telescope. Her whole body seemed to be trembling, but when she looked at her hands, at her legs beneath the blue cotton, there was no sign of movement. Alexander was leaning against the wall beside her.

'Lucy, I'm sorry . . . I didn't mean . . . I shouldn't have . . . you seemed so sad about poor Charity, I wanted to comfort you.'

Lucy pushed her long fair hair back from her forehead, and looked calmly up at Alexander, once again in command of herself.

'I suppose I must have wanted to be comforted. That explosion . . . brought the war so close to us all. Women expect the usual dangers of childbirth and getting ill. Accidents too, like a fire or drowning. But being blown to pieces or roasted alive . . . it's so terrible.'

A warning rattle on the ladder caused Lucy to stand quickly and move away along the parapet.

'Beg pardon, Sir Alexander, there's a message for you. Sir

William has taken a turn for the worse, and the doctor wonders if you would like to talk to him now.'

Before Alexander could reply Lucy was at the head of the ladder herself, preparing to follow the trooper down to the room below.

'Thank you so much for letting me try your telescope, Sir Alexander. It really is quite powerful, isn't it? Do enjoy the game pie, and if you like I'll bring you another, no ... something different. Tomorrow?'

'Tomorrow would be fine, Mistress Francis. If it's not too much trouble?'

'Until tomorrow then. My kindest regards to Sir William, and please give him our best wishes from Mr Francis and myself for a speedy recovery.'

Recovery was not what the doctor wanted to talk about. He met Alexander outside the door of Sir William's chamber and led him to one end of the landing, out of earshot of the sentries below.

'His fever is high and rising. I've bled him of course, several times, but ...' He spread his hands in a gesture of professional despair. 'Frankly, I am most worried. Those two weeks, after the news came of the disaster at Stratton, he did not spare himself by night or day. He would rise at four to spend every hour of daylight at his blessed redoubts, getting back at ten at night to labour by candlelight on reports to Parliament, and studies of manpower or supplies or pay for his men. Is it to be wondered at that the fever has taken such a hold on him?'

'Is he rational?'

'If you mean "Is he babbling or delirious?", the answer is, "No". But if you mean, "Is he resting quietly and trying to conserve his strength?", the answer is also, "No". He has insisted most strongly to me that he wants to talk to you.'

'Then here I am.'

'Indeed you are, sir. I should forbid you from the

sickroom, partly to protect my patient, but also for your own sake. Lord knows what miasma it is that has seized him, but he is burning up with it, and Plymouth can ill afford to have yourself struck down with it also, Sir Alexander. So when you go in you are to be brief, no more than five minutes, I beg you. And it is not necessary to embrace or approach so closely that you take his breath. A friendly handshake will be reassurance enough.'

'It's not plague? I heard some rumours in the town . . .'

'There is some plague in the town, just one house down by the dockside, and it seems to be a mild one this year. But Sir William's case, though puzzling, is definitely not the plague.'

Alexander opened the door into Sir William's sitting room, bright now with the afternoon sun. It was silent, as though awaiting a visitor.

'Who's there?'

'It's Alexander Carew, Sir William, you wanted me to come in I think?'

Alexander pushed open the bedroom door, and peered into the gloom. The thick red wool curtains were drawn across the window, and the air was fetid with the smell of sweat and stale linen. Sir William's simple bed was behind the door.

'Come in, come in, Sir Alexander. That damn doctor would have me perish in the stinking dark. Pull back the curtains, would you, and open a window to let some of God's glorious air into this place?'

Alexander obeyed, and the room was transformed from night into day. He turned to see the Garrison Commander sitting up in bed with a big feather pillow behind his back. His face was gaunt and drawn, and his usual outdoor sunburn had been replaced with a sickly pallor, except for a bright spot of colour on each cheek. Beads of perspiration plastered his thinning sandy hair to his forehead. There was a hollow-eyed look about him that reminded Alexander inexorably of his father's last hours. He tried to be cheerful and down to earth.

'The doctor seems to think you're over the worst now, Sir William. Is there anything I can get you? Some wine perhaps?

I have some excellent game pie. Mistress Francis brought it over, and it's more than I can manage.'

Sir William said nothing for a few long seconds, as though summoning his strength.

'Nothing, thank you Sir Alexander. I've been bled by that butcher till he's had all my powers, and now it's up to me I know. If I can just see the night through . . .' His voice faded, and he was obviously making a great effort to concentrate. 'Our defence . . . I know you've been taking my place these last days, and I thank you for it. Press them, press them hard to finish the redoubts properly and get the cannon mounted. You must arrange watches. And a system of checking on the watches. The biggest danger is a surprise attack that succeeds in capturing some part of our defence. If any redoubt or fort is taken it must, must be recaptured, no matter what the cost. No matter what, is that understood? It must be . . .'

His eyes closed and his head dropped abruptly to one side. For a moment Alexander thought he was dead, but he drew a huge gasping breath through his open mouth, then continued to breathe shallowly. Alexander took up the hand that hung down beside the bed, and folded it over Sir William's chest before stepping quietly from the room.

Sir William survived the night's crisis, but he was left considerably enfeebled, as the doctor reported to Alexander two days later.

'He's like a baby, Sir Alexander, a weak and helpless baby. I pray to God that he may live, but even if he does his days of soldiering are over, I'm sure of that.'

Alexander wrote a short report on the situation for Parliament's War Council, which concluded:

By general consent I have assumed the duties, but not the title, of Governor of Plymouth, and am well supported in this by our Mayor, Mr Philip Francis, and by Sir William's Captains of Foot, Horse, and Artillery, good men all. We are

confident that your army will crush Hopton's Cornish before he
can join with the Prince, and so you may proceed to relieve our
beleaguered position. You may be certain that your Bastion in
the West will be loyally and fiercely defended if the need arises.

The report went that night by ship to Portsmouth and on by
courier to Westminster, where it arrived on 27 June.
Alexander's half-brother, John Carew, read it amongst the
rest of the next day's correspondence for John Pym. John was
twenty years old, dark and rather sallow from long hours in
Parliament's service, with a thin face and close-cropped hair in
the Puritan fashion. He thought of his mother's letter which
had arrived a week previously, and wondered where the truth
lay. Was Alexander the dedicated 'Keeper of Parliament's
Bastion' as his report proclaimed? Or was he the callous
schemer his mother had described? Alexander had always been
a rather distant figure, being fourteen years older than himself.
Was he likely to turn traitor? John and his mother Grace, and
all her Rolle family were deeply committed to Parliament's
cause, and had been for many years. It was for that reason that
Pym had taken John as one of his secretaries. But the Carews
were much grander, connected by descent and marriage to the
Arundells, the Godolphins and the Edgcumbes, all great
Cornish families, all likely to favour the royalist cause. John
decided that, whatever the truth of the matter, his own
interests would be best served by cautiously following his
mother's lead. If Alexander were to go over, John's position
would be compromised unless he could distance himself in
advance. He pinned a note to Alexander's report:

> In view of Ruthin's illness we should appoint another
> Garrison Commander, and ensure that the garrison is paid.
> There are rumours locally of a plot to surrender the town. We
> should avoid the possibility of a situation similar to that just
> uncovered at Kingston upon Hull.

John Carew read and re-read his note, and concluded that it
struck just the right tone. He could imagine that Pym's

reaction to the report would be to want to publish selected parts of it as a pamphlet for general distribution, with the aim of fortifying London's morale with the story of heroic resistance in Plymouth. Alexander himself could be cast as a popular hero. He might even become the *Bastion* personified! His own little comment might just give them pause. The War Council, led by John Pym, seethed with personal rivalries, suspicions and fear of treachery. The Earl of Stamford had arrived only a week previously from Exeter, and was to be formally impeached as being responsible for the debacle at Stratton that had allowed Hopton's army to escape. John knew that, as a matter of standard practice, a new garrison commander would be instructed to put spies and agents provocateurs to work, so if his mother was right in her suspicions Alexander would certainly be trapped. Could he do anything more? He paced restlessly around his tiny room, then sat down again to write, rising again to call down the hallway.

'Messenger there! There will be a letter to catch the Plymouth ship in ten minutes.'

Westminster, 28 June 1643

My Dearest Mother,

Although your letter has only just arrived, I hasten to reply today as I know that a ship sails for Plymouth on this afternoon's tide.

I will not comment at length on the unforgivable way Alexander has conducted father's funeral – or should I say not conducted it? Suffice it to say that I have always thought that he resented you and our family, and now his actions confirm that he intends to keep you and us in a place subservient to his wife and his family. I need hardly tell you, mother, that we will do everything possible to resist such a shameful denial of your rightful heritage.

On the other matter you touched on, I understand absolutely your meaning, and its implications. You will be interested, therefore, to learn that it was reported in Council yesterday that Sir John Hotham, Governor of our town of Kingston upon Hull, was arrested two days ago with his son, and charged with conspiring to betray the town to the Royalist delinquents. You can perhaps imagine Mr Pym's attitude to the threatened loss of our stronghold in the County of Yorkshire! He swore that Hotham would lose his head, and his estates, as an example to others who might plot against us. Let Alexander beware!

No more now, as our man is come to take this to the ship. May God bless and keep you,

    Your loving son,
    John

A little sigh, and the sound of soft breathing – Alexander opened his eyes. A narrow shaft of light from the curtained window of his small bedroom fell onto the white shoulder and the slim curves of Lucy's naked back. She slept peacefully beside him, a hand shading her face beneath a tousled mane of blonde hair. Alexander's head felt fuddled still by the wine they had drunk. By the angle of the light it must be late in the afternoon – four or even five o'clock? What was it that had awakened him? Some noise . . . downstairs? As if to answer his question there was a thunderously urgent knocking on the sitting room door.

'Sir Alexander, sir! A most important message from Captain Hallsey, sir. Could you come up to the top of the tower at once, please sir.'

Alexander was immediately alert, and called out as he dressed, 'Tell the captain I will be there in three minutes.'

Beside him on the narrow bed Lucy stirred and awoke. She stared at him in confusion for a few seconds as he struggled into his clothes, then calmly sat up and stretched. 'Alexander? Alex, what is it? What time is it? Must you go?'

'There's some emergency, I don't know what it is, but it must be important for Hallsey to disturb me.'

He finished tying his shirt, and reached for her, cupping one small breast in his right hand as he kissed her. 'I have to go at once, Lucy. I would say it is certainly late now, and you must get dressed too. Pick up your basket and come up to the tower with it as though you had just arrived. I shall be surprised and delighted to see you.'

If Captain Hallsey knew of Alexander's visitor, he was careful not to show it. 'Ah, there you are, Sir Alexander. I was sure you would want to see this.' His telescope was now on the tower's eastern parapet, and he stood aside as he spoke to offer it to Alexander. 'If you look due east, sir, past Saltram, about a mile.'

'Plymstock?'

'Past that sir. The village is hidden in those trees, but look in the road beyond.'

'Yes, yes, I see. A long column. Men on horseback.'

'And farther back I think I caught a glimpse of flashes of light from the tips of pikes.'

'Not our reinforcements from Exeter?'

'No such luck, sir. I saw an officer at the front just now with the red sash. Royalists.'

'They've come sooner than we expected. As far as we know Bristol is still ours, and Parliament's army is still in the field. Do you think Hopton has turned back?'

'He may have, sir, but I doubt that's him. There will be about a thousand dragoons there, and a few hundred infantry following behind. Hopton's army is much bigger, and nearly all infantry. My guess would be that this is a newly-raised force, perhaps from Barnstaple and North Devon. Recruited after Hopton had marched through and put the fear of God into our people. They will have heard tell that we are fortifying Plymouth, and have decided on a quick strike before the town is made impregnable.'

'Most of the Earl's army must have got back to Exeter by now, those that escaped at least. We should send a boat urgently with a request for troops. If we hold the enemy up at Plymouth, and our friends come straight on down the road from Exeter, we should catch the Royalists nicely in a trap.'

'Fine tactical thinking, sir. Only I rather doubt if it can be done that way.'

'Why's that?'

'In the first place we know the Earl has been summoned to London to explain himself, and so his captains will have no regular commander – so who could take the decision to strip Exeter to save Plymouth? Secondly, it's well known that the folk in Exeter are nowhere near as firm for Parliament as we are here. Fifty-fifty, as I've heard, and no doubt the soldiers there are just as divided. Half will think the King is going to win now, so they'll be for joining him while there's still time. And the other half will be afraid that Exeter will be the next city to be attacked after Bristol, so they'll want to remain there to man the defences. I doubt you'll get much from Exeter. Could your boat sail to Portsmouth for help?'

'It would take a lot longer, but I see no reason why not. I'll get him on his way as soon as I can get a letter over to the Island. Meanwhile could you arrange for a continuous watch to be kept on those troops from here, and call a meeting in half an hour in my room – the other captains and Mr Francis? And Sir George Chudleigh of course.'

'Very good, sir. And I'll get the bells ringing, and put the garrison on full alert.'

As he turned to go the ladder gave its familiar warning rattle.

'Why, Mistress Francis! I'm sorry there's no time for dinner now, we have an emergency. But you could play a part if you would. May I ask you to find the Mayor most urgently, and ask him to attend a meeting of the War Council in my room as soon as may be? There is a regiment of the enemy sighted, coming through Plymstock.'

From below he heard the bell in the Castle Chapel begin to sound a thin, rapid note, to be taken up within a minute by more sonorous tones from St Andrews and from King Charles New Church. A babel of shouting arose in the narrow streets around the Castle, which gradually coalesced into a single cry across the whole town.

'To arms! To arms! TO ARMS!'

* * *

Philip Francis finished his plate of cold pork, and pulled on his coat in silence after Lucy had relayed her message.

'It's two weeks now that you've been taking Sir Alexander your pies and fruit and your new bread. Two weeks of climbing up to his tower and admiring the scenery. And what's 'e bin doin' all this time, I wonder? Admirin' you, no doubt. 'As 'e kissed you? More than that, perhaps? 'Ave you 'ad 'im?'

Lucy looked him straight in the face, and her voice was firm and quiet. 'If my father heard you speak to me like that you'd feel the weight of his arm for sure. I've just been doing what you told me to do, flirting a bit, encouraging his attentions. He's got London ways, hasn't he? He likes to amuse himself courting and flattering a girl, but he's easy to keep at arms length, and he knows not to press too hard and spoil the game. Because that's all it is, a game. Mind you, I could lead him on if you wanted?'

'No need for that, not yet at least. But you do understand what could happen if Plymouth was taken, I know you do. Sir Alexander is our lifeline, and he has to want to save you, and so he has to save both of us.'

He pulled her to him and kissed her long and affectionately. 'I suppose I must seem a bit rough and a bit old-fashioned after Sir Alexander, but I do love you. We must work 'arder at makin' that baby we talked about.'

He was grinning like a naughty schoolboy as he left, and Lucy felt a momentary pang of contrition. First flirtation, then deceit, and now adultery. Where would it end? Today had been the first time. There had been a cold wind up on top the tower, so it seemed the most natural thing in the world to take their picnic lunch in his sitting room. The wine had made her dizzy, and Alexander had put his arms around her from behind as she sat, nodding a little, at his table. His lips were warm on her neck, and friendly as he blew a curl from her eyes. Then she was turning her face up to his, and he was kissing her long and hard and deep, and she was melting as he half-led, half-carried her into the darkened bedroom. It

was all so easy – he was such a tender, considerate lover . . .
she could feel the weight of him still on her body. She ran a
hand over her belly – wouldn't it be funny if the first baby
she had was Sir Alexander's? She must remember to call him
'Alex' in private . . .

Her daydream was overwhelmed by the dissonant clanging
of big and small bells and the shouts of people outside. They
would be assembling now in the Fish Market, by Sutton
Pool, exchanging wild gossip and hungry for hard news. She
knew of something to tell them, and hurried out to join the
bustling crowd.

'Anything moving your side of the tower?'

'Quiet as a Puritan's wedding. Yours?'

'Quiet here too. Sky's getting lighter over Dartmoor
though.'

'Thank the Lord for that. It must be after four then. Still
too dark to see much, even with these blessed telescopes.'

There was no immediate attack from the Royalist troops, and
Alexander had been pleased to find, earlier that evening, that
the Captains of Horse and Foot were bristling with
confidence.

'That's not a real army out there. That's a force raised in
Devon by Acland or one of the other local squires, I
shouldn't wonder. No doubt they've stiffened them with a few
professional troopers borrowed from Hopton. Probably just
sent here to make sure we don't combine with Exeter to take
Hopton in the rear.'

'Let's hope they try an assault on the new ramparts, they'll
soon find out there are no easy pickings here. And who knows,
if we could give them a bloody nose, that might stir those shifty
doubters in Exeter to get back into the war on the right side.'

Gabriel Barnes, the Captain of Artillery, was older than the
other two and more circumspect.

'The redoubts are finished at last, and furnished with cannon, of a kind. But we have yet to test them with real powder and shot, and my men have not yet had the training they should. And just think about the assortment of weapons! There's culverins and demi-culverins and sakers and God knows what else. Some of them go back to Queen Bess, if not to King Henry. About the only thing we can be certain we can fire is a bag of grape-shot.'

Recalling Sir William's pleading, Alexander had insisted on a detailed plan of the watches, and on Corporals appointed to check that the watches were properly kept.

'Captain Hallsey is right, this is certainly no army sent to lay siege to Plymouth. They've come to probe our defences perhaps, and they'll either mount a quick assault or they'll march away to look for a softer target.'

'I am surprised that your uncle, Sir George, has not joined us, Sir Alexander. I trust he has not fallen victim to a fever, like poor Sir William?'

Alexander wondered if Philip's concern was genuine, or was he obliquely questioning Sir George's loyalty? He decided that frankness was his best safeguard.

'Sir George was certainly sent for, but was not found in his room. I am at a loss to suggest where to look for him.'

'If he were in Plymouth he would certainly have heard what's afoot, and in that case wouldn't he also know that his place was here at the War Council?'

'I take your meaning, Mr Francis, and I would not dispute your reasoning. We should assume that Sir George has left the town.'

It was Philip's turn to allow a long pause before he spoke again. 'There is no easy way to say this, Sir Alexander, but it must be said. Our lives may depend on it. It is unlikely that Sir George could ride or walk out of the Town Gate without being noticed, once the alarm had been raised. We have to assume therefore that he left early, before the alarm was raised. Would you all agree?'

They nodded, and Alexander saw all too clearly the looming inference.

'And if he left before the alarm, either there was a very great coincidence, or he already knew the enemy was coming?'

'But he knows the disposition of every cannon and every trooper!'

'So he does, Captain Hallsey, so he does. And probably the state of our food and powder supply, how much money we have, and where the weak points are in the old town walls.'

Alexander was now seriously alarmed. How long before the already assumed 'like son, like father' was extended to 'like uncle, like nephew'?

'If Sir George knows our weak points, then so do we, Mr Francis. No doubt our captains will know how to reinforce them, and how to turn them into traps. I have despatched my ship already to Portsmouth to ask for more troops, more powder and more shot. Mr Francis, can we leave it to you to convey this to the people, and also our firm conviction that there is no great army out there, but merely a scouting or probing party? Panic in our streets will serve no one.'

'What's that over there?'

'Where?'

'Eastward. Come on over to my side. There, beyond the Lipson redoubt, towards Compton. I'll swear I saw movement out of the corner of my eye. Damn this half light. Can you see anything?'

'Nooo, yes! Wait a minute, it could be a trick of the mist shifting . . .'

'I see them, I see them now! They're coming down the bank of the creek in line abreast and . . . and . . . they're just walking on the water! There, by Leery point! Horsemen, hundreds of them now, just trotting across the creek. Are they devils?'

'Not devils! It's the neap tide. There must be a ford there at dead low water. Shout down the trapdoor, sound the alarm!'

* * *

The original ditch and rampart had stopped at Lipson, because the ground for the remaining four hundred yards eastward to the creek was too boggy to allow passage, let alone digging to any depth. And the Lipson redoubt itself had been the slowest to be built, because of the continual problems caused by the soft ground. As a consequence the cannon had been hauled up only the previous day, and the ramp was still in place on the inside. Within ten minutes the bells ringing out from every tower had aroused the whole town, and ten minutes later Captain Hallsey was leading six hundred dragoons at the gallop out of the East Gate. But it was too late to save Lipson. The steeply sloping sides of the redoubt were not yet protected by the planned layers of sharpened stakes, and so could quickly be scaled by determined troops. And the ramp made an easy incline for the squadron of dragoons in breastplates and helmets, who took some casualties but stormed the crest through a hail of musket fire. The Royalists had their breach! Hallsey charged towards the redoubt, but was checked first by half a regiment of pikemen, who had followed the Royalist dragoons across the Leery Creek ford at the double, and arrived at the foot of the redoubt in good order. Then he found himself caught in a murderous cross-fire from the captured redoubt. Only muskets at the moment, he thought, but how long before they manoeuvred the cannon around to sweep his men away with grape-shot? He could not afford to take such losses amongst his best troops. The sun was now clear of the looming bulk of Dartmoor, and was shining full in his face, making it difficult for his men to pick out the enemy, but making perfect targets of themselves.

'Retreat! Bugler, sound the retreat.'

The thin tinny notes had hardly sounded when they were overwhelmed by a roar of shouting from the town behind him. He turned to see hundreds, no, thousands of men pouring out of the East Gate and the two adjacent gates in Resolution Fort, in the town wall. Leading the nearest group he recognised Sir Alexander Carew himself in a red cloak, coming out at a flat gallop on a fine black stallion, followed by a charging mob, a few armed with muskets, but mainly with pitchforks and pikes and ancient swords. The citizen army flooded past him still yelling, and he lost sight of Sir Alexander as they reached the ranks of the enemy pikemen. Could they break through? How much longer would it take the Royalists to service the cannon? Surely any minute now there would be a thunderous volley that would kill hundreds and likely deprive the town of its leader?

He waited for the impetus of their charge to be checked by those cool, disciplined pikemen with their red sashes, who had broken his own charge just moments before. But this time the balance of numbers was different. Held back in the centre, the men of Plymouth simply flowed around the flanks on both sides until a weak point was found on the right, where the pikemen were slipping in the mud beside the Cattwater, then they rushed in before the ranks of the enemy could be righted. Once inside the ring fence of pikes they tore into the enemy like men berserk to terrible effect, and within another five minutes every last man who stood his ground was butchered, and only the few who made a run for it back across the creek were spared. Hallsey had his bugler sound the 'Stand Firm', and advanced with a dozen men himself through the carnage. On every side the enemy lay where they had fallen, some staring sightlessly at the sky, some still breathing but skewered to the ground with pike or pitchfork and screaming with pain. Some of the civilians had taken it upon themselves to go from man to man, cutting throats, others were obsessively collecting muskets, pikes, pistols, swords and armour, but most were just standing still and silent as the morning sun glittered on their moment of triumph. Hallsey could see the enemy dragoons still on top of the redoubt. Why had they not fired the guns? By what act of Grace had they all escaped total annihilation?

At last he saw the black stallion, standing quietly amidst a thicket of dead and dying pikemen. As he ran towards it he saw crimson blood welling from a long wound across its haunches. Was Sir Alexander dead? Then, as he reached the horse, he glimpsed the red cloak just beyond. Sir Alexander was sitting on the grass with his eyes tight shut. His cloak and black leather jerkin were coated with congealing blood.

'Sir Alexander, sir, it's me, Hallsey. Are you badly hurt, sir?'

Alexander's eyes opened, and his face became boyish again as he managed a smile, 'Hallsey, good. I think I'm all right, or I will be in a minute. Poor horse was hit and threw me. Probably saved my life. I've been banged on the head with a pike, and trodden on by some very heavy men, but I'm all in one piece, thank the Lord.'

'But you're bleeding, sir!'

Alexander looked down at his jerkin, and saw the blood for the first time. The colour drained from his face as he felt for the wound.

'Let me get a couple of my men to carry you away from here, and quickly. We are a point-blank cannon shot away from the redoubt. I can't understand why they haven't already started firing.'

'Cannon? I can tell you why they haven't started firing.' Alexander levered himself shakily to his feet. 'Sir William left strict instructions that the armourers should not move powder and shot onto a redoubt until proper shelters were built, and Lipson hasn't got its shelter yet. So they have nothing up there to shoot at us. Lucky, aren't we?'

'Lucky we are, sir. But you should not stand with that wound, you'll start the bleeding again. Let me . . .'

Alexander waved him away, 'It's all right, Hallsey, I think this must be some other poor fellow's blood. Not mine, this time.' He sat down again abruptly, 'But my head still hurts. So what do we do about this redoubt? Sir William was most insistent that no effort should be spared to achieve an immediate recapture, at any cost.'

'He said as much to me, sir. And of course he's right. But I'm not anxious to get good men killed in an unnecessary assault. Do you feel up to talking them into surrender? I'd do it myself, but I think your name behind the promises will carry more persuasion.'

'Promises?'

'If they surrender now, without spiking the cannon, they keep their arms and may ride away with honour.'

'And if they refuse?'

'We'll starve them out, plus using them for some nasty cannon practice from the next redoubt at Holiwell. In short, they will all die for nothing.'

'With those alternatives on offer I think I can be quite persuasive, Captain Hallsey. May I borrow your horse, and a trooper with a flag of parley?'

Within the hour the bells were ringing out across Plymouth again, this time not with the wild jangle of alarm, but with the measured, intricate peals of victory. Philip donated two barrels of his best French wine, and Alexander joined him and his fellow councillors, together with all the commissioned and non-commissioned officers of the garrison, in getting solidly drunk in the Town Hall. Philip's toast was taken up everywhere:

'To Sir Alexander Carew, who has saved Plymouth by his leadership, so that Plymouth may by its example save the cause of freedom in our West Country.'

SIR ALEXANDER! CAREW! CAREW!

By mid-afternoon Alexander could drink no more. His head was aching too from the morning's blow. As he was being helped up the steep stairs to his chambers a trooper came out of the guardroom below. 'Beg pardon, sir, but I have a letter addressed to you. The girl found it in Sir George's room when she tidied up a few minutes ago.'

Alexander sat wearily on the edge of his bed and cracked the wax seal on the single folded sheet. Sir George wrote in a small but well-formed copperplate hand.

My dear Alexander,

By the time you read this I will have left the town to find Colonel Digby, whose troops you will doubtless encounter, and then to join James.

I think this will not come as a complete surprise to you, but I would have you believe that it has been the most difficult decision of my life. Our family has supported Parliament, its rights and its duties, for many generations, and I have deeply appreciated also the many kindnesses you have shown me, and also the trust you have placed in me. In that respect you may have absolute confidence that nothing of what I have learned in Plymouth will be passed on to Colonel Digby, or to anyone else.

In the end the choice became quite simple. Did I intend to make war against my own son?

If I have grieved you by this decision, I beg you to forgive me, if not for my sake then in remembrance of your dear mother, who loved me greatly I believe.

May God grant us all a speedy release from these times of peril and of bitter choices.

Your loving uncle,

George Chudleigh

The night was warm and sultry. Around the old four-poster bed the dark blue curtains hung motionless, the golden deer and lions for once suspending their endless chase, as the two tapers on the bedhead burned without a flicker. Jane Carew lay naked and asleep beside Alexander, a glorious woman now sated with his lovemaking. He quietly poured himself another glass of the wine and brandy mixture they had taken to bed with them. How simple, how pleasant life could be!

Beside him his wife stirred, and opened one sleepy eye to catch him inspecting her appreciatively. He saw a blush begin on the rounded curve of her belly, and swiftly suffuse her white breasts until it burst into her cheeks. Hastily she sat up and drew her knees up under her.

'Alexander! Have you no respect, that you stare at me as

though I were one of your prize heifers? Where's my night-dress? For shame! Is this some Roman orgy?'

Despite her indignation she could not prevent the little bubble of laughter from breaking through into her voice, and Alexander ignored the demand for her night-dress, handing her his glass instead.

'Here my love, take this. It will keep you warm. Why should you feel shy, when you are more beautiful than any of the Roman goddesses painted on the ceiling of the King's palace?'

Jane made a face at him and burrowed beneath the sheets to find her shift, which she hurried to pull over her head.

'There, I feel more comfortable now. I suppose I should feel flattered that you pay me compliments after we have made love. Especially now that you are the hero of Plymouth's celebrated defence.'

'To tell you the truth, Jane, I think I must have been more than a little mad. The result of being cooped up in the town for those weeks, I suppose. The people were all milling about in the marketplace, waving weapons and shouting, and I was just caught up in the excitement of doing something.'

Jane reached up to touch his chest, as though to reassure herself. 'You could have been killed. Then what would have happened to us all?'

The note of reproof in her voice was serious. Alexander filled the glass once more, and drank deeply.

'Who can say? What will happen to us all anyway? Perhaps we are like the bears, saved from the dogs today so that we can be baited again tomorrow?'

Sensitive to his change of mood, Jane sat up and put aside her playfulness too.

'I understand that your duty and obligations will call you back to Plymouth, Alex. But what about us here at Antony? Are we safe, do you think? Should we close up the house and join you in the town?'

'No!' Alexander's refusal was sudden, and almost violent, 'No, my love,' he said more quietly. 'At least, not yet. We have a plan, a way to escape, if ... if ...'

'A plan? We? Who's the "we" in this plan?'

Alexander leant back on his pillow, and looked up at his wife – sensible, practical Jane! Was it right, or necessary to keep the details from her? If something were to go wrong, she could be the one to rescue him! But he could not bring himself to talk about the pearls, now hidden in his father's coffin. Instead he talked of the boat.

'You have the essentials already, Jane, in that you bought and fitted out the boat with a cabin. That's now permanently on patrol off St Nicholas Island for us. The only thing you are not aware of is that I have promised to take with us Philip Francis and his wife. You remember them, I'm sure?'

'I was introduced to Mr Francis in Plymouth once, when your father took Grace and myself in, on a visit. People say he has Spanish blood, and I could see why. Sir Richard said he was a leader of an important faction in Plymouth, and he did go out of his way to make himself agreeable to us – he even sent over a barrel of wine. But I didn't like him that much. He was a widower, I remember, so this must be a second wife. Why have you involved them in this plan? Can they be trusted? Alex, this is our very lives we're talking about – couldn't you have kept it in the family, or at least among people we really know? Why Philip Francis?'

Why indeed? Alexander thought back to the time – could it be only a few weeks ago? – when Philip had come to see him in Plymouth, and made him see the dangers of their position. Those pearls had seemed a godsend then. How could the pearls have been obtained, to be the solid, easily portable foundation of a future life in some foreign country, if he had not promised to include Philip in the escape plan? And Lucy? He remembered the wit and intelligence of her mind as they talked long and soberly about how England should be governed if the war was won. He could still feel how her young and wiry body moved beneath him in the heat of sudden passion. How could Lucy be left behind?

'It's quite complicated to explain all the politics in Plymouth, Jane, but Philip is now mayor of course and has the leadership of the townspeople. I felt that I would surely need him as a friend if the town was likely to be taken. He is an out-and-out Parliament man, with no Royalist friends in high places to protect him. So he has the strongest possible reasons to be faithful to us, do you see?'

Jane saw, and agreed. And wondered why that niggling doubt at the back of her mind would not go away.

'Oh Alex, let's not talk about the war any more.'

Alexander was up soon after the summer dawn, and had spent an anxious hour in the rent-room with his steward, Walter Goodman, by the time Jane came down. He wondered if Walter would notice the dark rings under his wife's eyes, and decided this was not a time to be concerned about such niceties.

'Come in, Jane, come in. These days the estate rents are as much your concern as mine.'

He handed over a slip of paper with a list of names and amounts.

'You'd expect that, with wheat fetching forty-eight shillings a quarter in Plymouth, none of the tenants would have problems paying, but of course everything's on credit, No one seems to have cash now.'

'Will Plumley has been exchanging his wheat and turnips for salted mackerel. He's offered us a barrel for next Quarterday.'

'I think we might be well-advised to take it, rather than accept a note of hand, which is probably the only alternative. Try to get money if you can though, Walter. That will have to be enough for you now. I will need young Peter though, with the boat to take me back this afternoon – shall we say two o'clock?'

'Oh Alex, not so soon, please?'

'I must Jane. We've given them a bloody nose and a warning that we are not an easy target, but that King's colonel, what's his name?'

'Digby you said, Colonel Digby.'

'Right, Digby. He's only withdrawn to Plymstock, we heard. To lick his wounds, spy out our defences and await reinforcements no doubt. We heard from one of the prisoners that there was a report of a great battle between Hopton's army, now united with Prince Maurice, and our Sir William Waller, somewhere near Bath. Thousands killed on both sides, but no decisive victory either way. That would have been about two weeks ago, about 5 July.'

'Does that mean that Hopton will now come back against Plymouth?'

Alexander reached out a hand to his wife to reassure her. In the bright morning sunlight he could see the touches of grey that were creeping into her thick dark curls, and the lines of anxiety that knitted her forehead.

'Not likely for a good while yet, I'd say. He must give priority this summer to helping to take Bristol, if they can, and they can't move against Bristol safely until they've dealt with Waller. So Hopton will have his hands full this year without worrying about Plymouth.' He stood up and kissed her on the forehead. 'But we can take some precautions to protect our stock.'

'Our stock? You mean our cattle? Our pigs and chickens and so on?'

'Yes, well the cattle at least. I've asked Walter to change the brand.'

'Forgive me, Alex, but I don't understand.'

'Digby's troops are the best part of two days' march away, at Plymstock, the other side of Plymouth. But they are likely to get some reinforcements, perhaps men who come from Cornwall, and in time they are likely to spread out as far as Antony for their foraging. You remember last autumn, when they ran off half the cows and my prize bull.. But this year we'll be ready for them.'

'But how on earth . . .?'

'It's Walter's idea, and you must ask him to show you the work. Our brand is a letter "C", like this.' He picked up a

slate from his desk and drew the broad letter "C", for Carew,
'Now Walter is going to change the branding iron by adding
a bar through the middle of the "C", changing it to an "E".'
' "E"?'
' "E" for Edgcumbe.'
'Of course, Sir Peter, your old friend. But he's for the King.
Will he help us?'

The largest Edgcumbe estates bordered the Carews on the
south, and ran five miles down to the English Channel. The
house stood on a hill where it could be seen from the sea, a
great square stone building with turrets at each corner, said
to rival the Derbyshire mansion of Bess of Hardwick in its
magnificence. Sir Peter Edgcumbe had been born in the same
year as Alexander. They had played together as children,
hunted and hawked together, and gone up to Oxford
together. Peter had succeeded to his inheritance when he was
twenty-nine, five years before. Unlike the Carews, the
Edgcumbes had no tradition of political involvement; when
the war began, Sir Peter let it be known he was for King
rather for than Parliament, but took no action either way.
Alexander was confident that Sir Peter would be helpful, as
long as he was not personally compromised.

'I think Peter owes us a favour. If I had carried out those
instructions from Parliament to seize enemy property, I could
have ruined him. Even now, he has no troops at hand to
protect him if we wanted to make a raid from Plymouth.'

'You're going to ask for his help?'

'Yes. Or rather we both are. I must get back now to the
town, but I'll write a letter before I go, and you can ride over
with Walter to deliver it in person, either later today or
tomorrow.'

Jane was taken with the simplicity of the scheme, and put
her arms around Alexander's neck to deliver a warm, friendly
kiss. He was immediately on his guard.

'Now what have you thought of?'

'Don't you see Alex, if Peter will accept temporary
ownership of our cows, why shouldn't he extend his

protection to us as well? If the worst happens and Plymouth is taken, that is.'

'He couldn't, not even Peter Edgcumbe has the power. Not to protect me, I mean. There are treason warrants out for me and the town leaders like Philip Francis. That's the very reason for the plan . . .'

'Yes, of course darling. I appreciate that you have the ship, and the plan to get us away to France. But don't you see this might be a better idea?' She paced restlessly around the room, and returned to kiss him again. 'Now don't be angry. Of course you must have the ship to take you across to France, or back along the coast to Portsmouth, whichever looks safer. But remember, we have seven small children here, and the eldest, John, is only eight. And there's myself, and Grace, and two, no three maids at least. Can you imagine say twelve of us, plus Mr Francis and his wife, all in a small fishing boat, heading across the English Channel? And what if it was the night of a proper Channel storm as well?'

'Now look here, Jane, I am not a magician to work a miracle. The plan isn't perfect, but it will work, and could save . . .'

'Listen a minute, please Alex. I've tried to imagine for you some of the problems that might arise with the plan. The advantage of this idea is that it avoids those problems. If the town is to fall, you must take the boat with Mr Francis and his wife. But all of us at Antony can put ourselves under the protection of Peter Edgcumbe, and we will do our best to look after the house and the estates as well. Will he go that far for us, do you think?'

Alexander sat down in his chair and looked up at Jane. He hated the very thought of running away like a fugitive criminal, and leaving his family and lands under the protection of the Edgcumbes. Peter was a good friend, but the word was that his mother was pressing him to adopt a more active style to support the King. On the other hand Alexander could claim a blood tie. His great-grandfather, Thomas Carew, had married an Edgcumbe. If Jane asked for sanctuary, could they turn her away? Not without loss of all honour, and honour was very important to the Edgcumbes. He reached up to kiss her.

'I'll do it, Jane. I'll ask him to take care of you all.'

To Sir Peter Edgcumbe, at Mount Edgcumbe   18 July 1643
Dear Peter,

I trust that it is not necessary for me to tell you how deeply grieved I am that the harsh pressures of the quarrel between Parliament and the King's misguided advisers have come between us, and compelled us to interrupt the friendship of a lifetime. Certainly my affections for you and for your family are so unchangeable that the cannon's roar itself cannot violate them. You know that I must be true to the cause that I serve, and for my part I continue to respect most sincerely your own commitment to His Majesty our King.

I think we are both players upon a stage, who must now go on to act out the parts assigned to them in this Tragedy. Let us do that with honour, and with no personal animosities. No matter what the outcome may be, I shall never willingly relinquish the title of

Your most affectionate friend,
Alexander Carew

Alexander signed the letter with a final flourish, and gave it to Jane to read.

'Oh Alex, it's a beautiful letter. When Peter reads it he will certainly hear the sound of your own voice speaking through it to him.'

'I've had to be careful what I say, in case the letter should come into the wrong hands, but you'll be there in front of him when he reads it, able to explain exactly what we may need him to do. You must be ready to explain to Peter that there is mutual benefit, showing him, very delicately, that I have also been protecting him, and will continue to do so. I think that he will not, in all conscience, be able to refuse you, but try to see him alone, without his mother being present. Which reminds me, I've yet to see Grace. Is she likely to recover today from that headache that kept her from supper last night?'

'I don't know, Alex. She is certainly still determined that you are her enemy. Since the quarrel about the funeral she has been acting most strangely. Morose, withdrawn, secretive also. She has written to her eldest son John at Westminster.'

'He's working for John Pym?'

'Yes. Is that good or bad? She makes me nervous, Alex. I think she really hates me as well as you, because we've taken her place, and if she could do us harm she would. In fact I believe she would pull the roof down if she thought that in doing so one slate would fall on me or you.'

'And yet I wish her no harm, no harm at all. Quite the contrary, for father's sake I would like to see her honoured, safe and contented.'

Jane had learned of Grace's habit of taking the tea made with the herb 'Savin' from one of the maids who had suffered from the rough edge of Grace's tongue, and had complained to Jane at length about it. Guessing at its function, she had tried it in secret herself that morning, and it had made her head swim. She wondered what the cumulative effect might be, and decided to say nothing to Alexander.

'I think you'll just have to accept that Grace has strange moods that possess her at times, and hope that this one passes too. Frankly I don't think you will see her today. Shall I give her your warmest regards and sympathy?'

'If you would, please. And I think you should use every endeavour to ensure that Grace knows as little as possible about our plans and our business. That way she'll be less able to do us harm if this mood persists. And now I'd really like to have a look around the Home Farm before I leave. Will you ride with me?'

Despair and Hope

Alexander had barely had time to begin to read the week's situation reports in his room in Plymouth Castle when he heard a commotion below, followed by a knock at his door.

'Beg pardon, sir, it's Mr Francis below. Says he must see you. Most urgent.'

Alexander's heart filled his throat, as he had a sudden vision of an angry husband complaining that his innocent young wife had been taken advantage of by a man in a position of trust, who had abused the mayor's hospitality in a most dishonourable way, and so on and so on. The reality was quite different – much worse, but infinitely preferable. Philip was indeed very agitated, and the sweat was pouring off his dark forehead as he came up the stairs at a run and burst into the room.

'Sir Alexander, thank God you're back!'

He paused, drew a deep breath, and closed the door carefully behind him. Alexander was more relieved than alarmed by his tone, and offered him a glass of wine.

'Come and sit down at the table, Mr Francis. Whatever the problem, we'll survive it, I'm sure.'

Philip took a grateful gulp of the wine, and sat for a moment apparently examining the glass.

'I'm not so sure now, Sir Alexander, not so sure at all. A man came to see me last night.'

'A man?'

'A soldier. To be exact, a deserter from our army in Somerset, the one commanded by Sir William Waller. The army that was supposed to prevent Hopton and Prince Maurice attacking Bristol.'

'I don't understand. Why would you be receiving a deserter last night? How did he get to Plymouth?'

'It's not an easy thing to explain. He's a man of good family here in Plymouth. He is. . . was . . . very attached to Lucy, so much so that when she decided to marry me last spring he was almost out of his mind with disappointment, and his father came to me for advice. I knew the man already, and suggested that a complete break would be best. So I wrote him a couple of letters of introduction to some business friends of mine in London, and contributed twenty pounds out of my own pocket. You won't tell Lucy any of this, will you? She'd say I was going soft. But I did it out of friendship for his father.'

'Of course, Philip. I assume this man brought bad news?'

'The worst. It appears that, after that battle earlier this month near Bath, General Waller pushed the Royalists as far as Devizes, and had them besieged, as he thought, in the town. That's where my young friend deserted.'

'Do you know why?'

'I pressed him about that, but I couldn't get a sensible answer. Perhaps he should never have volunteered as a soldier in the first place. He was working as a clerk in the London offices of a wine importer, a close friend of mine, and got carried away with the London apprentices in their riots and political rallies. Be that as it may, he slipped away from our army one night, three days into the siege. He knew there were lots of Royalists to the south, so he headed north first, towards Marlborough. He says that, early the next morning, he realised that there was an army on the road ahead, coming down from Oxford he guessed, so he climbed up a hillside and watched. He saw them go past him, and then attack General Waller, who was caught between that army and the Royalists who came out of Devizes. He says our troops were just butchered, all of them. Our army has ceased to exist, so Bristol now stands alone. That was five days ago.'

'How did your man get here, in only five days? It must be over a hundred miles?'

'He stole a horse he found near the battlefield, and travelled at night.'

'Do you believe this story?'

'Why should he lie? As a self-confessed deserter he risked his life coming back into Plymouth.'

'From what you said, he could be fairly sure you would not betray him, for Lucy's sake as well as for his father. What does Lucy think of it, by the way?'

'With respect, Sir Alexander, I wonder if you are not trying to avoid facing the truth in this? Lucy was mistrusting at first, as I was, but if you'd heard the man tell the story in detail, if you'd seen for yourself the horror and the fear in his face as he talked of the battlefield, I think you would believe him.'

'Where is he now?'

'Safe in the attic of my house. I don't want his story going around Plymouth until we've decided what to do.'

'You won't have to keep him long. If there is truth in his tale it will reach Plymouth soon enough. I notice my ship is back from Portsmouth. Had the captain heard any of this?'

'He arrived early this morning. Of course he is waiting to report to you, but I think not. I saw him at midday, when I looked in to the "Grapes", and he was full only of cheering stories of the reinforcements we can expect soon from Portsmouth. But that's not surprising. He would have sailed from Portsmouth two, if not three days ago, and the report might well have not reached there by then. Anyway I'll keep my man out of sight until there's some confirmation one way or the other. The point is, Sir Alexander, that I believe we have advance news of the greatest disaster Parliament has suffered since the war began. Bristol will be next, and where does that leave us?'

Philip drained his glass, and did not demur when Alexander offered to refill it. It was clear that the Mayor was close to panic.

'I suppose you are already thinking of our escape plan, the pearls and the ship, is that it?'

Alexander's brutal question brought Philip up short.

'No, no, definitely not. Not at this stage, anyway. Of course I'm relieved to know that your ship is back . . .'

His voice trailed away on a note of enquiry.

'And that the pearls are absolutely safe, Mr Francis, and ready to be picked up the minute we need them. If that sets your mind at rest?'

'Exactly. I was sure of it. And Lucy sends her regards, by the way. She told me that you had been giving her some instruction, matters of finance and politics and so on. I think she's very grateful for your interest.'

Alexander wondered if he detected the slightest hint of innuendo in Philip's words, but responded directly.

'She's a charming, intelligent woman, well-read and thoughtful. Sometimes I agree with the Levellers you know, when they say that women make up half the world but take only the smallest share in the responsibility of managing it. Lucy is a case in point, as indeed is Lady Carew, my wife. Both very capable, I'd say.'

Philip seemed to regain some of his composure, perhaps drawing strength from Alexander's studied detachment. 'Do you think there is any action we should be taking immediately, Sir Alexander?'

Detecting the note of deference in Philip's tone, Alexander responded by becoming the leader again, 'Our first duty is to remain calm, knowing that many lives, as well as our own, depend on our good judgement. How is Sir William, by the way?'

'Much better, though still quite weak. He has let it be known that he accepts that he will not be able to resume active command, and suggested to his captains formally that they look to you for leadership, at least until Parliament sends us another officer in his place.'

'I will call a Council of War for ten o'clock tonight, and I will try to consult with Sir William in the meantime. Bring your man with you, but make sure he is wrapped up well so that he is not recognised. I'll ask the captains to listen to his story of the battle. They'll soon establish where the truth rests.'

'And on the last day I got onto Dartmoor, and felt it was safe to travel in the light, sticking to the old paths that I knew. I slipped into Plymouth just before dark, and Mr Francis 'ere took me in. I'm very grateful to Mr Francis, very grateful indeed.'

Tobias Fisher was about twenty, lean and gangling with black hair, cropped very short after the fashion of the London apprentices. His features were partly obscured by a dark stubbly beard, but he had bright blue eyes and a fine nose, so that Alexander thought he was probably quite handsome when cleaned up. His buff leather jerkin was stained black with sweat and mud, and there was a drawn, almost haggard look to him. As the night was warm, no fire had been lit in Alexander's room, and Tobias stood at the end of the long table, his face, like those of his questioners, illuminated now by the flickering candles which left the rest of the room in shadow. As he finished his account his head dropped, and he swayed as if about to fall.

'Captain Barnes, there's a stool by the fireplace. Let him be seated now. Mr Fisher, no doubt our captains will have many questions for you, but I have just two. Firstly, why did you desert?'

'It was the bullying, sir. I just couldn't stand it no more. I'm not naturally a strong man, but they 'ad me carryin' this pike more'n' twice as long as m'sel', an' drillin' with it an' pushin' with it. I tried, sir, really I tried, I wanted to be a good soldier for Parliament, but I'm just not that strong. And this Corporal Jason kept pickin' on me, and makin' fun of the way I talked, an' givin' me extra guard, until I couln' stand it no more. I didn' run away from no fightin', we was just sittin' there outside the town, and I thought they could do that without me . . .'

Alexander could see he was not far from tears. 'All right, so that's why you left the army. And why did you come to Mr Francis' house? Why not go to your father's?'

Tobias looked at Philip, who was sitting next to him at the end of the table, and Alexander thought he saw an almost imperceptible shake of Philip's head.

'I s'pose I was ashamed to face me father, sir. I'd be told I was a bloody fool to volunteer in the first place. I'll 'ave to face 'im sooner or later. But Mr Francis, e's bin that kind to me already, I thought 'e might understand and forgive one time more.'

Alexander guessed this answer was far from complete, but thought there was little advantage to be gained by pressing the point, and perhaps embarrassing Philip, or Lucy, or both of them.

'Captain Hallsey, would you like to start the military enquiry?'

'Just one matter of profesional interest. You say the whole of our army was destroyed – "butchered" was the word you used, I recall. In my experience the dragoons and cavalry usually escape from such a trap in some numbers. So how did it come about that this time they did not?'

There was a sharp edge to Hallsey's voice that made Tobias sit up.

'You're right sir, as soon as they saw our infantry was in trouble the cavalry and dragoons cut an' run for it, like cowards if you ask me, sir. But it didn' do them no good, no good at all.'

'Why was that? Were they caught by the army coming out from Devizes?'

'Not exackly, sir. You see I was up on 'igh ground, lookin' back the way I'd come. So I could see that our army was drawn up across this long narrow ridge, called Roundway, that led north from the town. The Royalists was comin'down from the north, so they was marchin' along it. So I saw them charge into our ranks, and I saw our men go down by the 'undred in the centre, where the fightin' was 'ardest. I saw the cavalry and the dragoons back off, an' then they gallops off towards the town. What they'd forgotten was that there's this steep slope down to the town with a ditch at the bottom, an' that's where most on 'em ended up, a mess of blood and 'orses. Then, like I said, the royalists comes chargin' out of the town to finish them off, an' to take our army from be'ind. The lucky ones that was still alive surrendered, an' I lay low until dark.'

'Did you see General Waller surrender?'

'I wasn't that close to see, sir. But if 'e didn't 'e's dead for sure.'

Hallsey looked at the other captains, but they shook their heads. It was obvious from the details that Tobias' story was the truth as he had seen it. Parliament's army no longer existed. Alexander allowed a decent pause, then asserted command again.

'Mr Francis, we'd be obliged if you would escort Mr Fisher back to his lodging with you, and keep him secure, and then return to us as soon as may be.'

'What do you recommend, please gentlemen?'

Alexander looked at his three captains – Horse, Foot and Artillery – and waited. First to speak was Captain Thomas Reever, a short wiry cavalryman with a bustling, aggressive personality to go with his fine black mustachios.

'I don't like it, Sir Alexander, I don't like it at all. I think we must accept that Sir William Waller's army has been destroyed, and the King is now free to turn on Bristol, as he surely will. Even more worrying, our army was not defeated by Hopton and Prince Maurice – they were still shut up in Devizes it seems, at least until the very end. So the King was able to send down a second army, powerful enough to crush General Waller's on its own. And now those two armies are free to attack Bristol, or to divide if they want to go for Exeter and ourselves as well. Meantime we're tied down here with Digby sitting on our doorstep. I have to say that the towns of the west looks like a row of sitting ducks, waiting to be picked off one by one. Forgive me, Sir Alexander, for speaking so bluntly, but those are my views.'

'I'm grateful for them, Captain Reever, and I welcome the utmost frankness at this moment, before Mr Francis returns. Once he comes back however I beg you to consider that he is not a military man, and may not appreciate your honest statement of the problems, even though it is the only way to arrive at the best course of action. Captain Hallsey?'

'Like yourself, sir, I wondered why this self-confessed deserter should be confident of finding sanctuary with our mayor?' Hallsey spoke quietly, in a slow, measured way that commanded respect. 'I'm sure we must accept that Mr Francis is totally loyal to our cause, sir, but nonetheless I agree that we should not involve him in all our military decisions, just to be on the safe side.'

'Do you have a plan?'

'One thing Captain Reever said struck me most forcibly, sir. We should not sit still in Plymouth and wait for the royalists in Plymstock to be reinforced.'

There were vigorous murmurs of support from the other two captains, which encouraged Alexander. 'You'll be interested to know that Sir William gave me exactly the same advice when I saw him earlier this evening. He suggested that, as long as the weather holds, a force could be despatched tomorrow night to move in secret north into Dartmoor, then east to find the Exeter road at, say, Ivybridge, then west again to take Digby in the rear and drive him onto our rampart and guns.'

'Sir William is a most cunning strategist. Obviously this is a task for horse, and I would be very happy to lead this force, if you will allow me, Sir Alexander.'

Captain Reever's confidence and enthusiasm infected them all.

'Do you agree, Captain Hallsey?'

'With pleasure, sir. Although I would suggest that Captain Reever should not risk it with horse alone. Digby has around a thousand men, mostly mounted, and no doubt they're licking their wounds after the losses they took at Lipson. We should attack them with two thousand men to be sure of crushing them with the smallest possible losses to ourselves – a thousand dragoons, five hundred cavalry, and five hundred of our best pikemen.'

Alexander paused, trying to understand the military logic, 'That would leave only Captain Barnes' guns, and the remaining thousand, no eight hundred infantry to protect the town. Nearly three miles of ramparts, and the five redoubts and the forts. Is that wise?'

'I think we have already seen the power of Plymouth's hidden army, those terrifying men who overwhelmed the pikemen at Lipson. I think you will be quite safe for the few days this sally will take, and as I said, the best guarantee of total success lies in striking at the enemy with a force large enough to crush them at the first blow.'

'Can you march north without the enemy scouts spotting you?'

'Provided we leave after dark . . .'

The captain was interrupted by a knock at the door, which was opened to reveal Philip Francis. There was a palpable moment's silence before Alexander could recover.

'Come in, please, Mr Francis. We were just discussing the desirability of putting out patrols north and east, not scouts but patrols in strength, to give us advance warning of any movement to reinforce the royalists at Plymstock.'

Philip looked bewildered and slightly suspicious as he took his place back at the table.

'That sounds most judicious, Sir Alexander, though I lay no claim to being a strategist. My concern, and that of my fellow citizens, must be for the very survival of Plymouth as Parliament's Bastion in the West. If Bristol falls, can our town be defended, with the King free to turn the whole weight of his power against us?'

There was silence around the table. Philip had asked the question each had asked himself, but none had dared voice.

Alexander thought that his three captains were honest professional soldiers, whose hearts were probably with the cause of Parliament, and who would give of their best as long as they thought there was a chance of victory. But they were realists too, and they knew that, if the town fell, their only hope would lie in negotiations for an honourable surrender, or even a change of sides. For the first time he felt the weight of being their leader.

'Our military advisers here are very confident that our fortifications, all equipped now with guns, will allow our men to give an excellent account of themselves. And we should not forget the truly magnificent power of Plymouth's citizens, as they recently demonstrated to the enemy at Lipson. Our immediate concern must be to maintain, and indeed strengthen that morale. It is the very key to survival.'

'No doubt, Sir Alexander, and a difficult task it will be once the news is abroad about the disaster at Devizes. And remember, it is only a few weeks since the disaster at Stratton that allowed Hopton to escape in the first place. Hardly the stuff to give our people confidence that the cause of Parliament is in good hands, is it? Do not mistake my meaning. Plymouth is staunch for Parliament, but they must have hope based on reason, not blind faith. You remember yourself, I believe, that Thomas Ceely was not altogether without support when he wanted to surrender the town back in January. This is the burden that I must carry. I trust that no one here doubts my loyalty to the cause?'

His abrupt switch to the offensive came suddenly and fiercely, as Philip lifted his head and looked into the eyes of each man around the table in turn, ending with a steady gaze fixed on Alexander. There was an uncomfortable silence, which Alexander eventually broke by picking up the pitcher of wine, and going around the table to fill each glass in turn, ending with the mayor's.

'A toast, gentlemen, our loyal toast: "Parliament and the King"!'

There was a rattle of bench and chairs as they rose.

'Parliament and the King!'

'I asked you to stand for a toast, gentlemen, so that we might remind ourselves of the cause we have all sworn to serve. No one's loyalty is in doubt tonight, Mr Francis, no one's. If there are some military matters in which we do not involve you fully, it is because, as you said yourself, you are no soldier. Sir William told me himself, back in January, that I should leave soldiering to the soldiers, and believe me, I am doing just that, as far as I may. So will you take my hand there, Mr Francis?'

Philip found himself for once outfaced, and took Alexander's hand almost obsequiously. 'I hope no one was offended by my outburst, Sir Alexander. It arose out of nothing more than a simple anxiety about our position, and a desire to assist in any way possible. That's if there is anything a poor civilian can contribute, of course?'

There were smiles all round the table as Philip's natural warmth relaxed the tension again. Alexander walked over to the empty fireplace, and finished his wine before he spoke. 'There is one task that only a poor civilian can accomplish, Mr Francis, only you in fact. That's to tell our people now the truth as we see it.'

'Sir Alexander?'

'The truth is, that three weeks ago there was a first battle, near Bath, which Sir William Waller won handsomely for us, seriously weakening Hopton's army, and forcing him to run away to Devizes. There he was reinforced by all the King's power, and in a second battle a week ago we were defeated. The King is now turning to attack Bristol, and we are sure that our commander there, Colonel Fiennes, will give Hopton and Prince Maurice a bloody nose, with the support of the loyal citizens of Bristol. Just as we crushed Colonel Digby at Lipson redoubt. Meanwhile we do not propose to sit idly by, but will be seeking to weaken the enemy in every way possible. And you have your own direct information from my ship's captain, Mr Amos, that we may expect strong reinforcements from Portsmouth. Parliament will support us, but we must look to help ourselves too. You should not play down the seriousness of the situation, but aim to reassure the people that, provided each plays his part, Plymouth can be defended. Do you believe and accept that certainty?'

Philip recognised that his role had been written for him, and responded with alacrity. 'I do, Sir Alexander, with all my heart. The strength of your leadership and the skills of our captains will guarantee our success, I know it. If you will excuse me now, it is important that we communicate the news before rumour makes it into a catastrophe. I must visit some of my friends tonight, to ensure that our message is properly understood.'

The night was warm and still, but a veil of cloud could be seen rising slowly from the west to cover the stars. 'Rain soon', thought Alexander as he climbed the ladder to step out onto the roof of the Castle Keep, and smelt the salt in the air. There was a movement at the north parapet.

'Who goes there? Ah, it's you, Sir Alexander. There's precious little to be seen tonight, sir, even with the telescope, it's a real dark one.'

'No matter, sentry, I just need a breath of air. Carry on.'

After the captains had left his room to make their preparations for the sally to take place the following night, Alexander had fallen into a deep, exhausted sleep. He had awoken to find himself shaking with a nameless dread, and soaked in perspiration. He breathed deeply after climbing back onto the rampart. Below the tall keep of the ancient castle the town spread out to the north and west, roofs and streets dark within the encircling ring of its old walls. He could see a watchfire burning on the north-east corner – Resolution Fort – and looking south across the Hoe he saw another, on his St. Nicholas Island. Everywhere else there was a foreboding stillness. He leaned against the parapet.

'What o'clock is it?'

The sentry looked up at Orion's Belt, 'After three, sir. Light in about an hour.'

What was the faceless terror that had gripped him in his sleep?
It would be natural to be afraid of capture and death, but in this
waking moment he could honestly say that he was not afraid of
death, as long as he had done his duty. But what was his duty?
He owed a loyalty to Parliament, which had given him rank and
a position of trust, and to the army and people in Plymouth,
who depended now so much on him. But how should that duty
be weighed and compared with the duty he owed to his wife and
children a few miles away in Antony, and to all the generations
of Carews, past present and future? What about his father,
buried but not laid to rest? He shivered. Was his duty truly
discharged by taking up arms against the King's evil advisers, as
official policy maintained? He thought of the words of Socrates
at the beginning of the great dialogue about The Republic:

'Our argument today is no casual debate. We are trying
to discover how a man should live.'

The two sentries had withdrawn discreetly to the far side
of the keep, and as Alexander watched, a burst of laughter
and the sound of a slap on the shoulder confirmed they were
good friends.

'What infinite heart's ease
Must Kings neglect, that private men enjoy!
'Tis not the balm, the sceptre and the ball
The sword, the mace, the crown imperial,
The throne he sits on, nor the tide of pomp
That beats upon the high shore of this world,
No, not all these, thrice gorgeous Ceremony,
Not all these, laid in bed majestical
Can sleep so soundly as the wretched slave
Who with body filled and vacant mind
Never sees horrid night, the child of Hell.'

The lines from the King's soliloquy came unbidden into
Alexander's mind. It must be ten years since he had seen the

play in London, and he had borrowed a printed copy so that he might read and commit to memory the words that had so moved him. Was this to be the eve of his own Agincourt? Would there be so miraculous a deliverance for Carew as there had been for King Harry?

'What's there?'

'Where?'

'Over to the east, towards Plymstock. I thought I caught a flash of light out of the corner of my eye. There's another, and another!'

The sound of gunfire reached and lapped up around them.

'Sound the alarm, they're attacking again! SOUND THE ALARM!'

Mount Batten Point and its Stanfort are on a narrow neck of land thrusting out into Plymouth Sound from its eastern shore. Between the Point and the town is the Cattwater creek, and the entrance to the harbour, known as the South Pool. From the batteries on the Point it is barely half a mile north-west across that harbour entrance to the Castle, and St Nicholas Island is a similar distance, due west.

In the deep darkness before the dawn there could be no certainty about events on the Point for the anxious watchers on top of the Castle keep, and still less for the crowds of men and women gathering in the narrow streets below, and in the Fish Market. It was clear that the enemy had attacked the Point. Flashes of pistol-shot and musket could be seen and heard, and the regular boom of cannon-fire confirmed that the defenders were still offering resistance behind their rampart. As the sky began to lighten in the east Captain Hallsey with a scouting party of troopers were ready to row across, but Alexander hesitated.

'I'd rather you did not risk your own life at this time, Captain Hallsey. You are needed here whether Mount Batten is held or lost.'

'No great risk, really sir. We'll not need to get closer than a hundred yards to get a report called to us, and I doubt if they've anyone that could hit me at that range. Besides . . .'

His voice trailed away. The gunfire had stopped!

'Does that mean the enemy has withdrawn?'

'I'm afraid not sir. If they were retreating our musket fire would gradually tail off, as the troopers realised they were out of range. A sudden stop like that can mean only one thing.'

'Surrender?'

'Almost certainly, sir. And if those cannon have not been spiked . . .'

'The ships! The fishing fleet, and all the transports in the harbour will be bottled in!'

'I'll get word to them immediately, sir. Everyone knows that if the ships can't get out Plymouth will starve. And your own boat, sir, Captain Amos on St Nicholas Island, he should get out to sea at once and act as a guard boat, warning any arriving ships away from the South Pool, and telling them to land their cargoes over on the west side of the Hoe, at Mill Bay.'

That was the dawn of 2 August. By a grim coincidence the only ship Captain Amos intercepted that day brought news of an even more significant disaster. Bristol, the best port and the greatest city west of London, had been stormed on 27 July. Captain Robert Adams told his story to a hastily reassembled War Council.

'In my opinion it was our own General that lost us Bristol, Sir William Waller. A month ago 'e ordered Colonel Fiennes, our Commander of Bristol, to send 'im every soldier that was fit to march, and we 'eard our men fought well at that battle at Lansdown, near Bath, where Waller 'ad the beating of the enemy. But then 'e goes chasing after 'em until they 'ides up in Devizes, an 'e gets properly beat in 'is turn. An' that leaves Colonel Fiennes with less than two thousand 'alf-trained militia to defend three miles of the city walls against a proper army of twenty thousand. You don't need to be a soldier to guess the result, and, to do 'im justice, the Colonel didn't tell 'is men that they 'ad to die on the walls or else. Just as well, I'd say, I mean what's the point in two thousand Englishmen getting killed at odds of ten to one? Anyway the enemy 'ad enough troops to attack at six points at once, an' it were all over in a couple of hours. As soon as the enemy was fairly inside the city the Colonel sent word to us to weigh anchor, which we was just waitin' for the tide to do anyway. Wind was from the north-west, so this seemed the obvious place to make for. I've a cargo of coal, sir, from Wales. Meant for Bristol, of course. Do you think I can sell it in Plymouth, or should I go all the way on to London?'

After Adams had taken his leave of Plymouth's War Council, a silence settled that no one seemed to want to break. Where was the benefit in stating the obvious, that if the King chose to attack Plymouth it could not hold out? At least not against the kind of force that had been unleashed against Bristol. Who wanted to be the first to raise the issue of negotiating a surrender, just a few months after Thomas Ceely had been brought down for proposing just that in the Council Chamber? Who was not now thinking of how his own safety might best be secured? Inevitably it was Alexander who felt driven to accept the burden of leadership.

'This is undoubtedly a situation where military judgement must have priority, so let's get to it. Nothing is so dark that a little consideration and planning cannot make it lighter. Captain Hallsey, please, may we have the benefit of your counsel?'

Hallsey leaned back from the table, and rubbed his face as though to massage some life back into his tired features.

'Let's start with the sally we were planning for tonight, to take Colonel Digby from behind. That should be abandoned, or at least postponed until Mount Batten Point is retaken. The enemy is now entrenched behind ramparts, which would certainly hold up our assault, and we might find ourselves caught from behind if, as I would expect, he has already sent for reinforcements.'

'How soon could he be reinforced?'

'From Bristol? A week perhaps, more likely two. The roads will be good and passable after the dry summer. Of course they might go for Exeter first. From what I've heard I'd expect it to surrender at the first shot, if not before.'

'I'm sure we can accept your advice not to divide our force and run the risk of getting caught from behind, while trying to lay siege to Mount Batten from the land. How about from the sea? We have boats enough in Plymouth, and I am conscious of the very strong advice from Sir William that if any of our forts are taken it must be immediately recaptured, no matter what the cost. I see Mount Batten Point like a sharp knife held an inch from the town's throat.'

'I believe Captain Reever has had experience of that kind of soldiering, in Holland?'

'Thank you for thinking of me, Captain Hallsey.' The note of mild sarcasm made it obvious that Captain Reever viewed the prospect of leading such an assault without enthusiasm. 'It's a tricky business, sir, a very tricky business. To carry across a thousand men, say, you have to imagine thirty, perhaps fifty boats being needed. Will they sail, or must they be poled or rowed? How are the tides running? They've got to move together, in the dark I presume. Needs practice and training, and even then there's no certainty in it. Could cost lives, many lives I'd say.'

Alexander looked around the table. He realised they were looking to him to make a decision.

'It seems to me that we must either try somehow to dislodge Digby now, or face the certainty of having to surrender . . .'

A sudden reverberating crash drowned his words, rattled the furniture beneath them, and shook a cloud of plaster dust from the ceiling, and was instantly followed by the deep boom of a cannon shot. Alexander, at the head of his table, was the first to the window. The sun had just set, but there was enough light still for the wisp of black smoke to be seen drifting slowly up from the earthworks on Mount Batten

Point. Barnes, the Captain of Artillery, offered a cool professional comment.

'That's a good half-mile! They must have an experienced man there to hit the Keep with the first shot. Brave, too. I wouldn't have cared to put a full charge into that sixteen-pounder. I recall inspecting it with Sir William six months ago. One of Queen Bess's guns, we thought, set up there before the Armada came.'

There was a note of admiration in his tone that Alexander was quick to notice. How big a step was it from professional regard to changing sides? His line of thought was interrupted by Philip Francis.

'If they can hit the Keep, they can surely hit the town, and how long do you think our people will bear that? Sir Alexander is right, we must surrender – which Heaven forbid – or recapture that point. So can you lead us, Captain Reever? I'm sure that cannon will produce a thousand volunteers for you – that's if us civilians have a part to play?'

As he spoke Alexander winced at the boom of a second cannon shot, but the only effect was seen in a fountain of water and widening circles in the darkening sea beneath the Hoe.

'Not so much expert as lucky with that first shot I'd say, Captain Barnes. The decision must be yours, Captain Reever. You understand well our position, but only you can imagine the difficulties and dangers involved in an assault from the sea, and it cannot be right for me to bid any man kill himself, no matter what the cause.'

'I'll lead, and proud to do it, Sir Alexander. My remarks about the difficulty were by way of a warning only, so that no one should expect a cheap victory like Lipson. As far as civilians are concerned, we could certainly do with as many as you can get of those wild men that put the fear of God into the Royalists at Lipson. Have them all assemble on the Hoe tomorrow at first light, and in the meantime I'll also need a good man to help me work out what boats and boatmen we can depend on?'

'Mr Francis?'

'Peter Keckwick's your man. I'll send him to you.'

After the soldiers had left to start their planning, Philip returned, and sank down unbidden into the leather-padded chair beside the empty fireplace.

'Brave words, Sir Alexander, and no doubt there will be brave deeds to match. Tomorrow night, I suppose?'

'Tomorrow night, yes. It's high tide early in the morning, so that will be the moment to land. I'm certain we can recover the Point, and destroy Digby into the bargain.'

'Pray God you are right. And then what?'

Alexander guessed where his thought was leading, but kept his answer deliberately non-committal. 'We carry on as before, I suppose, trying to make Plymouth as hard to take as we can, in the hope that no one will think us worth the pain.'

'But for how long can we keep up the bluff? With all due respect, Sir Alexander, I cannot believe you have not taken note of how easily they took Bristol. And that's a city with four or five times our population, even if the garrison was weakened. And who could find it surprising, when the King can put twenty thousand trained soldiers into the assault? We would exact some casualties for sure, but I doubt if our ramparts and forts would last an hour. This business at Mount Batten shows how vulnerable we really are. You have garrisoned St Nicholas Island in the middle of the Sound, but what about Cawsands and Edgcombe on the west side, for example? I've heard that Sir Peter Edgcumbe favours the King, and a battery there could close the Sound to shipping, just as well as anywhere else. Are we to defy now the whole of the west country and the King's army, alone? Is that a sensible, a prudent thing to do? I ask this, Sir Alexander, out of honest concern for myself of course, but also because these are the questions my fellow councillors and citizens will ask me, if not today then tomorrow or the day after. And when they ask I must be able to answer, and persuasively too, since I have no power to command their loyalty.'

Alexander knew Philip to be a natural intriguer and a deeply calculating politician, but that evening he could see only fear and uncertainty in his dark face. He seemed to have shed altogether the special ability to dominate that he usually exerted with his physical presence, and in its place was an engaging frankness that persuaded Alexander to be honest in return.

'I think you know already, Mr Francis, that I have no answer to your questions, except to respond to each situation as it comes. The loss of Bristol is a terrible blow, more for what it gives the King than for what it actually costs our cause. But Parliament will surely see the value of maintaining its Bastion in the West, so we should expect strong reinforcements from Portsmouth any day now.'

'Perhaps. Or perhaps Parliament will be concerned that, with a port now secured behind him, the King may strike at London itself next. In that case they will want to keep every soldier they can raise, to defend the capital. They may continue to praise our gallantry, but in reality treat us as expendable. Suppose you were sitting safe in Westminster, Sir Alexander, instead of worrying about your family and estates down here. Isn't that the advice you would be giving your esteemed kinsman, Mr John Pym?'

Out of political habit Alexander began to marshal in his mind the counter-arguments to Philip's cynical calculation. But even as he did so he realised in his heart that Philip was most likely right. The town could not be defended against a serious assault, nor could its lifeline to the sea be kept open if the enemy were able to occupy the shores of Plymouth Sound with cannon. Nor was it likely that Parliament would divert sufficient resources from the centre, where the war would be won and lost, to this point on the periphery where, at best, they could only be a minor irritant that the King might well ignore.

'Assuming, for the moment, that you are right, what would you propose that we do?'

Philip's eyes widened as his thoughts raced to comprehend the full implications of Alexander's apparently straightforward question. He knew that his own probings had been like those of a child, seeking reassurance from a parent that there was really no monster lurking in a dark corner of the bedroom – but confident that reassurance would indeed be forthcoming. But now? Was Alexander seriously inviting him to contemplate the probability of defeat? Might there be some trick, some test of loyalty? He kept his eyes averted as he replied.

'You mean, what should we do if we believe the town can no longer be defended?'

'Yes.'

There it was, out in the open, with no ifs or buts! Sir Alexander really did believe the town might be lost!

'I suppose it is up to us to consider what is best for our people. It can't be right to plough on blindly into a siege and an inevitable sack of the town. Nor to urge people to sacrifice their lives if we sincerely believe there is no hope. If Plymouth cannot be expected to hold out, our plain duty as leaders is to negotiate whilst we still have something to offer.'

'And what, in your view, is our negotiating position?'

'I imagine this is a case where us poor civilians should be asking the advice of the military, Sir Alexander. But let's suppose we save the King the trouble of diverting an army down from Bristol. We are saving them the expense of a long march – two hundred miles and more – perhaps the risk of hundreds of his soldiers' lives, the shot, powder and provisions they would expend, and of course the shot and powder that we would use as well. And I suppose they would expect to enlist a fair number of our troops, together with the cannon, muskets and pikes that go with them. When you think about it carefully, we do have a good deal to offer.'

'And what should we expect in return?'

There was something, a hint of challenge, in Alexander's quiet tone that made Philip feel distinctly uncomfortable. 'Sir Alexander, we are talking about treason here. Our intentions are of the best, but Parliament will call it treason none the less.'

Alexander was contrite. 'Mr Francis, I give you my word that we are not overheard here, and I hope you know me well enough now to know that I will never betray your trust, even if it costs my head. I need your honest counsel. Do you trust me?'

'Of course, sir, of course.'

'Then what should we expect, in return for peacefully surrendering the town?'

'For the town, simply that it be left in peace, with no more than a normal garrison, and no forced levy, either of tax or recruits. For ourselves and for our friends, I think we would need something more specific. Some kind of formal promise of reconciliation, perhaps.'

'A Royal Pardon? Warranted with the King's own seal?'

'That sounds exactly right, a Royal Pardon. I'd like to have that safely in my hands before we opened the gates. But could it be got?'

Alexander considered his own position. He was virtually a prisoner in Plymouth. It was impossible even to contemplate trying to leave the town at such a time, and the same was true for Philip. It would have to be done by letter. But who could be trusted with such a letter, that would put their very lives at stake? Some reliable intermediary perhaps . . .

'That young protégé of yours, the deserter?'

'Tobias Fisher?'

'Yes. Do you still have him safely locked away?'

'I let him go this afternoon, when it was clear the Point had been taken. I thought his news, if he wanted to tell it, would not be of much interest to our people now. And besides I felt that too long a stay would be embarrassing for Lucy . . .'

'Yes, of course . . . still, you could get hold of him easily?'

'He's at his father's now. Were you thinking of him as the messenger?'

'As the carrier of a letter. I was impressed with the way he made his way here from Devizes, apparently without difficulty. Can he be trusted?'

'Absolutely.'

'You seem very confident, Mr Francis. We are not talking here of trusting the man with twenty pounds, but with our lives. Your life, and my life.'

'Believe me, Sir Alexander, you have thought of the one man in Plymouth to whom I would entrust my life.'

'Despite the fact that he must be jealous still of your marriage to Lucy, and despite the fact that he has already deserted once from our army?'

'Despite all those things I know, with absolute certainty, that he would rather die himself than betray me.'

Alexander looked into Philip's deep-set eyes, beneath the bristling black brows, and saw only honest confidence. Obviously there was more to the relationship with young Tobias than had so far been revealed, but it was vital to minimise the risk.

'I would suggest then that you write a simple letter of introduction, and send Tobias with a verbal message to the home of Sir George Chudleigh. It's about thirty miles towards Exeter. I can give you exact directions. Sir George, if he's there, or Lady Chudleigh if he's not, will know how to get a message to the King's Commander in the field.'

'But surely Sir George's family connections are all for Parliament. I remember his son reciting the family tree, and the connection with John Pym himself, when I was introduced to him in this very room.'

'Perhaps their hearts are for Parliament, but their heads are for the King now. Remember that both father and son are in the field, in the King's army somewhere.'

Philip was silent for a moment. 'Excellent, Sir Alexander. I'll instruct Tobias this evening. Will mine be the only approach, or will you . . .?'

'I will be writing myself, but using another route. I think we will both feel safer if you know no more than that.'

Plymouth, 2 August 1643

My Dearest Jane,

It grieves me very much to have to tell you that the danger of an attack on Plymouth is now so imminent that I may not, in all conscience, leave my post to be with you. I hope that the sight and feel of my letter will recall to you a sweet remembrance of our happy times together, and so make up in a small way for this cruel separation.

I was so pleased to learn from Walter when he came over that our plans for you to be protected if the need arises are in good order – pray God there is no need! However, I must not conceal from you the gravity of our present state. We have just heard that Bristol has fallen, and Prince Maurice now has his army of twenty thousand free and no doubt able to attack us if he so chooses. Colonel Digby has seized Mount Batten Point, and there will be widows and orphans aplenty in the town after we have dislodged him, as we must. And we hear rumours that an advance guard of the royal army under Sir John Berkley is coming down to face Exeter.

The threats to our town are now so many and so great that it may not be sensible to continue to believe that it can be defended with our present resources. Nor is it prudent just to assume that Parliament will think us worth rescuing. The consequences of a storming and bloody sack of Plymouth are too terrible to contemplate.

Yet I cannot move directly myself, and must therefore depend on you, my sweet love, to approach our friend again, and ask him to speak to the King's Commander on our behalf – to Sir John Berkley that is – and seek for us all in the town a Royal Pardon, properly signed and sealed, if we are able to persuade our garrison and our citizens here that it is better to negotiate than to risk everything.

I beg you, as you value our lives, be very cautious and circumspect in every thing you do or say. Trust no one with more than is necessary, write nothing, and DESTROY THIS LETTER.

I love you. Kiss all my pretty darlings for me.

Your loving husband,

Alexander

Jane Carew could not suppress a small tear as she read and re-read the letter in her sunny upstairs drawing-room. She closed her eyes, and could see Alexander frowning at his table as he wrote. It was obvious, even though his words were guarded, that he thought the end of Plymouth's ability to resist was not far away. Was his own escape plan still in place, she wondered? Probably, but he was also taking thought for his friends in the town, and of how much better it would be for everyone if they could just stop fighting, and not have to run away and hide!

She stood up decisively, folded the letter and tore it across, then tore it again and again into small pieces, which she dropped tidily into the log box beside the empty fireplace.

'Bessie! Bessie! Tell Walter to get my horse saddled, would you? And then put out my boots and my riding cloak. I will be out for the rest of the day.'

Almost immediately after Jane had ridden off her elder sister, Grace, came quietly into the drawing room, leaning now on a stout cane. She opened the unlocked desk, and grunted with disappointment to find only the usual bills and accounts. Then her eye was caught by a small scrap of torn paper beside the logs, She could make out the writing – *istol*. 'Pistol', perhaps? Or 'Bristol'? She knelt down to remove the kindling and dry logs from the box, and to collect up all the torn scraps. If Jane had thought it worthwhile to shred the letter, then no doubt there would be advantage to be got from putting it back together!

John Carew, eldest son of the Dowager Lady Carew, sat behind his writing table in his tiny office. Behind him was a door that opened into John Pym's anteroom. There was a thin slit of a window on his right, beneath which one of Westminster's ever-busy clattering courtyards could be discerned. Even on a fine August morning like this one John usually had a candle or two burning when he was writing. Mr Pym took strong exception to inky mistakes. In front of his table, and almost filling the rest of the room, sat a large man in the dress uniform of a full Colonel, obviously impatient as he perched, without much dignity, on the small chair provided.

John finished his scratchy writing at last, and sat back with a small sigh of satisfaction. In marked contrast to the delicate good looks of his half-brother Alexander, John was a neat, scholarly young man, bony and dark, with his hair close-cropped in the style made fashionable by the London apprentices. His thick eyebrows knitted together as he read through the two closely-written pages, and then handed them carefully to the soldier.

'Those are your orders for Plymouth, Colonel Gould. Nothing exceptional, I would say. You have full command of the garrison and all enlisted militia, including of course all the six hundred men you will be taking with you from Portsmouth.'

Colonel William Gould was a career soldier. About thirty years old now, he was the youngest son of a wealthy London merchant family. A florid complexion and a heavy build suggested that his command had probably been earned in the salons of his father's powerful friends, rather than amongst the privations of the battlefield.

'I thank you, Mr Carew. If I may be so bold, you seem exceptionally young to be issuing Parliament's commission for so difficult and perilous a command. Am I not to see Mr Pym, even for a moment's private discussion?'

John gave no sign of being offended by this polite questioning of his competence, and replied in a straightforward way.

'See Mr Pym? I only wish you could, Colonel, I only wish it were possible. I think it would strengthen the resolve of every one of our commanders if they could get to know Mr Pym, and see for themselves how he exhausts himself day and night in Parliament's cause. But it really is not possible today, Colonel. The War Council has been in session since first light, trying to determine how we can find the money, men and supplies to make good the losses at Devizes and Bristol. And last night, at midnight, I was present to record the minutes of this very matter, the issue of saving, or abandoning the town of Plymouth. Perhaps you can imagine what was said?'

Colonel Gould was shrewd enough to recognise a young man aching to impress him with his importance.

'I'm afraid I do not have your experience of statecraft, Mr Carew. If it is not too confidential, what was said about Plymouth?'

'I can tell you that, with the exception of Mr Pym, every single member of the Council was against sending reinforcements to Plymouth. With Bristol taken, and our Army of the West no longer in existence, it was plain to them all that Plymouth could no longer have a serious role to play in the war. In fact there were strong arguments against dividing our forces into penny-packets, when the King had the rest of the summer now to concentrate and prepare to attack us in London.'

'And how did Mr Pym reply?'

'He waited until they had finished, and it seemed that the matter was already decided,' John riffled through the papers on his table, allowing time for the Colonel to appreciate the significance of his work. 'Yes, here it is. The actual note I took of his words as he spoke.' He cleared his throat, and produced a passable imitation of John Pym's style, if not of his measured delivery.

'Gentlemen, I see that you are all of the opinion that we should abandon Plymouth to its fate. If we were discussing Exeter, or Barnstaple, or Taunton, or indeed any other town in the west, I would have to agree with you. They are all touched with a fondness for the old religion, I fear, all too eager to doff the cap to any man with a title, let alone the King himself. But Plymouth is different, as I can vouch from personal knowledge. Down there they seem to breed sturdy Dissenters by the score. The men that Good Queen Bess relied on to beat the Spanish for her, and the men who risked everything to plant the new colonies for us in the Americas.

Only last month you may recall we printed a pamphlet about Plymouth's citizen militia, and how they were able utterly to defeat a regiment of the King's trained soldiers, which threatened their town by having captured one of their forts. We have made of Plymouth an example, a beacon held up for every citizen to follow. We celebrated the town as 'Our Bastion in the West'. And what will our people think of us if we allow that living torch to be snuffed out, without so much as lifting a finger to save it? Will this not be seen as an example of that cynicism without conscience that we say we are fighting against? How could we then prosecute Colonel Fiennes, as we have said we will, for his feeble defence of Bristol? If one can call his treachery there a defence at all! I say that we must reinforce Plymouth with every man, every gun we can spare. We should be able to encourage its men to come out into Devon, and harass the lines of connection to Cornwall, which is certainly the best recruiting ground for the King in the country. As long as our commander there is active, the King will have to protect those connections, which will cost him three men for every one we put into the town. And that, gentlemen, could be enough to hold him back from advancing against us here until we are ready once more to defend ourselves.'

'An impressive argument, which obviously persuaded his colleagues.'

'Indeed it did, and afterwards Mr Pym instructed me most closely in the specification of your orders, what should be written, and also what should not be written.'

Colonel Gould took the implication that any questioning of John Carew's competence was likely to get short shrift from Mr Pym himself, and turned the conversation hastily to practical matters.

'I understand of course that I am to succeed Sir William Ruthin as Commander of the Garrison, and I pray that he may recover his health in due course. I am puzzled though that I am to report directly to Parliament?'

'In practice that means to myself, Colonel. Though I hasten

to add that I am merely the instrument of the War Council, and your advocate there.'

'Of course. But is there to be no Governor of Plymouth? I remember that last year Sir Jacob Astley was promoted from Plymouth to be Parliament's General of Foot. Is he to have no successor? I have read that your own brother, Sir Alexander, has been doing splendid work there, and is Governor in all but name. How would you have me relate to him?'

'To be exact in these matters, Colonel, Sir Alexander is my half-brother. But yes, Parliament has taken note of his inspiring leadership, and it is to be hoped that you will be able to work successfully with him, for all our sakes. However . . .'

John let his voice trail away, shaking his head slowly, as though he had already said too much. Colonel Gould knew there was more to be heard.

'Come now, Mr Carew, Plymouth is a lion's den, as you well know. If I am to be asked to put my head in the lion's mouth I must be fairly warned of all the dangers. Is there something you have not told me?'

'Something more? Perhaps, perhaps not. The truth is that Plymouth is a long way off, and behind enemy lines. We have access by sea, of course, but really we know only as much as Sir Alexander tells us in his reports. And there are some disturbing rumours.'

'What do these rumours say?'

John sat in silence for a long moment, as he laced and unlaced his fingers on the table in front of him. Then he seemed to come to a decision.

'Colonel, may I have your promise that nothing I say now will ever be repeated, or even referred to by yourself?'

'My word as an officer and a gentleman.'

'Very well then. These rumours concern Sir Alexander himself.' He paused, as though searching for the right words. 'Sir Alexander, as you know, is a Member of Parliament, and a fierce defender of Parliament's rights and privileges.'

'And yet?'

'And yet he is also connected, through descent, with the Arundells, the Godolphins, the Courtenays and the Edgcumbes, all notorious for being the leading supporters of the King in Cornwall and in Devon. There have been rumours, just stories up to now, that someone in Plymouth, perhaps Sir Alexander, has kept contact with these great families. Recently we had the terrible news that our General James Chudleigh had turned traitor, and that his father, Sir George, had followed him. Not many people know up here in London that Sir George is the uncle of Sir Alexander Carew, being his mother's brother. So you see my difficulty?'

'I do, most certainly. You say not many people know that?'

'I had to remind Mr Pym of course, and it was his decision that we should hold back from the obvious course of naming Sir Alexander to be Governor. The damage to our cause if he should subsequently waver in his allegiance . . .'

'You need say no more, Mr Carew. I will take precautions against any possible treachery, and you may of course rely on my absolute discretion.'

'I am to ride tonight across Dartmoor to the Chudleigh house at Ashton, and ask to see Sir George, or if he's not there, Lady Chudleigh. No one else.'

'Mind you stick exactly to that, Tobias, no one else,' said Philip Francis with great emphasis. 'My life depends on it.'

'No one else, sir, I promise. I am to say to Sir George or Lady Chudleigh that I have a message for the King's General.'

'For Sir John Berkley. We know now that he is in command of the King's army in front of Exeter. We had a ship in only half an hour ago with the news.'

'A message for Sir John Berkley, at Exeter. If they ask "who from?", I'm to say it's from Plymouth, but I may not say who sends me nor what the message is.'

'Good. You were given the message with the most strict

instructions, to protect the very lives of the senders. You request the assistance of Sir George or his lady wife in obtaining a safe-conduct that will enable you to reach Sir John with a message from Plymouth.'

'And in the same way when I reach the Royal army I am to give the message only to Sir John. "For his ears only", you said.'

'Give your message only to Sir John. Say when you are alone with him that you have come on behalf of the citizens of Plymouth, including Sir Alexander Carew and the Mayor, Mr Philip Francis. Can you remember the rest now?'

'I'm to say that the leading citizens, including Sir Alexander and the Mayor, have no quarrel with the King and wish to be reconciled. Consequently they are willing to lay down their arms and open the gates, provided that:

Point one – Sir John promises to protect and maintain the town according to the Rules of War, and

Point two – each and every citizen, including and especially Sir Alexander Carew and Mr Philip Francis are given the Royal Pardon for any and all offences that may be alleged against them.'

'Excellent, Tobias, very well remembered. It will be dark in an hour. Get some food, and I will write you a pass for the gate. If you are questioned, you are a clerk in Mr Francis' employ, and you must go to your mother in Ashburton who is at death's door.'

Twenty-one years ago, just before he married his first wife, Philip Francis had been working in his father's wine-import business, and Tobias' mother, Ellen, had been a pretty little maid in his father's house. When she said she was pregnant his father had forbidden marriage, and instead had given Ellen a dowry of fifty pounds – five years' wages. Tom Fisher was just a labourer in the warehouse, and had been glad to marry her on such terms. He had used the money to start a business as a carter, which thrived with Philip's father as his first customer. Tobias seemed proud to know that Philip was his real father, though he would never say how he knew.

Philip had guessed that Ellen had told him, perhaps as part of the process of persauding him to give up his ambitions to marry Lucy, and he was devoted to him in his way, being his only natural child after the loss of his daughter in the plague.

'Good luck, Tobias. May God keep you safe. It is a brave thing you do now, for all our sakes.'

All the next day, and late into the evening Captain Reever laboured with his lieutenants and non-commissioned officers to teach his troopers and the civilian volunteer militia the rudiments of a night attack from the sea. He impressed on the sailors and fishermen who had the handling of the boats the importance of trimming sails so that the slowest kept up with the fastest. 'If a few get there ahead of the rest they will be dead before the full force can distract the enemy'. For security he kept them in Mill Bay, which lies on the west side of Plymouth and is completely hidden from Mount Batten Point by the swelling rise of The Hoe.

Alexander had announced his firm intention of joining the militia for the attack, and brooked no objection, 'I will concede that it is not appropriate for me to be amongst the first ashore, but I will be on my ship, we will land our forty men, and I will come ashore with them.'

Captain Reever felt that it was not his place to oppose the settled decision of the town's *de facto* Governor, and confined his comment to a sober appreciation of their chances.

'Surprise, or the lack of it, will determine how many of us will be killed. Even after they see us, they will not know which of our two landings is the main one, so if we can just catch them dozing, or off balance, we have the numbers to overwhelm them, and I would then expect them to make a run for it or surrender quickly rather than stand to be slaughtered. But if they are able to hold off our first attack and get behind ramparts, we must expect to take heavy casualties, as we must try to assault a fortified position. It will be particularly dangerous if they are able to bring the cannon to bear on us, loaded with grape-shot for example.'

Sufficient craft had been found to carry one thousand five hundred men. Divided into two groups, all were to be loaded in secrecy at Mill Bay. The first group would consist of a thousand experienced troopers, armed with pike and musket, who would be landed on the south shore of the Point, the side away from Plymouth; while the second, consisting of five hundred volunteer militia would assault the nearer north side. With no further need for concealment, the boats were then all to return to the South Pool to pick up a mixed force of a further thousand men. Captain Reever's planning was meticulous.

'It will take longer to sail to the south side of Mount Batten than to the north, so our troopers will embark thirty minutes before the militia, and will approach around the west side of St. Nicholas Island. I want the troopers under way three hours after midnight, and both should land at the same time, as close after four as possible. That way we should have the cover of the dark for landing, and first light for the assault. Is that clear, gentlemen?'

Following Alexander's lead, Philip Francis had also volunteered to lead a landing party, and offered a suggestion.

'You know I'm no strategist, Captain, but I was wondering if we couldn't give them back some cannon-fire? We have guns here in Plymouth and on St. Nicholas Island. Could they not support us?'

'A sensible thought, Mr Francis, but I'm sure Captain Barnes has some misgivings.'

'Indeed I do. You will have noticed that there have been only the two shots fired from the Point, which suggests to me that the weight of powder required to carry this far has damaged the gun. I do know that our guns here in Plymouth are of similar age, which makes them suspect, and in addition to shoot at Mount Batten Point would mean firing over the heads of our own militia as they are landing – not an acceptable risk, I'm sure you will agree.'

'And from the Island?'

'A much better prospect. There are two sixteen pounders there not more than twenty years old. The moment we see the first shots being fired at the landings, we could get off a couple of rounds of cannon that would enfilade the position between our two forces. Give them a very nasty shock, I'd say. Needs tight control, though. I could only recommend it if I was in charge myself.'

'Sir Alexander?'

'With all my heart. I'll write a note immediately, Captain Barnes. You will have command of the Island for tonight.'

Philip felt the tremble in Lucy's fingers as she buckled the old breastplate around his burly body.

'Now don't you worry yourself about me, my love. I'm no green lad to want to be first onto the beach or first up the ladder. I've done my duty by setting a good example and volunteering. We've bloodthirsty men a'plenty to do the killing.'

Lucy put her arms around his neck and kissed him hard. There were tears running down her cheeks when at last she broke away.

'There's something I've been meaning to tell you Philip. I was saving it for the right moment, but now . . . I wouldn't want you to go off fighting without knowing.'

Philip was immediately on his guard. 'If it's about Sir Alexander, I can tell you I've heard some stories already. I trusted . . .'

'Don't be so silly, Philip, of course it's not about Sir Alexander. He's just a kind friend, just like you said you wanted him to be. It's about us. Can't you guess?'

'You're not . . .?'

'Of course I am. At least I think so. I'm two weeks late, and I'm always as regular as the tide. My mother thinks we'll have the baby for Easter next year.'

Had he been cuckolded? How could any man know for

certain? With Beth, his first wife, they'd started a baby within the first couple of months of lovemaking, just like before with Tobias' mother, Ellen. But he'd been married more than a year now to Lucy, and there had been no baby. Until now, that is, a few weeks after he'd encouraged her to . . . to what? He rested his big hands on her shoulders. He could still feel that tremble in her body, but those wide-set tawny eyes looked firmly and lovingly back at him. What right had he to doubt her? He kissed her, gently at first, then with increasing passion, until she squealed beneath his grip.

'Softly, love, softly. You're wearing armour you know.'

'I'll come back, don't you worry, and I'll be the best father a baby ever had.'

The night was dark with a heavy overcast of low cloud, and no moon or stars to be seen. There was a soft, damp breeze from the south-west, promising something stronger by morning perhaps. The troopers had boarded already, and their motley flotilla, silent as ghosts, had set sail for the tack south, close-hauled down almost to the mouth of Plymouth Sound, and then the dead run back to their objective, the south side of Mount Batten Point.

Isaac Weaver the preacher waded waist deep into the water beside Alexander's converted fishing-boat, his gaunt features fitfully illuminated by the light of the flaring torch he carried.

'On, on then, you heroes of Plymouth! We have Sir Alexander here, we have Philip Francis, we have Peter Keckwick, we have every honest man in Plymouth with us. God is on our side! Let us teach these damned invaders a lesson that will be heard all across England!'

There were a few 'Hurrahs' in response, but for the most part the mood was one of silent determination as five hundred men waded through the dark ripples of the rising tide and climbed into thirty small boats, loading them down perilously close to the water in most cases. As each group climbed aboard the leader dropped his torch into the sea with a hiss and a shout of 'All on', and in a few minutes the bustle and lights on the beach had become stillness and darkness again. Alexander's boat had been renamed *Bridget*, after his mother, when Jane had it fitted out to carry passengers. He hoped the old superstition about bad luck following a new name did not hold true. Captain Amos looked grimly at the tense faces of the forty men now packed on board, mostly sitting hunched in the bottom, holding a pike, a broadsword, a pitchfork or occasionally a musket between their knees.

'We're fortunate the wind is light, Sir Alexander. One stiff gust and we'd be gunwales under, I'd say.'

Bridget was the largest and fastest of the fleet carrying the civilian militia, and so was one of the last to get under way. They were close-hauled for about two hundred yards, until they could see on their left the white necklace of foam all along the south shore of the Hoe, and then the helmsman eased her around to port until they were running due east, with the dark bulk of the Island on their right. The breeze seemed to strengthen, and Alexander felt the boat lift on the back of a roller and quicken. All around were the other boats now, silent except for the gurgle of water under the bows, the soft creak and slap of sail and rigging, and a cough and suppressed curse from below. For a few moments they seemed to hang suspended in the darkness of the night, then Alexander felt rather than saw on his left the walls of his fort on the eastern tip of the Hoe, and the sea sounds changed as they turned a few degrees starboard, across the entrance of the South Pool and directly towards the menacing loom of Mount Batten Point. Captain Amos' voice was whispering in Alexander's ear.

'About two hundred yards to go sir. We'll drive straight onto the beach a few yards left of the Point itself. After you're ashore the tide will lift me off easily enough.'

Captain Amos moved up into the bow to con *Bridget* ashore, aiming for a small strip of sand. There was one boat just behind them to the right, and away to his left Alexander heard crunch after crunch as the others ran ashore, dropping sail as they touched. It was so silent that Alexander wondered if the enemy had already abandoned the Point. A quiet order, and the sails came down as the boat touched sandy bottom and tipped over onto her side as she ran half her length onto the beach. A huge flash of light filled the sky ahead of them, and Alexander was thrown headlong onto the sand as a cannon ball tore into the boat with a thunderous roar. He lay on his back half-winded, and could see the flashes and bangs all along the shore as the line of boats was hit by cannon and musket. The night was filled with the shrieks of the wounded. He struggled to his feet beside the bow. There was a splintered gaping hole where the shot had entered the forepeak at a steep angle from above, and he guessed it had probably smashed its way through the keel. The beach around him was a maelstrom of men milling round in confusion.

'A Carew, A CAREW! Stand by me now. Now, quick as you can up the beach to the cliff. That will give you shelter from the cannon.'

There was another great flash and explosion from above them, and the sea boiled with myriad small splashes.

'Grape, they're loading grape-shot. For your lives now, press up against the foot of the cliff!' Alexander climbed back into the boat. 'Captain Amos, are you there? Captain . . .'

Alexander recognised the dark blue coat with the brass buttons. That first cannon-shot had taken off the Captain's head as neatly as a headsman's axe. Alexander leaped from the boat and sprinted for the cliff as the cannons roared again and a hail of grape-shot thrashed diagonally across the sand. He crouched low with his back pressed into the low cliff that afforded some protection against the gunfire.

'How many have we lost?'

There could be no certainty; in the darkness and confusion the men had run right and left and some had even dived into the sea to avoid death. He counted about thirty men beside him. Away to the east there was a flash and boom of cannon from the Island. Thank God, Captain Barnes had started to fire! From above he heard the thud and rattle as the ball skittled across the fort, producing mingled cries of alarm and screams of pain.

'That's one for us at least. Now men, our best chance is to get up off this beach and get those guns. Are you with me?'

Another salvo from above ploughed through the beach inches from them, and it was Isaac Weaver who spoke. 'We're with you, Sir Alexander. We remember the charge at Lipson, and know you are under the Lord's special care.'

'Good for you, Isaac. Tim Benson there, I recognise your honest face. Will you work your way along the cliff here, and tell the others to get up the cliff to just below the top, and then charge when they see us go.'

One, two, three flashes – a volley of cannon from the Island that produced a shower of earth and stone from the ramparts above, and more howls of agony. There was another sound too, muffled but unmistakable. Musket fire, from the other side of the Point!

'Captain Reever's men have landed! We go after the next volley from the Island!'

The two cannon on the rampart that had killed so many on the beach were now silent. The sounds of battle could be heard clearly now. The land sloped to the beach on the south side, so the enemy cannon would be even more effective if they could be brought to bear. A volley of musket crashed out, suggesting that the troopers were advancing in good order. It was still too early for the dawn, but Alexander's eyes had adjusted sufficiently to the darkness to be able to make out hordes of small boats raising sail on the Plymouth side. They would have reinforcements soon. A bugle sounded a tinny note from above – ours? – theirs? – what did it signify? Cheers, curses, the clang of weapon on armour, but no shot from the Island. Perhaps Barnes thought it was too dangerous now? Alexander looked at the dark, expectant faces on each side

'Charge, Charge, CHARGE! For King and Parliament!'
'FOR KING AND PARLIAMENT!'

All along the face of the low cliff the line of dark figures scrambled up onto the grassy slope of the fort, and then up to the top. Alexander had a sudden fear that they would meet their own troops charging the other way, perhaps even a volley of their musket fire. But there was no one. The cannon were abandoned in the embrasures, the ground, obviously torn up by cannon shot, was full of the dead and dying, both men and horses. In a moment dark silhouettes appeared over the south rampart.

'Don't fire, don't fire! They've gone! The Point is ours!'

All around men sank to their knees, and Alexander joined them as beside him Isaac Weaver began the *Te Deum Laudamus*. He thought of Jane, and as the anthem swelled he thought of his children, John, Richard, Bridget, Jane, Mary, Weymouth, and Thomas. In the strengthening light he saw Philip Francis with his head bowed, and he thought of Lucy, dear, sweet, fragile Lucy.

'Dear God, I thank you for my life.'

Antony, 7 August 1643

My Dearest Alexander,

We heard the rumble of guns two nights ago, and the next day Peter Goodman came back from Plymouth with the story of the assault on Mount Batten. A victory, for which we thank the Lord, but so many dead that I wept to hear of it. They say you are a hero again, but I take no joy of it. Have you no pity for your wife and your children, helpless here in Antony, that you must seek to squander your life in some trifling military adventure? If you love me, I beg you now to promise that you will never again gamble your life in such a way. God knows we have enough perils on every side.

The news from Exeter is that the King's army is being daily increased, and the city is expected to open its gates today or tomorrow. No doubt you will calculate what that will mean for Plymouth. Your messages have reached the right people, and

they are commanded to deal fairly with you. But you must
proceed urgently, my love, and contact the man at Plymstock. No
delay is possible. May God keep you and return you safely to us.
   Your loving wife,
   Jane

Peter Goodman had appeared at the Castle with Jane's
letter a few minutes before, and was waiting discreetly just
inside the doorway whilst Alexander sat in the window recess,
using the last of the evening light to read it. He admitted to
himself that, when he had announced his decision to take his
ship to Mount Batten, he had given no thought to Jane and
the children, nor any consideration to what would become of
them if he were killed, or wounded or captured. It had not
been vanity or vainglory. It was just that people saw him as
their leader, so he felt compelled to take the lead. Was his the
sin of Pride? If it was, God had been merciful on this
occasion, and he swore a silent oath that, for the future, he
would be as cautious as any family man should be.

The plain meaning of Jane's guarded letter was that Sir
John Berkley, who was about to accept the surrender of
Exeter, had delegated the negotiations for Plymouth to
Colonel Digby, the commander of the royalist army at
Plymstock. Alexander reread the words 'commanded to deal
fairly with you'. How much weight should be put on that?
Once negotiations were started, he and Philip would be
virtually at the mercy of this Digby, a man he did not know.

'There is no answer for now, Peter. I must consult with Mr.
Francis. Will you stay the night in the Castle, and come to
me after breakfast.'

'Very good, sir. High water is around eight, sir.'

'I'll be ready by seven.'

Alexander sent a soldier to ask Philip if he might call, and
was invited to supper.

'Mr. Francis ast' me to say most particular like that 'e

would be proud an' honoured if you would grace 'is table, as soon as you like sir.'

Despite the warmth of the invitation Alexander felt distinctly nervous as he reached for the heavy lion's head knocker on Philip's front door. In the euphoria of victory on Mount Batten Point they had slapped one another on the back and even wept together out of sheer relief at having survived. Philip had said something cryptic about 'having another reason to live now', but nothing had prepared Alexander for the scene that greeted him when the door was opened. Half the men of Plymouth seemed crammed into the parlour, some cutting thick slices of cold beef and drinking great gulps of Philip's best red wine from pewter tankards, some sitting on the board floor, beating time with their fists to a fiddler in the corner, some threatening life and limb in a reel, swirling, stamping, shouting and singing. Catching sight of Alexander, Philip stopped the fiddler dead with a word in his ear, and climbed on the table as the hubbub was hushed.

'Gentlemen, GENTLEMEN. Citizens of Plymouth, we are honoured now by the arrival of our leading citizen. I give you the toast: King and Parliament, coupled with the name of Sir Alexander Carew!'

'King and Parliament. PARLIAMENT AND CAREW!'

From somewhere inside the house Lucy appeared, dressed in white with a red bow tying back her fair hair. There was a sparkle in her eyes as the crowd parted to allow her through to offer Alexander a pot of wine from the tray she carried. She made a deep, slow curtsy that showed off the small breasts just beneath the low-cut neckline.

'Welcome, Sir Alexander, welcome to our celebration. Have you heard the news? I am to give Philip a child, my first, next Eastertide. Will you drink to my health?'

Speculations tumbled wildly through Alexander's head as he raised the brimming mug of Spanish wine in salutation, and then drank deeply. A child for Lucy! There was something in her smile, some challenge hidden behind that wide-eyed innocence . . .

'Your health, Mistress Lucy, and may you have a fine, healthy boy to carry forward the good name of my friend here, Philip Francis!'

Hands reached out on every side to shake his, or even just to touch him, as though he were some kind of good-luck charm. The fiddler struck up the wild reel, and the riotous dance began again. The din of excited talk had risen almost to a roar by the time Alexander had thrust his way across the room to Philip's side.

'Sir Alexander, welcome again to our house. You know Peter Keckwick of course, Lucy's father?'

'Good to see you, Mr. Keckwick. I heard a wonderful story of your courage, collecting wounded men on the beach while the grape-shot was still coming down from Mount Batten.'

'I was able to do something, and God decided I was not ready for him yet. To speak the truth, Sir Alexander, I lost too many friends to be in the mood for rejoicing tonight, much as I congratulate Philip here on his joyful news. I suspect you were beginning to worry if you might never be blessed with issue from Lucy, were you not Philip?'

Philip was too happy to be drawn by Peter's teasing, but replied seriously. 'I didn't hear the final counts, Peter. How many did you lose?'

'I had ten boats altogether in my group, and we have seventeen to bury tomorrow. And there are twice as many with wounds, so we must be prepared for more to die.'

The fiddler finished the last triumphant refrain, and the dancers cheered as they wiped the sweat from their brows and reached for their pots of wine or ale. Celebration, wake, thanksgiving, Philip's gathering combined all three, with a perceptible, darker undertone of sheer abandon.

'Philip, I've had a communication. Is there somewhere we can talk quietly for a few minutes?'

'Follow me.'

He led Alexander up the steep winding staircase and into the dinning room above, lit by a single candle. Alexander took a seat at the end of the table, in the big square bay window that jutted out over the dark street. The music and dancing began again below them, curiously filtered so that only the rhythmic stamping of boots on boards and the occasional high note from the fiddler came through. Philip lit more candles, and Alexander looked around the room as it came to life. The oak table with its strong carved legs could seat ten or twelve, and the high-backed chairs had a fine set of leather cushions, apparently embroidered in gold thread. The walls were panelled in linenfold as good as anything at Antony, and there was a handsome painted sculpture above the fireplace of Adam and Eve. Philip smiled as he followed Alexander's gaze.

'This was my father's house, and my grandfather built it. Everyone believes that the money came from one of the Armada shipwrecks, but grandfather always denied it, and said it was honest trade and hard work.' His expression became grim as he sat down heavily beside Alexander. 'I've had a communication too, Sir Alexander. Tobias came back an hour ago, no doubt with the same answer.'

'That we should treat with Colonel Digby?'

'Exactly.'

'What do you think of the proposal?'

'I'm not happy, Sir Alexander, not happy. Do you know this Colonel Digby?'

'Not at all, except that he is an energetic and dangerous enemy.'

'Dangerous indeed. I do not have a perfect count, but I believe we have lost the best part of two hundred men in recapturing Mount Batten, most of them from the civilian militia. There is such anger in the town too, as well as the grief. Did you feel it downstairs?'

'I sensed something, a wildness . . .'

'Well, enough of that. Our people will grieve in their own way now, but I have to tell you that I think it a great blessing that we did not take any prisoners . . . So, how should we proceed?'

'The letter to me stressed that we must proceed urgently and without delay.'

'No doubt our bargaining strength would be less once they have started to besiege the town again. And there is the more urgency now that we no longer have the *Bridget* to depend on. I was sorry to hear about your Captain Amos, by the way.'

Alexander shuddered to recall the headless body on the shattered foredeck, with the blood still welling thickly from the neck, amidst the darkness and terror of that beach. There was a tremor in his voice as he spoke.

'He was a good man, honest and reliable. I went to see his widow this afternoon. Three grown sons and two unmarried daughters.' Alexander paused to drink some more of the wine he had brought upstairs, 'How to proceed? It's obvious, the sooner we start talking, the less the likelihood of another attack. But how can we be certain of Digby's discretion?'

'Could we sound him out first? A letter perhaps?'

'A letter setting out our precise terms? Yes, that could do it. But my connections . . . the route I used to reach Sir John Berkley . . . I don't think they would be of use to reach Colonel Digby, at least not directly.'

'Leave the route to me, Sir Alexander. But the letter would carry more weight if it came from yourself, wouldn't you agree?'

Alexander looked up sharply from his wine. Was this a trap? Might Philip be intent after all on exacting revenge for the affair with Lucy? Yet when he looked into Philip's deeply shadowed eyes, dark beneath the bristling black brows, he recognised only concern and honest purpose.

'Of course I would want to put my own name beneath your own, but I'm sure it should come from you, Sir Alexander.'

'And you'll use Tobias again to deliver it?'

'He was successful last time, and Plymstock is no distance. He could go first thing in the morning, if your letter is ready.'

'I'll write tonight, and perhaps you could come to me in the morning to add your signature?' Alexander drained his mug. 'A fine wine, Mr. Francis. And may I add my congratulations on the good news about a child? You must be very pleased, and Mistress Lucy too of course.'

Philip led Alexander down a back staircase to avoid passing through the guests still roaring and stamping in the front parlour. 'And thank you again, Sir Alexander, for honouring our little celebration.'

Philip raised a hand in salute to Alexander as he left, but did not return immediately to his guests. Instead he took a walk in the opposite direction, where the street curved round to lead onto the waterside quay by the South Pool. Plymouth's harbour was less crowded than usual, because the larger ships had not yet come back from their refuge in Mill Bay. He had the quayside to himself as he sat with his legs over the harbour wall. There was no moon yet, but it was a clear, warm night, and the sky was alight with the familiar constellations he had learnt as a boy.

Philip had sensed at once the hesitation Alexander had felt when the letter had been suggested. If Sir Alexander suspected a trap, that meant he had some reason to doubt Philip's loyalty. Which could only mean that he thought Philip could have some reason to be treacherous. And what could that be, except for Lucy? Or perhaps the hesitation had only been the natural fear of the consequences if the letter were intercepted? How could a man really know who was the father? He thought of putting pressure on Lucy, but rejected the idea, at least for the present, because of the danger of making an enemy of Lucy's father, Peter Keckwick, his most important political ally. And Lucy had been so loving and affectionate when he had returned safely from Mount Batten, it was obvious she really loved him. He had entrusted those pearls to Sir Alexander to help ensure they had a safe escape if the need arose, and Lucy had only been doing his bidding when she devoted time and attention to Sir Alexander.

Still undecided, Philip was standing up to return to his guests when his eye was caught by a movement, away at the entrance to the harbour. Alarmed, he peered into the darkness, and recognised the dim silhouette of a large ship, now rounding Fishersness and ghosting on a faint breeze into the South Pool. There had been no alarm from the Island or the Fort, so it must be friendly. The reinforcements perhaps, from Portsmouth? He hurried back towards his house, wondering how that might affect the future.

Betrayal

'It was bravely done, Captain Hallsey, bravely done and boldly lead. And Captain Reever's planning was sound, and we may allow that Captain Barnes' fire from the Island was most precisely managed and signally effective. But the question that cannot be avoided, gentlemen, is 'Why was the action necessary in the first place?' Here we have a detachment of the enemy, known to be energetic and aggressive, based only three miles away at Plymstock. And here we have a fortified Point, equipped with cannon that could be used to close off Plymouth's harbour and bombard the town itself. So why did no one foresee the likelihood of an attack? How could the defences be so obviously taken by surprise and overwhelmed? Most importantly, how could those guns be taken without having been spiked first?'

Colonel Gould had arrived officially into Plymouth Castle at first light, and had lost no time in calling a meeting with his three principal subordinates. He wore a dark blue military jacket with silver facings, and sat behind Sir William Ruthin's dining table, with the three captains standing stiffly to attention in front of him. Receiving no reply to his questions, he continued.

'I have received good reports of all three of you, so we will proceed no further with what I had originally intended after I heard of this Mount Batten business this morning, which was a full Court Martial to enquire into the matter. But I think we should now be asking ourselves if there is a possibility that the Fort there was deliberately and treacherously surrendered. If so, the culprits were directly responsible for the deaths of the two hundred men of Plymouth who will be buried today. Captain Hallsey, do you know or suspect anything of the kind? Have there been any attempts by the enemy to suborn our men?'

Hallsey shifted his feet uncomfortably. As the senior captain, the responsibility for the defence had fallen mainly on him during Sir William's illness. He glanced at the closed bedroom door. Sir William was apparently still asleep, and so had not yet met his successor, but he had previously advised strongly against any excessive measures to uncover possible traitors. 'Our cause is just and honourable,' he had said, 'And we are well rid of any who want to leave.'

'If I may be allowed a comment, sir?'

'Please, Captain Barnes.'

'There was one case, soon after Colonel Digby was reported to have arrived at Plymstock. A man called Ellis Carkeet, a notorious rogue, approached one of my chief gunners, Corporal Kneebone, who has the responsibility for one of the forts on the rampart, at Magdalen. He offered my man ten pounds if he would hold back any order to fire when the fort was attacked.'

'What happened?'

'Kneebone reported the approach, and we laid a trap to catch Carkeet. Unfortunately he was too wary, and we never caught him.'

'I remember that,' said Hallsey. 'Then Carkeet and another man were reported missing from the town, and we thought later that they were the source of the local knowledge that made possible that first attack of Digby's, on our Lipson Fort.'

Colonel Gould sat back in his chair and closed his eyes for a few seconds, as though to commune with some inner enlightenment, than snapped forward with a new edge to his tone.

'The probability is, gentlemen, that you were not able to catch this traitor because he was forewarned by another traitor here in Plymouth. Let me paint a broader picture for you. At this very time Sir John Hotham and his son are in the Tower of London, awaiting trial and certain execution for handing our city of Kingston upon Hull over to the royalists. And we are about to charge Colonel Fiennes also with treason, for the feeble surrender of Bristol. We know that Exeter will not fight because it holds more royalist rogues than honest Parliament men, and Cornwall here is noted as the best recruiting ground for the King. Is it likely that Plymouth is altogether free of that foul infection?'

He stood up briskly, and walked to the window, where his expression suggested that he was singularly unimpressed by the fine view over the Sound.

'I think we may adjourn at this point. It is time for me to be meeting Sir Alexander Carew and some of the Plymouth worthies. We will assemble here again this afternoon, and you will acquaint me with the detail of our defences and the positions of the enemy.'

'With respect, sir.'

'Yes, Captain Hallsey?'

'There is to be a funeral service for our dead at midday, and then the official interment. With the parades and speeches that will follow ... and perhaps it would be appropriate for you also to attend ...'

'Of course, and I thank you for reminding me, Captain. You are all bidden instead to take supper with me here at five.'

Tobias Fisher sat on his narrow bed in the small whitewashed garret in Tom Fisher's house. The floor was bare, and the only other furniture was a chest of drawers with a washbasin. A small window looked out onto the South Pool, now filling up again with returning ships. Tobias however had no thought for the bustling world outside. Instead he sat

endlessly turning over and over in his hands the folded letter,
sealed on the red wax with Sir Alexander's coat of arms, the
three lions. He was trying to make a decision, but the
consequences were so momentous either way that deciding
was hard indeed.

His instructions from Philip Francis had been quite simple.
He was to leave the town that afternoon in a small sailing
boat, as though going fishing. No one would take any notice
anyway, because of the funerals. Once out in the harbour he
was to sail up the Catwater, and land on the west shore at
Saltram. From there it was just a mile to walk to Plymstock.
His letter was for the Royalist commander's eyes only, this
time Colonel Digby.

Simple enough. For Tobias however the whole activity had
become hateful, and he was torn between his deep affection
for his natural father and benefactor, Philip Francis, and his
equally deep dislike of what he seemed to be planning with
Sir Alexander. Not that politics entered very much into his
thinking. Of course he'd been carried away by the excitement
of joining the London apprentices in their marches and riots,
but he knew he'd been stupid to volunteer for the army, and
he'd found nothing in common with the rabid Levellers and
Diggers and Ranters who preached around every campfire.
Tobias understood simple patriotism, and loyalty to one's
friends. Most of his friends seemed to have been butchered
on Mount Batten Point. How could Philip now even
contemplate negotiating with their murderers? Wasn't it well
known that the King intended to bring back the old religion
if he won? That couldn't be right, could it?

And there was Lucy, dear sweet yellow-haired Lucy.
Tobias had been half-mad with anger and disappointment
when her father had told him of the marriage arranged with
Philip. It had seemed so cruel, so unfair that his own natural
father should take away his beloved Lucy. But his experiences
in London and in the army had brought him a surprising
maturity and peace of mind about his lost sweetheart.
Bitterness and resentment against Philip had been replaced

now by gratitude and respect and acceptance. He could see that Lucy herself had little choice in the business of the marriage, and he was genuinely pleased to see how fond they were of each other; which made the present situation all the harder to bear. Philip might be overjoyed that she was to give him a child, and determined to disregard the gossip about Lucy and Sir Alexander Carew. But Tobias knew better. He had a close friend who was a trooper in the Castle, and his stories of Lucy's regular visits, and of the door closed and the curtains drawn were evidence enough. Sir Alexander had taken advantage of his position to seduce his beloved Lucy, and so to betray the man to whom Tobias owed everything. Could it be that this letter had been given to him so that his might be the hand of vengeance that brought down Sir Alexander? That would silence too any slander that might question the parentage of Lucy's baby.

He ran his index finger thoughtfully over the Carew crest embossed now on the seal. Lions ... would Colonel Digby know what to look for? Probably not ... with a sudden decisive movement he cracked the wax, and smoothed the letter flat onto his knees.

Plymouth, 8 August

Dear Colonel Digby,

We have now endured almost a year of siege, with all the privation, disease and death that war brings in its train. And yet we have no quarrel with the King's majesty, but only with the policies foisted on him by a few of his misguided advisors.

We, therefore, think it wrong that more men should die on both sides, when it is clear that a little good sense can bring us peace. You will know, from your own experience that, once defended, Plymouth will not be taken cheaply, even if the King should send as great an army as that which fell upon Bristol. And to take our town, the King will have to march that great army across all Somerset and Devon, and consume great provisions of food and armament, and sacrifice many lives. On the other hand if we can reach agreement now, His Majesty will be spared that expense of men, material and time, and will also gain the advantage of our fine port, the support of its honest people for his cause, and the use of our stores of powder and our cannon.

WE PROPOSE, THEREFORE that, in return for the keys of Plymouth:

1. The town and all its people be honourably treated according to the Rules of War, and in particular all people and property should be protected from assault or offence, as though they were the King's own.

2. Only a modest garrison be placed here, for our defence.

3. A full and total Royal Pardon for any and all offences alleged against the King's Majesty be granted to myself, to all Members of our Council, and to all citizens whatsoever. This Pardon to be signed by the King himself, or failing that by his next most senior Commander in the West.

We believe that you are already empowered to agree these propositions.

With all due respects,
Alexander Carew, Baronet
Philip Francis, Mayor

Tobias slowly read through the letter for a second time, folded it carefully and went downstairs. The house was empty – they were all at the funeral service. He needed a knife . . . no, the Bible would do. He opened the heavy, copper-bound cover and, using it as a straight edge carefully tore off the bottom inch of the letter with Philip's signature on it. Fortunately that end had been folded inside, so it had no wax on it. He replaced Sir Alexander's seal with a larger blob of fresh wax, and a blurred impression from an old Spanish coin he kept as a talisman. He tried to look at the letter as though he were seeing it for the first time. Perhaps a little soot from the fireplace to conceal the creases made when he had broken the original seal . . . perfect!

Early the next morning, 9 August, Alexander had just finished shaving when he heard a sudden commotion below and the sound of heavy boots on his stairs. The door was flung open without ceremony by Colonel Gould, with half a dozen troopers behind him.

'Guard, wait outside on this landing. No one is to come up the stairs without my express permission.'

Alexander had taken a dislike to the new Commander of the garrison when they had met just before the funerals. There was a sneering arrogance in his manner which was evident in every contact with those he judged to be his military or social inferiors. To Alexander he had been coolly correct and polite, but he had barely bothered to conceal the implication that 'a professional had arrived so the amateurs could withdraw'.

'I must apologise that I am not ready to receive you, Colonel . . .'

'Never mind the niceties, sir, my business has nothing to do with politeness. This letter is for you, I believe?'

He pulled a folded sheet from his pocket, and dropped it on the table in front of Alexander with a little gesture of disgust. Alexander turned it over without unfolding it. 'Sir Alexander Carew, Personal' was written in a good hand. The seal had been broken.

'You've read it? You've broken the seal on a letter addressed to me personally? Is this . . .'

'Damn your manners, sir, I doubt if you will deserve any apology from me! Perhaps you will be good enough to read it?'

Alexander stood motionless confronting Colonel Gould, outwardly calm, but his heart was thudding as though to burst his chest.

'You are in no danger here, Colonel. Can we close that door and discuss this like gentlemen?'

Gould ran a nervous hand over the hilt of his sword, then turned to the troopers behind him, 'Close the door, but be ready to come in if I call.'

Alexander wiped his face slowly with the cloth that hung around his shoulders, and pulled on a shirt. The letter was quite short.

Plymstock, 8 August

To Sir Alexander Carew Bt. MP and his friends in Plymouth
Sir,
    Your messenger arrived a few minutes ago, and I reply in haste so that he may return with this.
    I have been commanded by Sir John Berkley to accept from you the surrender of Plymouth on the terms you propose. To satisfy your reasonable concern, I have already despatched a man to Exeter to obtain the Royal Pardon. His Royal Highness Prince Maurice is expected to arrive today in Exeter, and so I expect my man back tomorrow or the next day at the latest.
    I await your next communication, and in the meantime will avoid all unnecessary hostilities.
    My sincere respects,
    JOHN DIGBY, Colonel
    His Majesty's Army of the West

Alexander kept his voice very steady. 'May I ask you how you came by this letter?'

'What business is that of yours? Can you deny the plain implication of its content, that you have been engaged in treasonable correspondence, with the intention of handing over the town to the King?'

'Nevertheless I should like to know how you came by it?'

'If you must know, it was delivered to me. You were betrayed. The traitor is himself betrayed.'

'How do you mean, delivered to you? Do you have the messenger to confront me?'

'Not yet, but we soon will, no doubt of that. This little note was slipped under my door during the night. What do you make of that?'

'I think you have been the victim of a cunning deceiver. Someone who wants to see us divided, perhaps an enemy of yours who wants to see you make a fool of yourself by trying to arrest the very man who has led Plymouth's struggle for a year. Do you have an enemy in Plymouth, Colonel? Someone who came with you on the ship, perhaps? I heard you had told our captains yesterday of the great importance of catching spies and traitors. Perhaps this is someone's way of getting his own back?'

Colonel Gould was not used to being coolly baited by a prisoner, and kept control of his temper with difficulty.

'You're very clever, sir, but we'll see how clever you can be on Tower Hill. I was warned before I left London that the Carews might not have given up all their old connections with Royalists, and no doubt this letter will be just the first of the proofs against you. Guard!'

The door crashed open again.

'By the powers vested in me as Military Commander of Plymouth, a town under siege and under martial law, I arrest Sir Alexander Carew in the name of Parliament, on a charge of Treason. The accused is confined to these quarters, with six men on guard, day and night. No letters out or in, no personal communications except through me.'

The previous morning Alexander had watched while Philip signed his letter to Colonel Digby, and had been filled with apprehension as Philip left to send Tobias Fisher on his way. His fears had all been for the consequences if Tobias were caught – the possibility that he might turn traitor had never occurred to him. Philip had been so certain of his loyalty, and yet it must be Tobias who had delivered Digby's letter to Gould. He heard the voice of his steward's son, young Peter Goodman downstairs. He had decided that he would not write to Jane yesterday, but wait until there was some answer from Colonel Digby. And now it was too late, as he heard Peter turned away by the sergeant of the guard.

'Ah, it's you young Peter. If you've come to see Sir Alexander, this is not the time. He's under close arrest, charged with Treason, and only Colonel Gould can give permission for a visit. If you'll take my advice, you'll keep well away. Treason's like pitch. If you touch it you'll find it sticks to you. Get off back to Antony now, you can do no good here.'

As Peter emerged from the dark gateway of the Castle into the morning sunlight, a crowd was already starting to gather. Most seemed to be women who had lost sons or husbands on Mount Batten, and who had been grieving now for three days and nights. At first the hubbub was confused and divided, but those well-disposed to Alexander quickly found they were in the minority, as the shouting grew louder.

'Death to the traitor! A life for a life! Death for Carew! Hang him now! Throw him off the battlements! Death to Carew, death to Carew, hang Carew, HANG CAREW!'

The sergeant attempted to clear the drawbridge and the road in front, but his men were abused, shoved and spat upon by the howling mob of angry women, and then driven back inside by a rattling fusillade of cobblestones, whereupon he hastily dropped the portcullis.

'Give us Carew! Give us Carew! Give us Carew! Hang him, hang him, HANG HIM!'

At the front of the old stone house at Antony, Alexander's father had made a garden after the French model, a complex knot of paved paths lined with low hedges of green box, with roses growing in between. Beyond this was a closely clipped lawn, planted with sweet-smelling herbs, and protected on three sides by a tall yew hedge. There was a stone seat there, guarded by life-size figures of Apollo and Aphrodite, and it was a favourite place for Jane Carew to play with her children in the sunshine. She rose in alarm when Peter Goodman came out of the front door of the house at a run.

'They've arrested 'im, M'lady, they've arrested Sir Alexander for treason!'

Despite the warmth of the sun she felt her body grow

suddenly cold, and the voices of the children faded and faded as a thick shadow seemed to surround her. Peter took her arm as she swayed.

'M' lady, oh m' lady! 'Ere, sit down on the seat now.'

As he looked around for help his father, Walter, came hurrying out of the house, having heard Peter shouting as he ran through the house from back to front. He was followed more slowly by Grace Carew, leaning heavily on a stick as she moved.

'It's all right, Peter, I'll see to 'er Ladyship,' said his father, 'You go in and get Bessie. And bring out a cup of water when you come.'

When he returned Jane had recovered her composure, and waved away Grace's suggestion that they should go in out of the sun.

'Now then, Peter, I want you to sit here on the grass. Grace, you sit here by me. We'll get nowhere by panic, and it's important we know everything we can. So when you're ready, Peter, we'd like to hear everything you saw and heard, from the time you handed my letter to Sir Alexander.'

'. . . So when the sergeant told me that Sir Alexander 'ad been arrested by this new Colonel Gould for treason, I knew there was nothing I could do there, and that I should sail 'ome as quick as I could to tell you.'

'You've done well, Peter. The sergeant didn't question you at all?'

'Oh no, we're good friends. Sir Alexander often asked me to give 'im some of our salt venison. But the women were terrible frightenin', and I were glad to get away.'

'Which women?'

'There seemed like 'undreds of 'em. Outside the Castle gate. I recognised some of them from the big funeral yesterday. Then, they was all weepin' and tearin' their clothes an' rubbin' dirt in their faces. But this mornin' they was like dogs that 'ave smelt blood, all chantin' they wanted to 'ang

Carew. I think they'd 'ave torn the Castle down with their bare 'ands if they could.'

'But the soldiers kept them out?'

'Yes, a few of the soldiers got 'it with the stones they was throwin', and they ran back in an' dropped the portcullis. An' I ran off then to catch the flood.'

'Good, Peter. We may need you again soon, so you go indoors with your father, and get some food inside you.'

Jane leant back against the warm grey stone of the seat beside Grace, and attempted to make a plan. But try as she might her mind seemed to be paralysed by the suddenness of the blow. Arrested for treason! Threatened by the very people he was trying to save! Surprisingly, it was Grace who provided a plan of action.

'Well, you can't say you were not warned. I knew from the way he treated his poor father's body that Alexander was heading for a fall, and now it's come, hasn't it? Oh don't look so helpless, Jane, I'm not going to sit here and gloat. He may be a fool, but he is a Carew and the head of the family, so I will do everything possible to get him out of the Castle and to get this silly charge dropped. Your place now is in Plymouth, Jane, beside your husband, and Peter can take you in with Bessie this afternoon. I will write at once to Heanton Satchville. Henry and John are both members of Parliament after all, and I trust no one will dare question the loyalty of the Rolles to Parliament. If one or perhaps both of my brothers can come to Plymouth, I'm sure this Colonel Gould can be made to back down. And I'll write to the Colonel myself, to remind him of our family connections. Walter can take the letter to Heanton, and you can give Gould my other letter yourself.' There was almost a spring in her prematurely aged body as she pushed herself upright, 'Come on, Jane, there's a lot to be done!'

From the big upstairs window that overlooked Plymouth's High Street, Philip Francis could see and hear the mob that was building up in front of the Castle. Cautiously he sent a man to enquire what was happening.

'It's Sir Alexander Carew, sir. 'E's been arrested. For treason! They say 'e was plannin' to open the gates an' let those murderin' Papists in to slaughter us all in our beds.'

'Who's the leader there?'

'Couldn't say for sure, sir. Most of the shoutin' seems to be coming from yesterday's widows. I think they'd string 'im up on the spot if they could get 'old on 'im.'

'Has the Colonel said or done anything about the mob?'

'Not as far as I 'eard, no sir. But I did 'ear the Sergeant of the Guard shout through the portcullis that if they didn't clear off 'e'd let 'em 'ave a volley o' musket. But that didn't scare 'em one little bit, just made 'em scream all the louder "Gie us Carew, 'ang Carew!"'

After his servant had left, Philip stayed at his vantage point in the casement window, watching and listening as the mob flowed around the castle gate. Within a couple of minutes he was joined by Lucy, and he told her as much as he knew. Lucy knew most of Philip's manoeuvres, and immediately put her finger on the danger.

'What if Sir Alexander tries to save himself by trying to involve you, Philip? You did sign his letter yesterday morning, didn't you?'

'I did. But that can't be the source of the charge, or they would certainly have arrested me already. Sir Alexander has been making his own approaches, using his family connections I believe. Most likely it's one of those that has broken down. I respect him you know, Lucy, and I don't think he will involve us or let us be drawn into it.'

Impulsively Lucy put her arms round him and kissed him. 'Of course you can trust him. But you need to find out what these charges are all about, just in case they could lead back to you. You are the Mayor after all, and Sir Alexander has been closely . . .'

She broke off as her attention was caught by the sight of a man running through the street below them, towards the Castle. It was a tall, bony figure with a prominent bald head and a ragged black cloak that trailed behind him as he ran – Isaac Weaver! He reached the fringes of the crowd, and pushed his way towards the front, apparently driven by some desperate need. People cursed him as he elbowed them aside, but eventually he reached the gate to the drawbridge, which had not been closed. He climbed up onto the gatepost to obtain a precarious point from which to speak.

'Men and women of Plymouth! Fellow citizens! You know me, Isaac the Preacher. Will you listen to me now?'

He held up a hand, and gradually the screaming died down.

'Are we animals? Are we as the mad dogs and ravening wolves that we must gather together in a pack and howl for blood? Sir Alexander Carew is no special friend of mine, but you all know he has done good service to the town, as his father and grandfather did before him. If there be proofs against him, let him be brought to trial so that they can be tested in the light of day. Which of you here wants to come before his Maker with the blood of an innocent man on his hands? I beg . . .'

Afterwards, no one could say for certain who threw the stone. It struck Isaac full in the forehead, and he fell to the ground without a sound. In a moment the maddened crowd was surging around the place where he had fallen, and Lucy saw hand after hand rise up holding a stone and strike down, then come up again dripping with blood. She screamed and stood as though to go down to the scene, but she was held by Philip's restraining arm and quiet voice.

'Easy girl, easy now. You can't do nothing for Isaac. The soldiers will come and sort things out when the people calm down a bit. And nor can we do anything for Sir Alexander at this time, not without putting my own head on the block. Tobias has friends in the garrison, I know. I'll send for him to report on his meeting at Plymstock. In fact I'm surprised he hasn't come here already. He can find out more about these charges. Don't you worry yourself about Sir Alexander either. He has powerful friends in London, including John Pym himself. He'll come to no harm.'

Like most of the people of Plymouth, Lucy had participated in the mass funerals the previous day, and understood the overpowering grief and rage that still possessed the town. Philip and her own father, Peter Keckwick had risked their lives in the assault, and she knew at least by sight most of the men who had died in her father's boats. She watched in silence for a few minutes more with Philip's arm around her, then made an excuse to withdraw.

She was still feeling the shock of Alexander's arrest and the awful murder of Isaac Weaver as she sat down by herself in the big kitchen. The open fire had been banked up, but there were no servants around, and Lucy wondered vaguely if her own cook or kitchen maids might be amongst that terrifying mob. Perhaps one of them had even thrown the stone? Philip had said that Alexander was not in danger – could she be sure of that?

In the beginning the relationship with Alexander had been a game, played according to certain rules. He was a Carew, a great gentleman with a wife and family; she was the mayor's pretty young wife, well-educated and comfortably off. He was allowed to amuse himself and her by courting her in a playful way, she was allowed to be delighted by his courting as long as nothing serious developed. But Alexander was more than a great gentleman. He was sensitive, intelligent, thoughtful and kind. He was also very alone in Plymouth, and desperately in need of the kind of friendship that Lucy could provide. And Lucy herself was a vivacious young woman, eager for life and knowledge, well-educated and capable, but aware too that Philip's first need was for an heir.

She felt her belly. Too soon for any swelling to be apparent, but she had been horribly sick that morning, and she had no doubt that she was pregnant. Was Philip the father? How could she know for certain? After that first afternoon with Alexander, there had been four other such afternoons with him. He was a tender, considerate lover as well as a passionate one, and as a result Lucy's interest in the physical side of marriage had been sharply re-awakened. Had that led Philip in turn to respond with renewed enthusiasm? Or perhaps the awareness of the delicate game he had encouraged Lucy to play had itself produced an urge to compete? Was there even a kind of frenzy in the air, induced by the desperate state of their lives? Lucy shook her head irritably – what did it matter now? She was safely with child, and Philip was happy. She felt sorry though for Alexander. What must it be like to be shut up, with those ferocious women howling for his blood outside?

It was dusk by the time Jane Carew arrived at the castle, and the mob had long since dispersed of its own accord. The sergeant of the guard was polite.

'My orders are very exact, m'Lady. No visitors without the Colonel's express permission. But if young Peter would like to wait 'ere with your maid and the boxes, I can conduct you directly to the Colonel.'

When Jane was announced Colonel Gould was just concluding another meeting with his captains, who were determinedly pessimistic.

'So you see Colonel, in my opinion the situation is that, even with the reinforcements you have brought, we do not have the resources to defend the town for very long against a serious assault if it was on the scale of that used against Bristol. We must take note of the fact that Exeter has decided not to fight, which means the King can draw on troops, stores and cannon from there, and we have become aware of the problem of defending the shores of the Sound . . .'

Captain Hallsey was interrupted by the Sergeant's knock.

'Beg pardon, sir, but I thought you would want to be told that Lady Carew is 'ere. Requests leave to join 'er husband, sir.'

Colonel Gould was relieved at the opportunity to postpone the necessity of trying to dispel the gloom.

'Thank you, Sergeant. We were just finishing anyway. We will resume tomorrow, after breakfast please, gentlemen. Lady Carew, may I offer you a chair? You must be fatigued after the journey from Antony. Did you ride?'

'Thank you, Colonel. No, we have a young boy, my steward's son, who is very good with a boat, and he brought us here.'

'A glass of wine?'

'Thank you, not at this time. Now then, Colonel, what is this nonsense about charges laid against my husband? Treason? You have not been here long I know, but I am sure that your own captains, any councillor or any citizen you care to ask in the street will tell you of his outstanding services to the town and to Parliament. I myself have had to beg him not to risk his life in that cause, for fear that he would leave his children fatherless. So who are the villains that dare to accuse him of treason?'

Lady Carew was a small, pretty, well-made woman, with curly black hair just shading with grey now. She was wearing a pale blue silk dress in the new weave that appeared apple-green in streaks as she moved, with trimming of gold lace and buttons of pearl. Colonel Gould's expectation, when she was announced, was that he would be supporting or consoling a desperate wife. Instead he found himself on the receiving end of her fierce temper, and was forced to defend his actions.

'No villains, I assure you, m'Lady. I am myself his accuser, on the basis of written proofs that came into my hands this morning.'

'What written proofs?'

'I am not at liberty to show you, Lady Carew, but Sir Alexander knows. A letter, from the enemy, addressed to him, and proving that he has been conspiring to surrender the town.'

'A letter? Rubbish! It must be a forgery. A cheap fraud. An

attempt to sow dissension in the town, knowing you are fresh-arrived from London. Is that the sum of your "proofs"? I doubt my husband would arrest a poacher on such flimsy "proofs".'

'Nevertheless, Lady Carew, my decision was that he should be arrested, and held in his rooms whilst this letter is investigated.'

'No doubt you have the power and authority to act in this way, but I feel I should warn you, Colonel Gould, that we are not without friends and influence. My elder sister, who is the Dowager Lady Carew, has written already to our brothers Henry and John Rolle, who are both Members of Parliament, of impeccable standing. Do you know them?'

'I have heard of them, of course. Doughty fighters for the rights of Parliament.'

'Indeed, and you will no doubt hear from them shortly. We have a family connection to John Pym himself as well. Here is a letter my sister has written to you, to remind you of our family, and of what we have done for the cause of freedom under the law.'

She handed to the Colonel the packet Grace had pressed into her hand as she was leaving Antony. The Colonel's manner became distinctly conciliatory.

'Believe me, Lady Carew, nothing would give me greater pleasure than for Sir Alexander to be proven innocent, and so able to resume his fine work for our cause. Nothing. But I am just a simple soldier, and I must do my duty as I see it. You do understand, I trust?' Jane did not answer. 'Just a few days, Lady Carew, and everything should be sorted out. In the meantime I will have one of my men conduct you to Sir Alexander. You will find his quarters quite spartan, I'm afraid, but not too uncomfortable.'

After Jane had left the Colonel dropped back into his chair with a sigh of relief. What an Amazon! At first glance she was the pretty little wife in an elegant blue dress. But what an absolute tigress in defence of her mate! He lit the candles on his table, and casually cracked the seal on the letter from the

Dowager Lady Carew. He began to read, and sat up sharply.
Inside the packet were two sheets. One consisted of dozens of
small pieces of paper, apparently torn up then meticulously
re-assembled and stuck onto another sheet. The other was a
short letter:

Colonel William Gould at Plymouth   9 August
Sir,
     The letter enclosed will show you the planned connection
between Alexander Carew and our enemies. For further proof,
you will find that Carew's cattle and sheep have been
re-branded 'E' for Edgcumbe, a family whose adherence to the
King is notorious.

There was no signature.
'Sergeant!'
'Sir?'
'My compliments to the captain of the *Felicity*, that
brought us from Portsmouth.'
     'Captain Hoare, sir.'
     'Yes, Captain Hoare. Ask the captain to be good enough
to attend me here as soon as possible. And Sergeant,'
     'Sir?'
     'I will need a reliable corporal and ten men as guard for Sir
Alexander on his journey to Portsmouth. They will be leaving
on *Felicity* as soon as Captain Hoare can be ready.'

Trial

Alexander had afterwards only a few recollections of the journey from Plymouth to London. The Sergeant of the Guard had been peremptory and stony-faced.

'I am commanded, sir, to convey you tonight under strict guard to the ship *Felicity*, which sails on the tide two hours after midnight. My corporal and ten men will accompany you to Portsmouth, where the Governor will provide you with an escort to the Tower of London. Sir.'

'And my wife?'

'Lady Carew and her maid may accompany you. Sir.'

'Am I to see the Colonel before being packed off like this?'

'I have no instructions in that respect. Sir.'

The transfer from Castle to ship was accomplished at midnight without incident, though it was obvious that the escort were in great fear that some breach of security might have alerted the mob to the removal of its prey. Aboard, Captain Hoare was surprisingly sympathetic, and insisted that Jane and Alexander should take his cabin.

'I know you've been accused, sir, but to be frank, I didn't take too much to that Colonel when I brought him. And it will be for Parliament to decide if you're guilty or not.'

During the peaceful two nights and days of the sea journey, Alexander seemed to sink into a daze of introspection from which Jane could only occasionally rouse him. He told her of the contents of the letter from Colonel Digby.

'It's just as I said to Colonel Gould, Alex, you must say it's a communication from the enemy, designed to blacken your name. You did not receive it, and the messenger has disappeared, so no one can prove that it is your letter. If you just maintain that position they must acquit you.'

'There's no "must" about it, Jane. I will be tried by a military tribunal under military law. Niceties of evidence and proof go out of the window in time of war. And I don't believe that Gould would have dared to send me off to London so quickly if that was all the evidence he had. There has to be something else, something more damning.'

'What could there be?'

'How can I guess? Perhaps Philip . . .'

'What about Mr Francis? I never really liked that man you know.'

'I can't think what. Perhaps he has been threatened and has made some statement accusing me.'

'Could he do that without implicating himself?'

'I don't know, Jane, I just don't know. Let's leave it for now, can we please?'

From Portsmouth it was two days with an overnight stop on the road, and then the coach with its mounted escort was rattling into the streets of London. Jane, who had never been farther east than Exeter, looked around curiously.

'It's no better than Plymouth really, there's just more of it.'

They were slowed by the press of people and wagons on London Bridge, then past the great spire of St. Paul's, and so eventually to Tower Hill, where the coach stopped. After a few moments the young lieutenant in charge of their guard rode up to the door.

'We will be delayed here a few minutes sir, until the crowd has dispersed. It's for Sir John Hotham. Caught trying to hand over Kingston upon Hull to the enemy.'

They heard a quavering voice attempting to be heard above the catcalls, and then the crowd fell silent, as though holding its breath. The silence was broken by a heavy thud, and a great cheer went up. Then hordes of bullet-headed apprentices were streaming past the coach. A few paused to look in, but most were too busy to bother.

'One blow, William, just like I told you. One blow was enough for that scraggy neck. That's a penny you owes me.'

The coach and its escort clattered over the cobbles down the Hill to the Lion Gate. A sentry cast a perfunctory glance at the lieutenant's warrant, and waved them across the causeway to the Lion Tower, where they waited again, apparently for an officer to accept the prisoner. During his years in London, Alexander had frequently joined the crowds that came to see the King's menagerie on a Sunday. Now he looked down on the mangy back of a lion that paced like an automaton up and down the small iron-railed pit in the dry outer moat below them.

'He's just like the pictures in that book in Sir Richard's library,' Jane murmured, 'except that he's so big.'

'I'm beginning to understand just how he must feel.'

A spruce young Captain of the Guard appeared at the carriage door.

'Good evening, sir, ma'am. I have been given a properly signed warrant from Colonel William Gould, Military Commander of Plymouth for your arrest and detention in the Tower of London, pending trial on a charge of Treason. I have also received a package for the War Council, which I will pass on immediately. If you look over my shoulder, you can just see the top of the Beauchamp Tower, where you will be lodged. Two of our guests have just vacated their chambers there, and they had no complaints about their accommodation – in fact I believe they were quite reluctant to leave, although you could say the same of most of our guests.'

Alexander managed a wan smile, 'My brother, John Carew, is one of Mr Pym's secretaries. Could he be informed that we are here, please?'

'I will see to it. Though I note that this package is in fact addressed to him personally, so I imagine he will have the full information.'

The lieutenant of the Portsmouth guard raised his hat in

polite farewell, and the coach rumbled forward through the
Lion Tower, across the bridge, and under the Byward Gate.
Alexander thought of Dante's vision of Hell.

'Abandon hope all ye who enter,' he whispered to himself,
so quietly that not even Jane heard the words.

All that evening and far into the night John Carew was
totally absorbed in his secretarial responsibilities, and he did
not see Colonel Gould's report until the next morning, by
which time he found with it a letter from his mother, which
had travelled on the same ship. He opened them both, and
spread the papers on the table before him.

Antony, 9 August

My dearest John,

We hear that Alexander is to be taken to Portsmouth, and
presumably on to London, charged with Treason. I have no
doubt of his guilt, and the proofs will come into your hands
and will persuade you altogether of the truth of my fears.

NOTHING is more important now than that you separate
yourself totally from all danger that might arise, from the
inescapable connections that the Tribunal will make between
Alexander and every member of his family. Beyond any
question, he will be condemned and Antony will be forfeit.
Your opportunity must be to convince Mr Pym that your
loyalty, like that of our Rolle ancestors, is absolute and
beyond question. Then if the estates are transferred to you and
so to our side of the family, Parliament will be able to secure
for itself important and influential supporters in a County
where all others are coming out for the King.

Before she left, Jane cut Alexander's portrait from its frame,
and hid it beneath the carrots in the cellar! I do not think they
will find it so easy to hide their guilt from Parliament's justice!

May God bless and preserve you. <u>Burn this letter</u>.

Your deeply loving mother

John's heart beat faster as he grasped the implications of his
mother's letter, and he turned eagerly to the Colonel's report.

It was true! The re-assembled letter from Alexander to Jane, he recognised the writing immediately. 'To approach our friend again, and ask him to speak to the King's Commander on our behalf' – simple, undeniable treason! Who was this friend? Perhaps that would emerge during the trial, and they would get a whole nest of traitors! There was also the letter from Colonel Digby to Alexander, which proved that Alexander's instruction to Jane had been carried out. And the anonymous letter to Gould, with the strange information about re-branding the cattle for Edgcumbe . . . did that imply that Sir Peter Edgcumbe was the 'friend'? He scanned through Gould's report.

'. . . For fear of Civil Riot I have determined that Sir Alexander should be sent this night to Portsmouth and so on to you. We are enquiring most vigorously to discover his accomplices, for it is certain that he has not acted alone in this matter. In order to fulfil his promise to "open the gates" he must expect to have the aid of one or more of the captains, and sundry councillors and so on. We have been informed that his connection with the Edgcumbes – a most notorious Royalist family – is sufficiently cordial for him to have had his cattle re-branded for Edgcumbe, and I have sent a patrol to investigate.'

How would Parliament, and particularly John Pym, react to these proofs of treason? Colonel Fiennes had feebly surrendered Bristol, and had been condemned for it. He had been saved from the block only by the protecting hand of the Earl of Essex, Parliament's Commander in Chief. On the other hand Sir John Hotham had been exposed as a traitor before he could actually hand over Kingston upon Hull, and had been executed after the merest pretence of a trial. Pym was obsessed now with his plan to bring the Scots in on Parliament's side, to offset the advantage the King now had from having captured Bristol, and so having been able to land his army from Ireland. After the way Pym had intervened personally to ensure that Plymouth was reinforced and not abandoned, he might well feel a strong sense of personal betrayal. And he too might need to distance himself from Alexander, especially if the family connection through the Chudleighs were known. Pym needed to be above suspicion. Yet he was a man who took family obligations very seriously – John Carew's own advancement being a case in point.

John read through the papers again. 'Separate yourself totally from all danger' – that phrase of his mother's caught his eye again. Of course! The priority was to set in motion the trial, without himself being drawn into the net. He folded the Colonel's package carefully back together, and took it into the equally small office next door that housed his fellow secretary, Peter Winchmore.

'I've opened this packet, Peter, but because of the family connection I feel I should not be further involved. It's a matter of producing a summary for the Council and setting the trial in motion.'

Peter was a chubby, rubicund young man with a mop of fair curls, who made a habit of hiding his sharp wits behind a lazy, foppish manner. He looked casually at first through the letter Grace Carew had so laboriously pieced together.

'But this is a personal letter! From your brother to Lady Carew! Who provided this? Some disaffected chamber-maid?'

'Colonel Gould says only "supplied by an impeccable source". It's Alexander's writing all right, and Alexander has ruined himself. My concern is for the family, to ensure that he doesn't pull us all down with him.'

Peter had never much liked John Carew. He thought him to be a typical ambitious provincial – too intense, too wrapped up in his own affairs to be good company. But he was disarmed by this glimpse of the anxiety that lay behind the cool façade.

'Don't worry, John, I'll take this on. That way you can be doing your best to save your brother without a conflict of loyalties.'

'I am most grateful, Peter. He isn't my brother by the way, we are only half-brothers.'

In the days that followed, Alexander became very familiar with his prison. The Beauchamp Tower was built on the west side of the fortress, in the centre of the inner of the Tower of London's double skin of walls. It was semi-circular, projecting six paces into the fifty-foot gap between the two walls. His room had a small passage at the rear, which allowed him to take the air along the inner battlement walkway, north to the Devereux Tower, and south to the Bell Tower, which adjoined the Lieutenant-Governor's residence. From the windows there was a fine view across London's smoky chimneys to the massive spire of St Paul's, and more ominously, to the open space on nearby Tower Hill where the executions were carried out. Alexander was allowed out onto the battlements during daylight hours, and Jane could come and go as she pleased.

'The most urgent thing is to find out what evidence will be brought against me at the trial, Jane. I'm convinced that Gould must have more than that letter from Digby. If John does not come in the next day or two, I have to ask you to go to Westminster to find him. We will need to prepare an approach to John Pym, but not until we know for sure what their case against me contains, so that I can decide between denying everything and pleading innocence, and admitting everything and throwing myself on his mercy.'

It was two days later, and Jane had just finished dressing and making preparations for the journey by boat to Westminster, when John Carew was announced. He was full of apologies and anxious solicitations, and embraced them both warmly.

'Alexander, and dear Jane, I am so sorry you have been almost a week in this place before I could get to you. I heard only yesterday that you were here, and only then from a letter from my mother saying you had been arrested and taken to London. I immediately made enquiries, to find the case being handled by one of my colleagues, who had not taken the trouble to keep me informed. Of course I'm going to do all I can to help. But I have to say that, from what I have seen, the case against you looks terribly strong.'

John Carew had not been back to Antony since the time he had come down from Oxford, and then gone on to London to start his training in the law. Jane could see a remarkable change in those last three years. Then he had been not much more than a scrawny schoolboy, who had inherited his father's fondness for books, but none of the Carew spirit and confidence that made Alexander so charismatic. Now he was a typical successful bureaucrat, dressed in black throughout, with just the gold buttons on his long jacket to indicate that modesty rather than poverty was the reason for his sober appearance. He was not quite twenty-one, but appeared much older, and although he was four inches shorter than Alex there was a quiet authority in his manner that made them seem equals in every way.

'What we have to say should not be overheard. Shall we walk out onto the rampart?'

Jane had been dreading the journey to Westminster. The choppy waters of the Thames were only marginally preferable to the city's stinking streets, and she had expected then to have to spend a tiresome day pursuing Alexander's case from one flunkey's office to another. Perversely, John's arrival loosed on her a blinding headache that her determination had previously kept at bay.

'You two carry on outside, please. I'm going to rest for a few minutes.'

'It must be terrible for Jane, cooped up here with you, wondering desperately what the future will bring, and hundreds of miles away from Antony and her children.'

Alexander murmured agreement as they stepped out from the dark doorway into the bright morning sunshine. He was finding it difficult to decide how he should talk to this poised, confident young man, so different from the awkward youth he remembered.

'I hear you are Pym's right-hand man now, John. Father would have been very proud of you.'

John nodded. 'Since Mr Hampden died so tragically of his wounds, the burden of government has fallen to Mr Pym, and I do whatever I can to help.'

'Is he easy to work for?'

'He's very good-hearted. But he drives himself so hard, and the rest of us even harder sometimes. Just recently I came upon him in his chamber, doubled up with some pain in his belly. He swore at me for allowing him no privacy, and gave me work to keep me up and busy all night. And then another time he found me at my desk on a Sunday, when the sun was shining, and sent me out into the air, saying "No business of State is worth a young man's health".'

'What does he think of my case?'

John paused, and leaned back against the sun-warmed battlement, looking down inside onto the Tower Green in front of St Peter-within-the-Tower, where Anne Boleyn, Katherine Howard and Lady Jane Grey had been executed. It looked so peaceful and innocent in the sunshine.

'Mr Pym has been totally involved these last two weeks in the assembling and equipping of an army to raise the siege of Gloucester. And now he labours all day and all night on his great scheme to forge an alliance between Parliament and the Scots. Your case is likely to be left to the clerks and lawyers to put together the charges and evidence against you. One of Mr Pym's other secretaries has the matter in hand. When the case is ready, the War Council will be given a summary before the trial begins, so that any issue of political significance can be weighed and debated if necessary.'

'You have no part in this?'

'No. When the papers came in last week they were, I believe, kept away from me deliberately because of our family kinship. I was told only yesterday that you were in the Tower.'

'But you said the case against me was strong. So you do know what it consists of?

'I have been allowed only to glance at the papers, Alex, and I must not be seen to press too hard, for fear of compromising myself and so losing all chance of being able to help. There are two letters . . .'

'*Two* letters?'

'One addressed to you from a Royalist Commander . . .'

'Colonel Digby?'

'That was the signature. You obviously know the name.'

'Gould showed it to me, but it was he that received it, not me. I never saw it until he showed it to me, and I told him it was fraudulent.'

'Indeed. But there is another letter, from you to Lady Jane, undoubtedly yours, because the handwriting has been compared with your confidential reports.'

At that moment it seemed to Alexander that the world fell silent, and the heat of the late summer sun failed altogether, to be replaced by a cold emanation flowing from the grey walls of the Tower that chilled him through.

'What letter was this?

'I couldn't recall it all, but something about despairing for the defence of the town, and asking Jane to approach the enemy on your behalf for a promise of a Royal Pardon if you opened the gates. I think you must know the letter?'

John watched Alexander closely as he spoke. He observed the slight trembling in the hands, the beads of perspiration on his forehead. 'He can see already the block and the headsman', he thought, and waited.

Alexander remembered vividly the pool of light from the candle that flickered over the letter, as he wrote in the darkness of his room. And he recalled the emphasis he had put on his instruction that the letter must be destroyed. Why had Jane kept it? And how had it come into the hands of Colonel Gould? He went over the last few hours in Plymouth. Gould had burst into his room early in the morning waving Digby's letter, and had arrested him, but without any real confidence. Late in the day Jane had arrived, and an hour later Gould had announced that Alexander was to be sent to London at once. Jane had arrived ... cause and effect? Alexander looked down onto Tower Green, onto the very spot where King Henry had disposed of the wives who had deceived or displeased him. Was this Jane's terrible revenge for his affair with Lucy? She had been so strong and loving during the journey from Plymouth, and over this first week of imprisonment. Had that all been a cold pretence? Alexander shook his head angrily, as though to dismiss such stupid suspicions

'Forgive me, John. That letter to Jane ... it was private. I never thought ... you've no idea how desperate we felt down in Plymouth, especially after we heard that Bristol had been taken. We seemed to be facing the whole royal army by ourselves. I was just considering what might have to be done if ... if ...'

'Of course, Alex. I understand perfectly. You don't have to justify yourself to me, I'm only too grateful to have been spared those dangers, at least up to now.' His voice was calm and reassuring. 'I've always looked up to you, Alex. I remember you taking the lead in the impeachment of Strafford, and thinking how fine and brave that was. And of course your reports from Plymouth created a wonderful impression, when the War Council had great need of encouragement. Mr Pym himself ...'

'Yes?'

'When Bristol fell, the Council wanted to abandon Plymouth. It was Mr Pym who fought and personally insisted that it would be an unacceptable act of betrayal, and persuaded them to send Colonel Gould with the extra troops.'

'Then that's the answer! I'll write now directly to Pym. Throw myself on his mercy. Remind him of my record, and of the service our family has given Parliament.'

They turned back as they came to the Devereux Tower, at the north-west corner, and John screwed his eyes as the midday sun came full onto his face. His tone was firm and purposeful.

'You're right, you should write to Pym. Assuming you are charged under martial law, you'll be judged as a soldier would be judged who has been caught negotiating a treasonable surrender to the enemy. Legally, I can see only one possible verdict and sentence.'

'Guilty, and death?'

'Guilty and death. However Essex had the power to save Fiennes, who was guilty of surrendering Bristol with hardly a fight. So there's precedent. Certainly you have done greater service, and in more desperate circumstances than his. But you must take the political circumstances into account too.'

'Go on, please.'

'Forgive me if I seem to be teaching you things you know already, but I am supposing you are out of touch with affairs in Parliament . . .'

'Of course I am. Help me, John, please.'

'Well, on the one side, Mr Pym may feel personally embarrassed. I mean he has exposed himself to criticism by diverting forces to Plymouth, yet here we have the leading citizen of Plymouth apparently conspiring with the enemy to frustrate Pym's intentions. He may feel a natural anger about that, wouldn't you say?'

'I suppose so. To be honest, we never expected Parliament to send reinforcements, not after the fall of Bristol.'

'Just so, but they were sent. Another point. Quite a few people here know that Pym's mother married for a second time into one of our local families.'

'The Rouses. Great friends of Father and Grandfather.'

'Too close for comfort. Pym is a Member for Devon, but he must be seen to be impartial. He has plenty of enemies too, you know. People who think he is too anxious to find a compromise with the King. People who really hate his plan to bring in the Scots. If he's seen to go out of his way to protect you, it could really damage his standing in Parliament, and then he couldn't help you at all.'

'So what's your advice?'

'Write to Pym, of course. But don't be surprised or disappointed if he doesn't answer straight away, or if his answer seems cool. He is a good, honest man, and you can trust him to do what he can.'

'And what about yourself, John, can you see any way to help?'

They walked now through the cool shadowed passageway of the Beauchamp Tower, and then out again onto the sunny battlement that overlooked the lodgings of the Lieutenant-Governor.

'Have you met the Lieutenant of the Tower yet?'

'Sir Isaac Pennington? No, not yet. He sent word soon after we arrived to say he was engaged day and night in the business of the city, but that he looked forward to our company at dinner next Sunday.'

'A good man, and by all accounts he's proving to be a good Lord Mayor. Made his money dealing in fish, you know, so he has personal connections with Plymouth. Typical of him to invite you to dinner, despite the charges against you.' They reached the shadow of the Bell Tower.

'I want to help, Alex, really I do. But I have been excluded already from any participation in preparing the case, and I must be very careful.'

He paused, and kept his eyes away from Alexander, looking out through an embrasure at the huge bulk of St Paul's, looming over the clusters of houses that clung to its skirts.

'There have been Carews at Antony for as long as St Paul's has stood, and, please God, there always will be.'

'Amen to that.'

'I believe there is a way, Alex, that we can work together to make it certain.'

'I don't understand.'

John turned to face his half-brother, looking up to his greater height, but firmly in control at that moment, 'Let's consider the possibilities. First, you may be acquitted, and allowed back to Antony.'

'I believe that is not a realistic hope.'

'I agree. Second you may be found guilty. What then happens to Antony?'

'Forfeit, I suppose.'

'Forfeit, indeed. We may hope that Pym can save you from the axe, as Essex saved Fiennes, but you yourself were appointed a Parliamentary Commissioner earlier this year, charged with siezing the lands and goods of Royalists, which would certainly include Antony.'

Alexander looked long and hard at the young man who stood so confidently before him. Soberly dressed, with his dark hair close-cropped, he was the very epitome of a mild, harmless clerk, one of the thousands who laboured for the great merchant houses of London. But there was a fierce, concentrated intensity in the tone of his voice, and a tension in the thin, bony fingers he used for emphasis.

'It seems we must lose Antony whatever happens.'

'We may, but not if I can help it, Alex. I think our best chance lies in our being seen to be on opposite sides.'

'A foot in both camps?'

'More than that. We've agreed already that I can do nothing to help you directly in the trial. Needless to say I will do nothing that could harm you either. I will simply keep myself apart. If I am asked about you, I will say that your record of service to Parliament speaks for itself, and that those who have not been exposed to the rigours of the war, as you have, should be careful how they exercise judgement.'

'So if the worst happens . . .'

'If Antony is seized, I will be in a position to apply to Pym for it, even if I have to pledge our future revenues to pay for it. And I give you my solemn oath that I will be holding it in trust for your son, young John, and he will be my heir.'

'And what happens if the King should prevail?'

'No doubt my position then will be similar to yours now. I would be required to hand back Antony to Jane and young John. Don't you see, Alex, it's the only way?'

When Alexander returned to his rooms he found that Jane was asleep on the bed, and he sat down quietly without waking her, glad of the chance to compose his thoughts.

He could see no way to hide from his wife the fact that somehow she had provided the proof that might send him to the block on Tower Hill. And yet he knew she would be utterly devastated with remorse. Could that guilt be turned into determination? Because he needed her to be strong. He guessed that, sooner or later, she would have to make that journey to Westminster to find Pym, and to beg for his life. Probably this was not the right moment, but if he delayed he was really gambling that, at some time before the final verdict, Parliament and Pym would find some relief from the pressures now consuming them. Was that rational? Would his chances be less if there was another defeat? He concluded that, at least for the present, nothing was lost by waiting.

Then there was the enigma of John Carew. Was he honest? Certainly he had lied when he said that he had not seen the package from Plymouth until yesterday, and then only fleetingly. The Lieutenant of the Guard when they arrived had clearly said that it was addressed to John, so obviously no one could have kept it from him. But perhaps John had lied simply because he was embarrassed that he had not come into the Tower at once. Perhaps he was more fearful for his own safety than he cared to admit. Alexander heard a sigh beside him, and Jane opened her eyes.

'Feeling better?'

'Yes, thank the Lord. That pain was like a knife going into my temple. Has John gone?'

'Just a few minutes ago.'

'I'm not sorry to have missed him, I might have found it difficult to pretend that I trusted him. From living these last few months with Grace I can tell you she is half out of her mind with resentment against you. And John is her eldest. It's only sensible to assume that she has at least tried to enlist him into some scheme to harm you.'

'Jane, I'm glad you're feeling better. I have some bad news to give you, and I can't think of an easy way to say it.'

He told her that the letter he had trusted her to destroy was the chief proof against him, and that a 'Guilty' verdict, with the inevitable sentence of 'Death' to follow, were now inevitable. As he feared, her first reactions were guilt and remorse, but then the practical side that he loved so much took over.

'Oh Alex, it's my fault that you're here, it's my fault if they . . . if they . . . God damn Grace and her meddling! It was her, it has to be her! I know I tore your letter up into small pieces, and then I put the pieces into the log-box, thinking they'd be burnt on the next fire. She must have got them out and put them back together and . . . and . . . oh my dear Lord, it was me that gave Colonel Gould a letter from her. She said it was to remind him about our family connections . . . and all the time . . .'

She flung herself down onto the bed, and her body was shaken with great heaving sobs as though her heart would break. Alexander could only put an arm about her shoulders and murmur.

'There, there, my sweet love, no one could foresee her wickedness. And if Parliament is determined to make an example of me they will do it with or without your letter. Jane, my love, you have to be strong for me, I've no one else, my darling heart.'

She sat up and wiped her eyes with a handkerchief, 'You're right. We must make a plan. Let's start with John, and work on the assumption that he's a rogue, made worse by his mother. What exactly did he say?'

A few weeks later Alexander and Jane were spending the afternoon in bed together, as had become their habit. Waking from a dream of sailing again down the Lynher river,

Alexander lay back on the coarse linen pillow and looked up at the stone ceiling of the chamber. It was said that there was no fuel to be had now in London – might they still be in this cold Beauchamp Tower when winter came? What was that outside? Church bells! Ringing a warning of attack? He listened again . . . no, St Paul's at least was ringing out a peal, a celebration! He shook Jane awake, and they dressed hastily. He opened the chamber door onto the passage outside, and called down the stairs.

'Sergeant, is there some news? Is it peace?'

There was a pause, then the Sergeant of the Guard appeared, slowly climbing the winding stairs from the Guardroom. He was correct and respectful as always.

'I don't know about peace, sir. But there's news that Gloucester 'as bin relieved like, an' there's bin a vict'ry at Newbury, wherever that is. Anyways, the King's bin beaten, an' 'undreds of 'is blasted soldiers 'ave bin killed an' they've retreated back to Oxford.'

Jane was immediately alert to the implications.

'What day is it today?'

Alexander had kept a careful calendar and diary, to help pass the time, 'The twenty-second of September.'

'From what you said before, that's probably the end of fighting for the year then, and they'll be settling in for the winter. So London is safe from attack for six months, and when Pym gets the army the Scots have promised him King Charles will be beaten, won't he?'

'I'll write to Pym tomorrow. Can you send out for some good beef? I'm feeling really hungry.'

Early the next morning Alexander's good intentions were interrupted when a visitor was announced.

'Good morning, Sir Alexander, so good of you to receive me. May I express my deepest sympathy at your present unfortunate and no doubt undeserved imprisonment? I watched your career at Westminster with huge admiration, and earlier this year London was agog with the story of your truly heroic deeds at Plymouth. I said to a friend at the time that the real "Bastion in the West" was undoubtedly Sir Alexander Carew.'

He was a tall, thin, ascetic looking man in his fifties, with fine-drawn features, a sandy complexion and long fair hair that touched the lace collar of his elegantly-cut doublet made of pale blue silk. He looked about him with interest.

'This old chamber could tell some stories, Sir Alexander, if only walls could speak. These carvings by the fireplace, they record the time when there were five Dudleys kept here together. Fascinating, don't you think? And Lady Jane Grey, she was here, and was beheaded just outside ... terrible times, to be sure ... I was told ... yes, here it is, her name, "Jane", carved in the stone. Probably by her husband, poor fellow, before he had his own assignment with the headsman. But that's enough of the gloomy stuff, eh? Of course you don't really know who I am, do you?'

'Only the name, Mr Nicholas Gould? Will you take a seat, Mr Gould? Here in the window is comfortable. Lady Carew is asleep still, but may be with us shortly.'

'Thank you. Now to business. I am actually the uncle of Colonel William Gould, who is responsible for your being here.'

'I don't suppose he's sent you to enquire after my health?'

'No indeed, though I am pleased to see you retain your spirit. In fact William has only a minor role in this matter. I have come, in fact, on an errand, on behalf of no less a personage than our Lord High Admiral, the Earl of Warwick.'

He paused to allow the effect of the name to sink in, but Alexander merely looked puzzled.

'My enquiry has to do with some pearls, some very valuable pearls, that have disappeared. A few months ago a gentleman whose name still escapes me, came up to London from Plymouth with a box of pearls, which had been sequestrated, and which he was selling on behalf of the town.

He was directed to me, as I flatter myself that our trading house has the most distinguished reputation in London for experience and honest dealing in precious gems. For many years we had been entrusted with the King's favour in this regard.'

'You valued them?'

'Yes. Or to be more precise, I told him that they were literally priceless at that time. With the Court being absent from London, the demand for items of such quality was severely reduced, and therefore it made no sense to offer them on the market. I did give him an indication of their value under normal circumstances, a very large sum indeed.'

'I don't begin to comprehend how this involves the Earl of Warwick?'

'Quite a complex connection. I had mentioned the story of these pearls in conversations, as one does you know, to illustrate the abominable fall-off there's been in business. And yet Parliament expects us to pay taxes as though nothing had happened.'

'Quite.'

'Anyway apparently this tale eventually reached the Earl, and he wrote to me last month asking for my help in tracing the pearls. He said that his father had left them with the Earl of Marleborough as security for a loan, and if, as he'd heard, they had been sequestrated, he had as valid a claim to them as anybody. I though that might be a difficult issue at law, but as my nephew William was about to take up the command in Plymouth, I asked him to make the appropriate enquiries.'

'And how has he reported?'

'I have his letter here. He has enquired carefully of a Mr Keckwick, who says he entrusted the pearls to a Mr Vaughan, who says that he in turn entrusted the pearls to the mayor himself, a Mr Francis.'

'And Mr Francis says . . .?'

'He says that you have them as security for a loan you made the town to enable wages to be paid to the garrison.'

'There I would say he has had a lapse of memory.'

'In what way?'

'It appeared that the amount of actual funds that I could offer the town was just two hundred pounds, and that was so far below the value of the pearls as to be not worth considering as a fair security against them, and so it was simply left that, as and when the pearls could be sold, I would be repaid from the proceeds.'

'I see . . . So to the best of your knowledge Mr Francis has the pearls?'

'Or if not, he knows where they are.'

'Yes . . . I see. Well, thank you, Sir Alexander, I think that concludes our business, at least for now, and I must thank you for your patience and co-operation. May I ask you please to tell no one of our little discussion? The fewer that know the better, I'm sure you will agree. I am sorry not to have had the pleasure of meeting Lady Carew on this occasion, it must be a great comfort to you to have her with you in your hour of testing. Please give her my felicitations, and my sincerest wishes to you both for a happy outcome.'

Alexander opened the bedroom door carefully. Jane was still asleep, and he decided that there was no need for her to know anything of his visitor for the present. He took the seat by the window, and began to draft the letter.

The Tower of London, 23 September 1643

Dear Mr Pym,

I rejoiced yesterday to hear of the wonderful triumph of our army under the Earl of Essex at Newbury. Gloucester, it seems, is finally safe, and we may hope that, with the coming of spring, and the arrival of our new allies from Scotland, it may be possible to advance into the west, and so relieve my town of Plymouth from the terrible pressure of the siege which now afflicts it.

It is the weight of this pressure, and my responsibility for the lives of our citizens that have combined to bring me to my present distressing situation. After the fall of Bristol, I took counsel of my fellow leaders of the town, and of the captains of the garrison, who alone could offer military advice, due to the illness of Sir William Ruthin. Together we came to the conclusion that, with our available resources, Plymouth could not be defended against the kind of assault suffered by Bristol, nor indeed against half that force. T he town is remote from the centres of the war, contains no valuable strategic resource, and is surrounded by royalist sympathisers, so we concluded that it was not realistic to hope that Parliament would divert troops to reinforce us, still less that a campaign would be mounted to relieve us. In these circumstances we felt that our Christian duty was to attempt to spare our citizens the horror of a sack which would inevitably follow a siege and assault. Should I be condemned for such an attempt to spare English lives? Bear in mind that, under my leadership, Plymouth has stood alone as Parliament's 'Bastion in the West' for a full twelve months now. How much more should its people be expected to endure and sacrifice? Soldiers who have fought bravely may, when faced with overwhelming force and certain defeat, arrange parley with the enemy, and obtain honourable terms of surrender. Can it be wrong for a civilian to attempt the same?

I write therefore to beg you to intervene on my behalf, so that Parliament may be seen to be as generous and understanding in defeat as it is glorious in victory.

Your Humble Servant,

Alexander Carew, Baronet

Alexander read through his draft three times, and was starting to correct a phrase or two when Jane emerged from the bedroom.

'You shouldn't have let me sleep so long, it must be almost midday!'

'Not so late. Come and read this, you have a good head for meaning. This must be the most important letter I have ever written.'

The sun was beginning to fill the mullioned window with light, and as she sat there, pursing her lips and frowning over his work he felt a sudden welling up of affection. She deserved a better reward for her love and loyalty than to be shut up with him in this awful place, whilst his life ground towards some inevitable end, on Tower Hill perhaps.

'It's very fine, Alex, it has a strong appeal. One or two changes . . .'

He stood beside her as she ran a finger over the draft.

'You should be a little less commanding in your style here and there. For instance, where you say "Bear in mind", you could say "I beg you to bear in mind", and there may be one or two other places, where humility will do no harm. And at the end here, "generous" implies you want him to give you something. How about "magnanimous"? But there is one problem I worry about, Alex. How can you ensure that Mr Pym gets the letter directly? I wouldn't want to take the risk that it might be intercepted or held up by John.'

'There's only one secure way I can think of, and that's for you to deliver it for me. Put it personally into his hands, and wait while he reads it, that's if he'll see you.'

The sunlight picked out the increasing grey in her dark curls, and the heavy circles now evident beneath her eyes. She rested her hand on Alexander's shoulder as he sat down, and she handed him a fresh sheet of paper and a knife to sharpen his pen.

'He'll see me, Alex, even if I have to sit outside his office night and day for a month.'

Nicholas Gould was in full flow 'So you see, Mr Pym, there is a huge fortune at stake in that small box of pearls. The Lord Admiral had expressed a legitimate interest in them, and no doubt you would wish to oblige him, at least to the point where some tribunal is empowered to review the provenance of the gems and apportion ownership. But we have an obstacle to this desirable procedure that must be removed, namely the contradiction between the testimony of Sir Alexander Carew, and that of Mr Philip Francis.'

'And what line of action do you recommend to the Council?'

John Pym was almost sixty. A short pudgy figure with a pointed beard, dressed in his usual plain brown doublet and hose, his dowdy appearance and restrained style were in total contrast to the merchant who paced so excitedly about his office.

'Obviously the two should be brought face to face, and questioned closely until the pearls are forthcoming.'

'Here in London?'

Gould could see a pitfall looming ahead, and began to temporise. 'Well, you have Sir Alexander safely in the Tower. Perhaps a commissioner could be sent to Plymouth, with Parliament's authority to question, and if necessary arrest Mr Francis there?'

'On what possible charge?'

'Withholding sequestrated goods.'

'But you say yourself that Mr Francis has already made a statement to your nephew, Colonel Gould, to the effect that the pearls are no longer in his possession. Presumably you have established that Sir Alexander's modest loan was indeed received and accounted for?'

'It was, but . . .'

'No "buts", Mr Gould. Mr Francis is the elected, and by all accounts popular mayor of our bravest town. Over all the year we have had only the most exemplary accounts of his courage and commitment to our cause. Can you imagine the damage to morale if he were arrested, in addition to Sir Alexander? We need everyone in Plymouth, as well as here in London, to believe that Sir Alexander's case is one of a single weakness, not a general infection. Do you understand me, Mr Gould?'

'I do sir, very well.'

Pym pressed his hand to his mouth as though to hold back a cry.

'You are not well, sir. Shall I call for assistance?'

Pym stood up, and leant with two hands on his desk. His

face was drawn and ashen with pain. 'No, no, do not alarm
yourself, Mr Gould. I suffer from a periodic colic or
indigestion which . . . which incommodes me now and again.
There . . . there the spasm has passed.'

There were beads of perspiration on his forehead beneath
the wispy grey locks, but his voice was firm again.

'You may inform the Lord Admiral that I will do what I
can in his matter, short of endangering the defence of
Plymouth. Perhaps you would be kind enough to ask my
secretary, Mr Winchmore, to step in here as you pass through
his office?'

Nicholas Gould noticed the small, pretty woman in the
gold silk dress, sitting with her eyes downcast in a dim corner
of the secretary's office, but was too pre-occupied with his
own thoughts to pay much attention.

Pym kept Jane waiting another half hour after Gould had
left, not for the sake of exhibiting petty authority, but to
allow him to recover from the agonising attack. That was the
third in a week, and the worst so far. Last week he had been
inclined to accept the doctor's diagnosis, 'a colic, probably
the result of some summer infection'. But this time the pain
had been so severe, like a wild beast tearing at his insides,
that he feared it must be an ulcer. He vowed to put himself
on a diet of bread and milk, and prayed to God that he might
be spared to complete at least the work of finalising the
agreement to bring the Scots Covenanters down into England
as allies.

'Lady Carew, do please accept my apologies for keeping
you waiting. Has my secretary offered you refreshment? How
are your family, do you hear from them? Your brothers and
I were very close you know, when our shout of protest was
still only a feeble whisper. Let me set you a chair here by the
window, where you may see the river. I see I have just a few
papers that I must deal with, and then I will want to hear all
your news from the west.'

Jane sat in the window, but hardly looked out. She had seen plenty of the bustling life on the Thames on her journey upstream from the Tower. Her boatman had stood at the stern and sculled with a single oar, and seemed to feel it was his duty to point out the sights.

'That's Billin'sgate, ma'am, where all the fish comes in. Then this in front of us is Lunnon Bridge. You can see 'ow fast the flood is runnin' now, we'll 'ave you at Wes'minster in no time. That great spire up on the right there is St Paul's. 'Ave you bin in? Finest church in the country they say. This is Paul's wharf we're passin' now.'

And so it had continued, passing Baynard's Castle, Blackfriars, Bridewell. 'I gotta cousin in there. Bad lot, 'e is.' the Temple, Somerset House, the Savoy Palace, Whitehall Palace, and finally Westminster Stairs, where the crowded houses began to thin out to green fields again. 'It's just as I said before,' she thought, 'London is just like Plymouth, with a few big houses added, and a lot more of it. Even that St Paul's is no better than the cathedral in Exeter.'

She tried to study John Pym as he frowned over a draft, and then scribbled furiously in the margin. He looked like a perfectly ordinary farmer or tradesman, rather than the man chiefly responsible for bringing down a king. He had redefined Parliament's ancient privileges, at least that was what he said. The talk she had heard in London was so much wilder than the wildest Leveller or Digger in Plymouth. Here they talked of Revolution, and of doing away with the King altogether to have a Republic instead – whatever that might mean.

'Now, Lady Carew, that's finished for now. What's the news from Devon?'

She tried to explain to him how it was, being unable to leave Antony to visit friends, about not giving Alexander's father a proper funeral, about the constant fear of marauding troops of either side.

'If you can imagine a country without law, Mr Pym, where every man must fend for himself? That is how we live.'

He listened intently, then spoke seriously, 'I am of course

familiar with the facts of Sir Alexander's case, Lady Carew, and I have to say to you now that, if you have come to plead his case with me, it would be quite impossible for me to intervene while the matter is *sub judice*. No matter how much I might want to help personally.'

'Alex specifically asked me not to plead his case today, but simply to place this letter in your hands, and ask only for your help when you judge the time is opportune.'

Pym looked with curiosity at Jane as he ran a broad thumbnail across the seal of Alexander's letter. There was a quality about her, so calm and so direct, that reminded him of his own dear Anne, dead twenty years and more now. 'She was just about the same age as Lady Carew here when I lost her.' He read Alexander's letter through twice.

'You know what he has written here?'

'Yes.'

'Frankly it comes down to an admission of guilt, but a plea of necessity and justification.'

'I suppose so.'

He read it for a third time, then leaned back in his chair, his eyes apparently fixed on one of the badges in the coffered ceiling. It seemed an age before he spoke, and Jane had to will herself to wait in silence. Eventually he leaned forward, and collected both her hands into his own.

'Judge not lest ye be judged. I cannot say for sure what the Court will decide, but you would be wise to prepare yourself for the worst.'

He held her trembling fingers tightly as she fought against the tears.

'Be strong, my dear, be strong for his sake, won't you? I will do what I can, but I need help also from Alexander. Listen carefully, because I must speak in a riddle, and you must give him this message. Tell him that if he has it in his power to oblige another great man, he should do so, and so gain another friend. Have you memorised that?'

'Yes, he's to oblige a great man and gain a friend, if he can.'

'Just so. Now, you won't want to await the turn of the tide, so you must have my carriage take you back to Alexander. And may God bless you both.'

Alexander questioned Jane closely on every aspect of her journey and her interview, as though through her eyes he could continue to have a life outside of his prison. He pursed his lips when she mentioned the man who had emerged from Pym's office while she waited – 'tall, thin, with long fair hair, in a most elegant blue silk doublet'.

'Middle fifties, would you say, with a fine-drawn face?'

'Yes, I suppose so. Do you know him?'

'Possibly, but it's not important now. Would you say Pym's message to me just once more, please?'

'If you have it in your power to oblige a certain great man, you should do so, and thus gain another friend. Do you know what it's all about?'

Alexander made no answer, but instead stood behind her and nuzzled the nape of her neck until she began to wriggle in his grasp. As she turned around he kissed her, long and hard until she was gasping to draw a breath.

'Oh Alex, I'm . . .'

'Ssh, not a word now.' He drew her upright, and kissed her again, then began slowly to unlace the front of her best golden silk gown.

Afterwards they finished the cold beef in friendly silence. Jane sensed that Alexander was turning something over in his mind, but she felt sleepy and relaxed, for the first time since they had come to London, and she was content to wait for him to speak. Eventually he drained the last of a cup of wine, and sat back. It was almost dark outside, and the first cool airs of autumn were arriving. He got up to drop a cloak around her bare shoulders.

'I've come to a decision, Jane. It's the most difficult decision I've ever had to make in my life, but I'm sure it's the right one, it's for the best. I want you to go back to Antony.'

'Not until after the trial, Alex, you'll need me . . .'

'NO!'

His voice was raised as though in anger, but he lifted a hand quickly to apologise.

'No, Jane, please, please don't argue. This is so difficult for me as it is. You must go back. You said yourself that Grace is half-mad, or worse. Yet she has possession of all our children, as well as Antony. Who knows what she might do? I'm not suggesting it's going to be easy for you at Antony. Far from it, especially if Colonel Hopton brings the Cornish back to attack Plymouth. But I've decided that's where you should be. It's been a wonderful blessing having you with me, but you can do little more than comfort me now, and I worry so much about the children. Will you do this for me, my love?'

'When?' Her voice was hardly more than a whisper.

'The Sergeant has made enquiries for me today. There is a coach leaving for Portsmouth tomorrow afternoon. Well-escorted, because it's carrying the money to pay the garrison there. Our friendly Captain Hoare said he expected to sail again for Plymouth at the end of the month or early in October, depending on the weather.'

Tears brimmed in Jane's dark eyes as she reached across the table to take his hands convulsively in hers.

'Oh Alex, I may never see you again.'

'Sir Alexander, you have now heard all the evidence against you. Do you still think it necessary, or wise, to persist in your plea of "Not guilty"?'

Alexander had expected to be brought to trial very soon after he had sent Jane back to Plymouth. Instead he had been kept waiting through long, weary months in the Tower, and only now, on a gloomy mid-winter morning, had he been brought to London's Guildhall to face his accusers. The seven

Assessors of the Court Martial sat on a dais at one end of the bare room, lit only by the weak daylight that filtered in through the narrow windows. Alexander stood before them in a raised dock, with a guard of two dozen soldiers around him. Because this was a military tribunal there was no public gallery, and just a few privileged observers, among them Nicholas Gould. There were also three young men Alexander did not know at first, but then recognised as the three younger brothers of John Carew – Thomas, Wymond and Anthony.

The Court President was Sir John Corbet, and Alexander reflected at length before answering his question. The months of captivity had been hard for him to bear, especially after Jane had gone. His long hair was now streaked with grey, and his bearing had lost that easy, athletic spring that had helped to make him such a magnetic figure. More than once he had come close to despair, had even thought of suicide. Now he summoned all his strength for one last effort. Perhaps his judges might find room for pity in their hearts?

'Gentlemen, although I studied the law in my youth, my training was only academic, and I trust therefore you will forgive me if I do not always speak as a professional lawyer might. At least though you will know that my argument comes from the heart, and not from a manual of pleadings.

'The charges against me may be summarised into one of Treason, in that I am said to have attempted to open our town of Plymouth to the enemy, having been given responsibility by Parliament for part of its defences, and having out of necessity accepted the responsibility for the rest, until a new commander had arrived.

'My answer is that I am not guilty of Treason for two reasons :

'First, and most important in my defence, no witness or proof has been produced to show that I actually betrayed one inch of our town, or one soldier or citizen, to the enemy. On the contrary I have brought to your attention, from the official records, my own intervention to prevent Thomas

Ceely, then Mayor, from surrendering the town. When one of
our forts, at Lipson, was taken, it was I who organised and
led some of Plymouth's bravest to recapture it. And most
recently, when an enemy attack on Mount Batten threatened
to cut off our way to the sea, it was I again who organised
the night attack from the sea to recapture it, and I who led
our men up the cliffs, at a cost of two hundred dead. Is there
any man here who has done more?'

There was a ringing challenge in his voice as he lifted his
head, and gazed at his judges one after the other. Most
dropped their eyes, and there was some nervous shuffling of
papers.

'Sir Alexander we are not here to review your career, but
to hear your answer to the charge of Treason.'

'Thank you, Sir John, but my point is valid, nonetheless.
Did not our Lord say "By their fruits shall you know them"?
I wish to bring to the Court's attention the fact that all my
actions, my fruits if you will, have been of signal benefit to
our Parliamentary cause.'

'The answer to that, Sir Alexander, may be *corruptio optimi
pessima* – which we might translate as "the greatest evil is
done when the greatest men fail". Can you deny this falling
away, as our evidence has testified?'

'I can, and I do, and this is my second reason. There was
no "falling away", as you put it. Rather you have before the
Court the absolute proof of my continuing concern for the
people of Plymouth. Consider if you please our situation, and
bear in mind please that Plymouth is hundreds of miles away
from this safe place, deep into country where Parliament's
writ no longer runs.

'During the course of successive weeks we received news of
that overwhelming defeat at Devizes of our Army in the
West, followed by the terrible blow of the loss of Bristol.
Soon after, our town was closely besieged again, and we knew
there could be no expeditionary force from London to relieve
us. Indeed the most likely outcome was that the King would
sweep up every city in Devon, Dorset, Somerset and

Gloucester, and would then march irresistibly on London itself. Would it be sensible to continue to stand alone against so great a power? We were short of food, and there was little prospect that a harvest could be got in. Both powder and shot were limited, again with no certainty of supply. Our hearts were strong, and twice we repelled determined assaults, as I have said. But these were just small detachments of the enemy. Military opinion was unanimous that we could not survive long against a larger force, such as was already before Exeter.'

'Are you now admitting that you advised surrender?'

'Not in the least. I was for resistance as long as resisting seemed sensible. But I was also concerned, as any Englishman must be, for the thousands of men, women and children in Plymouth who had no part in the making of our quarrel with the King. What would be their fate if we resisted on until that bitter moment when the enemy bursts through our gates in hot blood? I beg you, gentlemen, to consider your own consciences in this matter. We shall all come before God's judgement, some sooner, some later. Would you have me stand in that dreadful day and have to admit that I could have saved these and these and these, but I did not because I feared a charge of Treason at today's tribunal? It is one thing, I submit in all due respect to be here in London, considering the niceties of the Law, or the requirements of public policy. It is quite another to be trapped behind the walls of a closely besieged town, and to know that today you must take a decision which will mean life or death tomorrow to thousands of your friends and fellow-citizens. Plymouth grieved in ways beyond your imagining for the two hundred who gave their lives that we might recover Mount Batten. I tell you that, no matter how certain or terrible the earthly punishment that might follow, I would not dare to have on my conscience the black stain that would come from handing over our town to the certainty of sack and pillage.'

Alexander paused, and knew from the absolute stillness that he had their hearts on his side. If he could only win their minds as well!

'We all suffered a tragic loss with the recent death of Mr Pym, but he left behind for us, as his legacy, clear thinking about our purpose in fighting this war. He said that our intention was not to make a revolution, but to defend our Protestant faith, and to restore the ancient rights and liberties of our Parliament. In such a war there are no enemies, but only fellow Englishmen who have been misled. None of us, I suggest, would be so full of pride as to claim to have a monopoly of truth or right or justice on his side.

'I repeat that no one was betrayed by my action, and I am guilty only of taking proper thought for the welfare of those committed to my care. I remain Parliament's most loyal servant, and I therefore beg the Court's pity for my circumstance, and mercy for all my faults.'

Alexander slowly dropped his head in submission, and seemed to relax his body. A close observer however might have deduced the power of the tension that possessed him from the whitening of the knuckles on the hands that gripped the sides of the dock for support.

'We are grateful to you, Sir Alexander, for your clear and concise statement of your case as you see it. The Court will now adjourn to consider its verdict.'

Alexander remained standing in the dock, and noted that Nicholas Gould walked purposefully across the floor to catch up with the President as he was withdrawing. But his attention was then absorbed by the three young men who came up to the dock.

'These are my brothers,' he said to the Sergeant. 'I have not seen them for several years. May they speak with me?'

'They may, sir, but they must not enter or touch the dock.'

Thomas was the eldest of the three. A year younger than John, he was also studying the law. Tall and fair, he seemed open and unguarded, where John had been close and cautious. He reached up between two troopers to grasp Alexander's hands.

'It must be two years, Alex, since we met at Antony. Of course John told us all about you, but he insisted we should not come to see you in the Tower. I found out about the trial this morning though.'

Alexander reached down to take the hands of the other two boys. Wymond was eighteen and Anthony seventeen – grave, shy young men with the small build and dark colouring of the eldest brother, and clearly nervous at being so close to a man accused of Treason. It was Thomas who took the lead again.

'I thought your speech was very fine, Alex. To my mind it opened up a new concept in military law, namely "Does the duty of a soldier go beyond that of obeying a legal command?" I must say I would love to hear that properly debated. Your case could . . .'

Alexander's anxiety was too great for this academic discussion to be bearable.

'Do you think they will acquit me?'

Thomas looked at his brothers, at the troopers who stolidy ringed the dock, and back at Alexander.

'I don't know, Alex. This is a military tribunal . . . they may consider the possible precedent if . . . There is a tag we hear quite often in the Courts these days, *Inter arma silent leges . . .*'

'When cannons roar justice is dumb.'

'A nice translation. I . . . I don't need to explain the implications, do I? Is there anything at all we can do to help?'

'There may be one thing . . . Do you remember there was a tall, thin gentleman standing near you -- middle-aged, long fair hair, wearing a pale blue doublet and hose, with gold trimmings?'

'Yes, of course, quite a magnificent sight. I think I've seen him before somewhere.'

'Possibly. That is Nicholas Gould, a wealthy merchant. Would you ask him to come and see me today please?'

'Of course. Is there any message . . .'

'SILENCE in Court.'

The members of the tribunal filed slowly back into their tall chairs. Nicholas Gould emerged last and slipped quietly along the panelled wall to resume his place at the side of the room. The President remained standing above Alexander, and read from his notes.

'Sir Alexander Carew, we find you guilty on the clearest possible evidence of Treason against the Ordinances of Parliament for Martial Law. In your plea of justification, you claimed that your approaches to the enemy were merely by way of parley, and that no actual betrayal took place. On the contrary the Court finds that your intention to betray your trust is obvious, and Parliament is fortunate in that you were apprehended before it could be put into effect. We cannot for one moment either allow the principle that you propose, namely that a commander in the field may take precautions to surrender his command so as to save bloodshed, other than *in extremis*.

'Sir Alexander Carew, Member of Parliament and Baronet, you have been arraigned and duly convicted before this honourable Court Martial that you, being a Commander in the service of Parliament, have traitorously deserted your trust and perfidiously plotted and combined and endeavoured to betray that trust to the enemy. For this the honourable Court Martial now sentences you to death, by having your head severed from your body. Sentence to be carried out on Tower Hill at noon tomorrow, the twenty-third of December. May God have mercy on you.'

For the first time in his life Alexander knew the fear of death, a choking, paralysing shaking fear that sat deep and icy-cold in his heart and overwhelmed his whole being. After the verdict of the court martial he was in a numb stupor as he was taken back to the Tower. It was only when the coach jerked to a halt at the Byward Tower that he returned to reality.

'Will you step down, sir?'

The captain of his guard was polite, almost friendly, but

Alexander needed all his concentration to keep his legs from buckling under him as he was escorted back to the Beauchamp Tower. In the quickly falling dusk the grey stone walls of his rooms, covered with those carvings done by long-dead previous inhabitants, seemed even harsher and more hostile. He thought of the warm, friendly walls of Antony, full of life and purposeful activity. He thought of Jane, and of Lucy, and the sound of children's laughter as they rampaged down a long corridor, and he sank onto his bed in deep despair.

Midday! Tomorrow! Midday! Tomorrow!

He was aroused from a fitful sleep, by a gentle but persistent tapping at his door. As he sat up he immediately felt sick, and was swallowing back the bile as he opened the door and peered at the figure holding up a candle in the darkness of the landing.

'Sir Alexander, it's Mr Gould, Mr Nicholas Gould. A Mr Thomas Carew said you had asked to see me. I had some business that would not wait, otherwise I would have come earlier. I offer you my sincere condolences for the verdict of that tribunal. Very dubious in law, very dubious, but of course a military court . . .' He allowed his voice to trail away, and with a great effort of will Alexander recovered his wits sufficiently to usher him into the chamber, and to light a few more candles to relieve the gloom.

'I see that, like my own house, you have no fire. Not surprising I suppose, they say there is no coal to be had in London at any price. But the news from the north is encouraging. Our new Scots allies promise to push the King out of Newcastle very soon, so perhaps we shall have coal before the worst of the winter. Now then, how may I be of service?' He sat down expectantly by the empty grate, and wrapped a thick black cloak around himself.

'I saw you in the Guildhall today, Mr Gould. I also noticed that you followed the president closely when he withdrew to

... to ... to consider the verdict. You must have some connection to this court, and you must know that I am a desperate man now. What time is it, please?'

'A little after seven.'

'That gives me just ... seventeen hours to live. Is there any way at all that you can help me?'

Nicholas looked at him in silence for a few moments. The ravages of months of imprisonment in the Tower were only too visible on Alexander. The fine blonde hair was now unkempt and streaked with grey, the handsome features were now white and pinched, the perceptible body-tremor was due to something other than the cold. He contrasted in his mind the haggard figure before him now with the man he had met previously, and shuddered. It could happen to any of us! All the more reason for them both to be of service to the Lord Admiral, if opportunity offered.

'I am just the intermediary in the matter, Sir Alexander, as I told you before. The Earl of Warwick, our great admiral, has retained my services in the business of his late father's pearls, so naturally I attended the trial to see if any more evidence might be forthcoming. I was disappointed, of course.'

'Have you heard any more from Plymouth? From Mr Francis, for instance?'

'Unfortunately not. These last months communications with Plymouth have been most difficult, and up to the time of his most regrettable death Mr Pym was resolutely opposed to any further arrests for questioning. The necessities of war ...' He made an elegant little gesture that made light of those necessities, and Alexander thought that the war had still not touched the likes of Nicholas Gould very closely.

'You were wondering if I could be more helpful, especially now in the shadow of the axe, as it were?'

'Something like that, yes. I will be quite frank with you, Sir Alexander, I wished to pursue your Mr Francis with the full rigour of the law, but was prevented from doing so by Mr Pym, who claimed the authority of the Council. The Earl was seriously displeased, but did not care to challenge Mr Pym at the time.'

'Mr Pym's death was a terrible loss for me personally, Mr Gould. I had hoped . . .' He left the thought unspoken. Was Gould a friend or an enemy? Could he really help? 'So you have only Mr Francis' original statement, that he put the pearls into my hands?'

'It seems that any further progress in that direction will have to await the end of hostilities, which, please God, will not be long now. However, I am sure there could be a road forward for yourself, that is if you could find some way in which the Earl could anticipate the recovery of his pearls.'

Nicholas had carefully avoided anything so vulgar as suggesting that Alexander had lied in his previous statement. Rather he was dangling a slender thread of hope.

'Please go on, Mr Gould. It must be obvious that there is little enough that I can do in the next few hours, which is all that seem to remain to me.'

'Yes, indeed. Well, I took the opportunity this afternoon to ask Sir John if the court was totally committed to parting your head from your body tomorrow, or whether, to oblige the Earl, they might be prepared to postpone sentence, or even, in view of your many past services, whether they might be prepared to commute sentence to something altogether less unpleasant.'

'What was his answer?'

'Much what one might expect. "On the one hand this custom and that precedent and these issues of public policy, and on the other hand mercy, and consideration of your past career, and a deep desire to oblige the Admiral." '

Alexander recognised that Gould enjoyed playing with him, as an angler enjoys playing a big salmon, but the stakes were too high for any show of pride. 'What was the outcome of this debate, please?'

'That if the Earl intercedes on your behalf – which means if I intercede on your behalf – the sentence may be postponed *sine die*. In effect you would be released into the Earl's, which means my custody.'

Alexander felt a huge upswelling of relief, and paced excitedly about the room. 'But that's wonderful, just wonderful, Mr Gould! As I said, the pearls are not in my possession, but I guarantee that, once I am face to face again with Mr Francis, I will have no difficulty in recovering them, on the Earl's behalf.'

Nicholas Gould sat unmoved by Alexander's enthusiasm. 'There is just one condition, Sir Alexander. I tried to get it removed or modified, but Sir John was adamant. Unless you fulfil this condition, the sentence must be carried out tomorrow as arranged.'

'What is this condition? I am in no position to bargain, I know.'

'During the course of your imprisonment here, and again during your trial, you were asked to name those whom the charges call "your fellow-conspirators". It seems that Parliament is certain you could not have been acting alone, and is deeply concerned that Plymouth may yet be betrayed from within. I would not have you deceive yourself in this, Sir Alexander. This is no time for bargaining, as you said, nor for temporising, nor half-measures. Only a total and frank confession of the names of all those involved with you, the route or routes by which messages were transmitted, and any related matters, will save you. Are you now ready for this?'

Alexander sat down in his chair, and closed his eyes, so that Nicholas Gould might not see the disappointment, and the invading fear that welled up irresistibly. It was not enough that he would have to reveal that he had used his father's coffin to hide the pearls. That seemed almost trivial now. But he would have to involve Philip Francis directly, which would bring down Lucy too – dear, sweet, fragile Lucy, with the new baby. His baby? And their messenger, Tobias Fisher, and the connection with the Chudleigh family. Jane of course would be accused, and Walter Goodman his steward together with his son Peter, and Sir Peter Edgcumbe would be dragged in too. The list seemed endless. Alexander tried to imagine the witchunt that Nicholas' nephew, Colonel William Gould, would enjoy conducting, especially once a victory for Parliament's army had removed the King's troops from the scene. The trials could be endless too. But he would live! In the gloom of a winter evening in the Tower of London, his home at Antony beckoned, as a distant lighted window beckons a weary traveller. Home! Peace at last . . .

'I . . . I'm not sure how much I have to offer, and whether what I can offer would satisfy Sir John and the Court Martial.'

'Perhaps you would like to use me as your sounding board?'

'Yes . . . I'm grateful for your help, Mr Gould, but I must have time to compose my thoughts, to consider the various implications. Forgive me, Mr Gould, but I must have some time.'

'Please, Sir Alexander, do not think of me as some pressing inquisitor. I am merely a sort of messenger. I could return at say, eight o'clock tomorrow?'

'I will be ready by then.'

'But no later, Sir Alexander, not a minute's delay. By eight you must have the essentials of your information, written out in enough detail for me to take to Sir John and have him issue the stay of execution. If you could do that, I will visit Sir John this evening and ask that he be prepared to receive me early tomorrow.'

'I will be ready for you.'

Nicholas rose and shook Alexander's hand. 'There is one other matter. The Captain of the Guard said that the minister from St. Peter's was standing by this evening to hear your confession. If you wish it, that is. And would you like some supper?'

'My compliments to the Captain, Mr Gould, and I would be delighted to have some supper. But perhaps we could put off troubling the minister?'

'Bravely said, Sir Alexander. Until tomorrow at eight, then.'

Nicholas Gould returned to the Tower promptly at eight, confident that Alexander had been sufficiently reduced in strength by the months of imprisonment and the imminence of public execution. He found that an astonishing transformation had taken place. Alexander had trimmed and washed his long hair, so that it fell elegantly to the shoulders of his fine red silk doublet, with its shirt trimmed in white lace. His clean-shaven features were still pale, but there was a certain perceptible vigour again in his bearing and movements.

'I am deeply sorry to disappoint you in this way, Mr Gould, particularly after you have worked so hard on my behalf. But I cannot comply with the court's conditions, and there's an end of it.'

Nicholas could see the anticipated large commission the earl had promised disappearing for good on Tower Hill, together with the invaluable benefit of the earl's good opinion, and made a last effort.

'I beg you, Sir Alexander, please reconsider. The Lord Admiral is a powerful man, and the court will not lightly disoblige him. All you have to do is produce a token list, say two or three obvious connections, and I am sure I can persuade Sir John to accept that as adequate justification to grant a stay of execution. It's such a small thing, don't you agree?'

'Not one name, not one connection. I am grateful, Mr Gould, for the efforts you have made, but I will not yield in this respect.'

'Then you are intent on condemning yourself to death?'

'If you care to put it that way, yes.'

'And there is no message, no alternative you would like me to put to the court?'

'You may say that I forgive them, if you would be so kind. And you could also say to the captain of the guard that I am ready now for God's minister, please?'

The previous night, Alexander had found the process of thinking what he should do totally overwhelming. Now that it might actually be possible to escape the headsman, his mind filled with a thousand pictures of life, which whirled round in his mind and blotted out the chill gloom of the Beauchamp Tower. Visions of Antony, of Jane and the children, of Parliament and of London's society. All at once he found his whole being was galvanised by the realisation that he was no longer the helpless victim of judicial process – his future was in his own hands. He felt too that the strength that was re-awakened in his body was not just physical. There was moral power as well, and there lay the problem. His whole being cried out, 'Choose life!' But try as he might, he could not come to terms with the images of how that life would be after he had complied with the court's conditions. He was not so naive as to believe that Parliament would be satisfied with a token confession of conspiracy. The questioning would go on and on, more and more people would be drawn into the net, and Alexander would be required, under pain of death, to give evidence in court after court against acquaintance, friend and relative. The innocent would be drawn down with the guilty, and nothing would ever be right again.

In the end, the decision had become simple. How could he choose life, if it meant destroying the very image of himself that made life worth living?

When the decision had been made, he felt suddenly lighter and at ease. It was as though some vital part of himself had been terrified that he might choose to suppress or even destroy it, and now it could emerge again into the light, proud and unashamed.

Alexander's greatest concern was that Jane might come to know that he could have escaped, and might feel herself betrayed or abandoned, might feel that he had in some way rejected her. He spent some time carefully composing a will, which left the majority of the estate under Jane's control, until young John should reach his majority and each of his children had received five hundred pounds. He could only pray that Parliament would leave Antony alone. Then he wrote a last letter to Jane.

The Tower of London, 22 December

Dearest Jane,

This is the most difficult letter I have ever written, because I must say goodbye finally to you and to our children.

You will doubtless receive from others a report of my trial this morning. I thought I gave a good account of myself – indeed I am certain the tribunal was persuaded that I had the right on my side. But, without Mr Pym to intercede on my behalf, the verdict was assured before the hearing began. Parliament must have its 'traitors' to parade on Tower Hill, so that others may be deterred.

As soon as the situation allows, place my father's remains in a new coffin, and bury him with all due ceremony in Antony church.

I have composed a will, which I am sending to you with this letter. Until our young John reaches his maturity – you are learning to call him 'Sir John' now no doubt – you are the trustee, and I have endeavoured to provide for all our children fairly. I understand your reasoned concern about Grace and her family. I talked this morning to the second son, Thomas. I found him open and honest, and I know he is well-regarded as a future lawyer. If a need arises I believe you could trust him.

You may be told that there was some possibility that I could have escaped the axe, if I had been willing to implicate in a charge of treason our friends and family. Dearest Jane, if anything could tempt me to do that, it would be the promise of seeing you again and holding you against my heart. But I could not do it, and beg you to forgive me for the choice I had to make.

I send you all my love, until we meet in Christ.

Alexander

Epilogue

Sir Alexander Carew was executed on Tower Hill on 23 December, and buried in St Augustine's Churchyard, Hackney. After the Restoration in 1660, Charles I was virtually sanctified as the 'Martyr King', and Alexander was celebrated also amongst those deemed to have been martyred in the Royal cause. His picture at Antony was sewn back into its frame, and the baronet's helm was painted in. He was succeeded by his son John.

Jane Carew gave birth to her youngest son, christened Alexander, after Sir Alexander had been executed, and lived on at Antony until 1679.

John Carew, the eldest son of Grace, the Dowager Lady Carew, became a significant political figure during the Commonwealth. He was selected to be one of the judges at the trial of King Charles, and he signed the Death Warrant in January 1649. A member of the Council of State during 1651–1653, he became concerned that Cromwell's personal ambitions were a threat to republican ideals. He was twice imprisoned for refusing to keep quiet, in 1655 and 1658, and was fined £100 in 1659. Most of the surviving regicides withdrew quietly from England in 1660, but John seems to have been driven to stay and be tried. He was hung, drawn and quartered on 15 October 1660.

No trace now remains of the Antony of this period – probably its stones were used in the building, by Alexander's grandson, of the beautiful Antony House that the National Trust now shows to the public.

Curiously for so famous a family, there is no exact record of the death of Alexander's father, Sir Richard Carew – no will, no tomb, no memorial even.

The location of his coffin is unknown.